THE THIEF
STEALS HER EARL

Christina McKnight

La Loma Elite Publishing

Dedication
To Angie~

You are the thief who stole my heart in Vegas. Our
friendship has been a true blessing.
Thank you for all you do for the indie community!

Prologue

London, England
March 1818

Miss Judith Pengarden should be anywhere but edging down the darkened halls of Lord Gunther's London townhouse, the chilled wall pressed to her back. Possibly having a late meal with her siblings or trying her hand at yet another card game her youngest sister insisted she learn. Or even attending the opera house. However, she was, indeed, sneaking through the drafty interior of a home long past needing a complete renovation. It was difficult to understand why her twin sister, Samantha, thought there was anything of value in this long-forgotten, ramshackle house.

In the hour Jude had scoured the musty second floor by candlelight, she'd discovered nothing but molding draperies, neglected family heirlooms, and unpolished wooden furniture. It was impossible to envision someone living within these walls, let alone storing a precious, ancient, and very valuable vase, carelessly placed on an end table.

"Oh, I should have known better than to trust you," Jude mumbled, cursing her own inability to see past her twin's many fables. It was more likely Sam hadn't even met Lord Gunther, nor overheard him boasting about his prized vase.

She searched the all-but-abandoned townhouse with only the current wing left to explore. Making one final turn, Jude looked down the short, dim corridor, knowing this was her last hope of finding what she'd come for; what she'd risked her neck to procure.

Immediately, she noticed that this hall was better kept than the rest of the home; the floors were swept clean, if not polished to shine, the long draperies were held back by finely tied lengths of cord, and a small table sat just to the left of a set of double doors.

Jude had found the lord's private chambers.

Finally.

She grasped her long skirt in her hand and sprinted to the end of the hall, pausing before the table.

Nestled securely on it was what she'd risked all to find; its porcelain surface recently wiped clean, removing any dust that may have gathered to dull its fine colors and artfully crafted exterior.

Her breath left her as she admired the piece's eternal beauty—only overshadowed by its worth.

It became increasingly difficult to draw air in as she lifted her fingers and gently touched the vase, feeling the slight ripples of the artist's brushstrokes as he—or she—used delicate hands to paint the piece. Or so she imagined.

The thought of taking the artifact in her hands and descending the flight of stairs to scurry to her carriage, which was waiting several houses down the street and around the corner, terrified her.

Not that she—and Sam—hadn't planned this ruse carefully, but never had Jude imagined herself breaking into another's home to steal something of great import. Once she held the vase, removed it from Lord Gunther's home, and traded it for enough pounds to settle her family's debts and feed all of Craven House's occupants for many years, a weight would be added to her shoulders. A line would be crossed and it wouldn't be easy to step back over.

Jude pulled her hand back as if the vase had burned her.

Maybe she could tell Sam that she hadn't found the piece, convince her it likely never existed, that their plan had been flawed from the start and they'd find another way to help their family. But she knew their options were limited and their time quickly running out.

Jude shook her head, casting out any lingering doubts. Her family needed help, and if she and Sam could provide their eldest sister with a fraction of financial security, then they owed her that.

And that safeguard, the answer to Craven House's dilemma, sat before her—waiting to be taken…all but calling to Jude to remove it from this dusty, dilapidated house and transport it to a new owner who would worship its delicacy as was deserving.

The vase was practically begging her to take hold and liberate it from its cruel circumstances.

The intricately crafted piece belonged in a museum; a place where the public could admire its beauty and historical worth, not hidden away in this dusty old house.

That Jude would also gain something from the transaction was a bonus she could live with.

Not one to turn down the opportunity to give something a freedom formerly denied, Jude grabbed the vase, surprised at its weightlessness in her hands.

She wondered if she let the vase go if it would float to the floor, gliding like a feather.

When images of it shattering as it hit the ground flooded her mind, Jude tucked the piece under her arm securely and retraced her steps to the servants' stairs.

Holding her breath once more, she descended the stairs two at a time before halting at the closed door that separated the stairwell from the hall that led from the front of the house to the kitchen.

Jude set her ear to the dull, cold door and listened.

Not a sound could be heard beyond.

No footsteps, no quiet whispers, no closing doors.

Not even a clock sounded anywhere in the house.

A shiver went through her. Her body was alert to the oddness of it all, but she pushed the door open and made her way to the room right off the main foyer. There, a window still stood ajar, waiting for her to crawl back through and lower herself to the shrubs below.

She was horrified at the exhilaration she felt as she moved through the abandoned house.

Jude only prayed she made it home safely—and that Marce, her eldest sister, appreciated all Jude did to help support everyone who sought refuge at Craven House. Not that Marce could *ever* know where the money came from, only that it appeared in her private chambers—as if from thin air.

The cool night breeze brushed across Jude's face as she stared out the open window.

It was her last opportunity to turn around, return the vase to its rightful place, and depart with no one the wiser.

And her conscience clear of any wrongdoing.

With a deep breath, Jude made the only decision that made sense for her and her family's future; she held the vase out of the window and released it, allowing it to fall.

...Directly into her twin sister's waiting hands below.

Chapter One

London, England
May 1818

Jude plucked at the sturdy wool of her filth-streaked pinafore as she held her breath to keep the wretched smells at bay. The stink of unwashed bodies, moldy, forgotten food, and wet animal was overpowered only by the stench of a coppery odor she knew to be spilled blood. She'd certainly need to burn her current garment as soon as she was released and able to return to Craven House—if one of her siblings ever saw fit to collect her.

To do away with such a precious thing as a dress was not something she'd always had the liberty to do. For many years, she counted herself lucky to possess several dresses—even though she shared each with Samantha. The time she and her siblings had spent at Craven House should have prepared Jude for this night; men angered by too much drink, which turned into arguing, which led to fisticuffs and blood—the smell of which was something she'd never forget, though her family had tried to keep her far from it as much as possible.

A sliver of the rising sun outside the narrow window of her cell allowed a slice of light to penetrate her dank enclosure; though Jude would have been happy to remain ignorant of her despicable surroundings. Her dress, though made from a thick material, still snagged on the rough, splintering bench below her. But after hours of standing—and pacing—Jude had to rest her aching legs. It was either the sticky, grimy, wooden bench or the more intolerable hard-packed dirt floor littered with discarded food and a pail filled with what she was told was water but appeared murkier than the River Thames.

Actually, she'd prefer a swim in the Thames as opposed to her current predicament. She only hoped her elder brother, Garrett, didn't ship her to the country for all the trouble she'd caused. The trouble she presumed herself in. A sojourn to the country would be preferable to what Marce, her imperious sister, would do to her if she found out about Jude's escapades.

She'd seen herself as invincible; above being caught—so much so that Jude should be in a complete panic. But the surreal nature of her position hadn't faded to allow in the stark actuality she faced.

It was supposed to be only once—the vase from Lord Gunther's townhouse. They were to sell the piece, give the money to Marce, and be free to live with some semblance of peace knowing their home was safe. But the vase remained at Craven House and now their family's future was in jeopardy. They should have known that a stolen vase would not go unnoticed and unreported in the post. They should not have been so delusional as to think they could take the vase and gain coin for it as easily as selling wares inside the marketplace.

As of now, she'd been left unaccompanied in this darkened room, the door securely locked, for hours. No one had come to inquire about her well-being; no offers of refreshment or fare, no blanket to ward off the night chill. She hadn't heard another person since the constable had slammed the door shut on her with his sharp reprimand to not cause him further grievance or he'd make her sorry.

She was unsure how much longer she'd be locked in this room—her stomach let out a loud growl in protest at the thought—or even if her twin, Samantha, knew where she'd been taken.

One thing Jude was certain of; she didn't relish spending another moment alone here. The window was too narrow for her to wiggle through and the door was bolted from the outside.

This led her to hours of pondering how she'd ended up here—what path she could have taken to deliver herself from such a wretched circumstance.

Her night had started off simple enough, with she and her twin devising a plan to remove fourteenth century Bible leaves from Lord Asherton's townhouse—a far less notable and traceable antiquity than the vase from Lord Gunther, but almost as valuable. It should have been easy. Samantha was to meet the lord in question at a dinner party she was attending with friends while Jude slipped into his home, collected the ancient papers, and disappeared as if she'd never been there. They'd heard during a recent outing that the man's house was light on servants as many had traveled to Lord Asherton's country estate ahead of his scheduled departure on the morrow. The perfect time for their heist.

But little had gone as planned.

After searching a study on the ground floor, Jude had fled down a dark hallway when she'd heard voices coming from the kitchen, growing louder as she rushed in the opposite direction. It hadn't been difficult to slip into an empty room, rush to a door, and flee—that was until her cap was ripped from her head as she bolted by a coat rack positioned inside what appeared to be a lady's sitting room. Jude had quickly retrieved the cap, tugged it back into place to hide her red hair, and continued toward a door she hoped would open to a garden sitting area...and her freedom.

She was mere steps from the door when the alarm sounded behind her.

Not the shouts of an infuriated lord or the call to halt by a faithful servant, but rather the searing shriek of a child. Jude barely glanced over her shoulder to see her identifier before rushing through the door, along the side of the house, and around to the narrow lane behind the row of townhouses.

Several hours later, her ears still rung from the high-pitched screech.

She would never forget the rounded, frightened eyes of the young girl who'd peered at Jude from her seat on the lounge, a throw blanket lying haphazardly across her lap as she read a book. Her tousled hair fell around her shoulders, still crimped from her plaits. A pristine white night shift gathered at her throat in a bow.

Jude couldn't accurately describe the girl beyond her long, dark hair and frightened look.

All she'd thought about at that moment was getting as far away from Lord Asherton's home as possible, the valuable Bible leaves be damned.

Fleeing from the house and gaining a block's distance hadn't stopped an alarm being sounded. The night watchman was rushing around the corner, his lamp held high to illuminate his way.

The burly man, dressed in merchant's trousers and coat, was only identifiable by the shiny tin star pinned to his jacket pocket. The swinging lamp sent light reflecting off the dinted piece of metal as they both stood stock-still, staring at one another. The pair was caught in the small circle of light given off by the uplighter. His expression was likely a mirror image of hers; fright.

She hadn't expected to be caught and it was probable he had never apprehended a suspected criminal on his nightly watch.

She was an unchaperoned woman, dressed in a less than fashionable gown with a cap hiding her hair. It was reasonable for the constable to question her on principle alone, for what woman would be traversing the deserted London streets at close to midnight?

Maybe she should have run. Sam would have vouched for this course of action.

Certainly, she should not have agreed to the harebrained notion in the first place. Marce would have counseled against it.

The man wasn't armed. Most night watchmen took to their route with nothing more than a billy club as protection.

And so, the standoff continued. Jude was analyzing the watchman's size and strength; concluding he would easily outrun her on foot in a section of London she was unfamiliar with.

There'd been little else for her to do but employ her twin's claimed talent for charming men. Unfortunately, her voice didn't hold the sultry depth of Sam's, nor was Jude adept at the coy behavior needed to lull a man into feeling secure enough to allow his guard to fall.

And so, she'd relented and allowed the watchman to lock her in this room—as any criminal would deserve.

Jude gave in to her exhaustion and leaned back against the grimy wall, needing to forget her many mistakes. She settled against the cold wall of her locked cell and drew her knees to her chest, allowing her dress to cover her chilled feet. As her head met the hard surface of the stone, she closed her eyes, begging her tears to stay where they belonged, unshed.

She would not cry. That right had been taken from her when she and her twin had decided to help bring extra income to Craven House—they'd known the risk they'd agreed to take with their actions.

She breathed deeply, allowing the stench of her surroundings to invade her nostrils and then expelled gradually, slowing her pulse. If she could calm herself, maybe sleep would take over and she'd wake to find it had all been an unpleasant nightmare. She'd awaken in her warm bed with Sam nestled in her matching one a few feet away, both tucked deeply under their soft, peach eyelet, down blankets. Jude would share her horrid dream with Sam. They'd laugh as they crawled from the warmth of their well-sprung beds and rang for their maid to help them prepare for their day of shopping and entertainments.

Except, Sam and Jude shared one bed, hadn't the luxury of a maid, nor the spare funds for as much as even a new pair of gloves.

Marce reminded her younger sisters, daily, each time they offered their complaints, that many women were much less fortunate than they. At least they had a roof over their heads, food in their pantry, and some hope for a more fruitful future if they minded their behavior and attracted fine suitors.

And they had love.

They undoubtedly had an abundance of love.

But love would not keep the debt collectors at bay, nor garner additional food for their table.

And a new dress or two for them all would be appreciated, especially since Lady Haversham had been so kind as to sponsor their societal debut.

Jude huffed. It was a trivial, selfish thought, especially when she was perched on a splintered bench with her head leaning against a grime-covered wall in a room that hadn't been properly swept in Lord knew how long.

From somewhere outside the cell, Jude heard loud, angry voices. They were muffled by the wall and door separating her from other parts of the building housing her, but the aggression in the dominant voice was unmistakable.

Jude would prefer a large hole open in the room and swallow her, as opposed to the force of nature currently headed her way. Only moments would pass before the ire presently unleashed on the night watchman who dared keep Miss Judith Pengarden locked in a room, would be refocused on Jude herself.

"I will not stand for this, Garrett," Marce, Jude's eldest sister and only motherly figure, bit out harshly as a key was slid into the lock. "I will have this door opened at once or I will bring the fires of Hades down on this *establishment*." Marce's emphasis on the word left no doubt in anyone's mind what her family's matriarch thought of the night watchman and his lodgings.

"Dear sister," Garrett coaxed. "The man is only doing his job, earning a respectable salary while keeping the night streets free of vagabonds."

"Judith is most certainly not a vagabond." Marce's voice rose three octaves until it was almost a shrill scream. "Now, release her at once or I will be forced to call on Lord Haversham or Lord Chastain. I am certain you know both the earl and the duke. They will quickly settle all this once and for all."

Jude could picture her sister stamping her foot, her fury intensifying with each word.

No one dared defy Marce—not at Craven House or anywhere else she'd witnessed her sister in action.

"Ma'am," the night watchman stammered, clearly resigned to following Marce's orders. "My apologies for the mistake. The alarm was sounded and the butler in the household gave a description matching Miss Judith's appearance."

"And when you found nothing incriminating on her person, you decided the best course of action was to lock her up for hours in this flea-infested room? Most certainly not proper accommodations for a woman of her status."

"Calm yourself, Marce." Garrett attempted to soothe his sister's wrath. "I know Mr. Newman would not purposely apprehend an innocent young woman."

"I can assure you it was not—" Newman tried unsuccessfully to interject.

"I will not calm down." The door was wrenched open, its hinges groaning in protest at the swift movement. "If one hair on her head is harmed, I will have *you* drawn and quartered!"

Marce, her blonde hair falling down her back unrestrained and her coat buttoned down her front, stormed into the room with Garrett close on her heels. The night watchman remained outside, likely knowing it's safer for him to stay out of Jude's eldest sister's reach.

"Again," said Mr. Newman. "I was also worried about her being out late at night. She could have been set upon by any sort of unsavory character. She was without a chaperone and was unwilling to give me any information about herself beyond your direction, Lord Garrett."

Jude would have laughed at the use of Garrett's name spoken so formally, but that would draw Marce's attention far sooner than Jude was prepared for.

Her sister may be vehemently protective of her siblings, but that in no way meant she coddled them.

"That will be all, Mr. Newman." Retreating footsteps sounded as the poor man heeded Marce's curt dismissal. But with his retreating steps, Marce's concern also fled. "What exactly were you doing wandering London at midnight?"

Jude knew better than to speak. It was a rhetorical question meant to keep her silent, for Marce was in no way finished talking.

"I can tell you where you were *not* last night. You were not attending the Buckhams' soiree with Lady Haversham and Mrs. Jakeston, as you should have been. You also did not arrive home with Samantha. I dare say you did not so much as depart with your twin at the start of your evening." Marce's brow rose, daring Jude to refute her. "What do you have to say for yourself, Judith Pengarden?"

Marce only used the siblings' full names when trouble was afoot and she knew it could tarnish their family—as much as their scandal-ridden clan could be tarnished where they hung on the fringes of London's proper *ton*.

"Is there something you'd like to hear from me?" Jude retorted, any calm she may have achieved disappearing.

It irked Jude to no end that Marce viewed her as a mere child—always the girl in plaits and kid boots—not a mature, educated woman, old enough by society's standards to marry and start her own home and family. However, here Jude sat: in a dank room when any proper lady should be abed, accused of stealing into the home of a member of the *beau monde*.

And all because she was attempting to help her family.

Garrett stepped between his sisters. "I beg the both of you, finish this conversation in a less public," he paused, looking at the filth overtaking the room, as if seeing it for the first time, "and certainly more hygienic, place. After Jude is allowed a hot—very hot—bath to cleanse this awful stink from her."

Mockingly, he brought a loose tendril of her hair to his nose and sniffed, disgust masking his teasing nature.

She swatted at his hand and allowed her curl to fall from his grasp.

Jude looked to her sister, silently pleading for Marce to take Garrett's suggestion.

Marce's narrowed stare said she wasn't convinced they need move their conversation. "I have a mind to leave you here."

"Leave me here?" Jude gulped.

"Leave her here?" Garrett said at the same time.

"Why not?" Marce set her hand on her hip as she stepped around her younger brother to face Jude once more. "I am unsure what you—and likely Sam—are up to, but I will not allow you to run about London with no regard for the consequences. Both for you and our family as a whole."

"I despise when you speak rationally." Jude crossed her arms and stood, signaling her desire to depart. "It would be best to return home before we are spotted leaving a place of such ill repute."

"Thank you for thinking of someone and something other than your own pleasures," Marce said before turning on her heels and leaving the room with as much fanfare as she'd entered it. She left Garrett and Jude staring blankly at one another. "Come along, you two."

The comment stung, but the truth in Marce's words was undeniable. Her sister may not admit when she needed help, but Jude's actions were risky and not as thought out as she'd hoped. It was highly likely Jude would never be adept at such things. Thankfully, she had no interest in repeating her actions. Not until their financial situation became increasingly dire, at least.

She vowed to refocus on being rid of the vase and not entangling herself in any more harrowing escapades about London.

"I have no doubt your reasoning for tarrying about after the midnight hour is very compelling, yet less than savory." Garrett took Jude's elbow and guided her from the dirty room, both of them squeezing through the doorway. "Sam's note of warning did not find me abed either." He winked with his words, letting Jude know he was concerned about her but would not pry—as he loathed his siblings prying into his affairs.

Jude turned rounded eyes on her elder brother—the lone wolf of a family full of females. She'd often wondered what occupied his many leisurely hours, but her need to respect his privacy outweighed her interest.

"Do not dally." Marce's call floated down the long corridor leading to the front of the establishment, her sure footsteps keeping time. "I have no qualms about leaving the pair of you to secure your own transport home."

Jude allowed Garrett to walk her down the hall as she suppressed a sigh at her sister's ire.

The situation seemed drastically less dreadful now that she was among the free again.

She and Garrett nodded to the watchman as they crossed the threshold into the cool morning air. A little bird chirped in the tree bordering the front walk.

"You will owe her answers when you arrive home," Garrett confided.

"I am aware."

"I hope you have thought up a plausible explanation in your hours spent locked down."

"I have not," Jude said.

Both remained quiet as a man came down the path before them. The stranger removed his hat and nodded to Marce in greeting. If her sister issued any response, it was too quiet for Jude to hear.

"Good morn," the man greeted Jude and Garrett, a grim smile on his face as he looked away. His hair fell across his forehead at the movement, but he quickly brushed it aside. As he did, Jude noticed the youthfulness of his face.

She glanced over her shoulder as the man pushed his spectacles farther onto the bridge of his nose and strode into the night watchman's home, his trousers and coat wrinkled as if he'd either slept in them or was against bothering his valet this early in the day.

"And to you, good sir," Garrett called as the door closed behind the man, her brother's shoulders lifting as he steered Jude toward their waiting carriage. It was very much like Garrett to puff his chest when faced with a gentleman of peerage, something he longed to be but had given up on years before—the forgotten younger son of a deceased lord.

Garrett's horse stood tethered to a post nearby.

Jude's heart sank. "You will not return to Craven House with us?"

"I fear not, mop," he said, handing her up into the carriage where Marce was already arranging her skirts. "I have much to attend to."

Marce chuckled softly from inside. "I'm certain he does."

He turned a peeved look at their eldest sister inside the dim conveyance before continuing, "However, I will be round this afternoon to discuss…things."

Jude hoped they could discuss "things" without her present, for she was certain she would be excluded from any and all talks of punishment due her.

"I shall be canceling my trip," Marce said when Jude seated herself across from her. "There is something afoot and I will not let this family go to ruins in my absence."

There was certainly something happening, but it was far more concerning than Sam's and Jude's antics.

"It is one week, Marce." Garrett entered the carriage, his own transport forgotten as he motioned Jude to scoot over and allow him room to sit.

Their sister left her siblings for only one short week every year. Sometimes it was immediately following the holiday season, other times it was during the summer months, but she always returned a bit lighter in nature. They'd come to relish the short time Marce was gone, never asking her destination. But Payton—Jude's youngest sister—had assumed for years that Marce traveled to Bath for several days of rest before returning to her obligations. Jude's sisters envied Marce's travels, thinking they were excluded from something enjoyable, but Jude could only imagine the weight on her sister's shoulders. She cared for so many—receiving nothing in return. If she sought a few days to live a normal, carefree life then Jude could not blame her for taking it.

Many days, Jude wished she had the fortitude to do the same.

Take her life and future into her own hands, provide for herself instead of partaking in what Marce worked tirelessly to provide for them. Instead, she'd been told continually that at her tender age, she was still to be taken care of. Far too young and innocent to take on any further responsibilities.

And that had led to finding another way around Marce's ban on Jude being anything more than a debutante—protected, sheltered, and treated as a delicate thing.

A way to help support their large household and push the debt collectors back. One time. That was to be the end of it, but when they'd been unable to sell the stolen vase, they'd had to alter their plans slightly, which included Jude taking the Bible leaves.

Another failure and setback for them.

"I can handle things at Craven House in your absence."

Garrett's declaration snapped Jude back to the present.

"That is not necessary," Jude snapped. "We are of an age to care for ourselves."

"In a fashion similar to last night?" Marce asked. "I think not."

"Then it is settled—" Garrett started.

"Nothing is settled," Marce refuted, turning a sharp look on the pair. "I no more trust you to keep Craven House from burning to the ground than I trust the twins. It's bloody insane, but I think Payton has a better handle on herself than the lot of you."

"Payton?" Jude and Garrett said at the same time, once again.

"Do stop doing that," Jude hissed at her brother. "People will think you and I are more closely related than Samantha and me."

"Is that so awful?" he teased. "I am undoubtedly more attractive than she."

"We look identical, you cad!" Jude felt her temper rising as it did on most occasions when she and Garrett were in the same place.

"Then I will be the pretty twin." Garrett fluttered his eyes, his long lashes being one of his most notable features—if not as manly as he'd like. "I am certain to have many offers for my hand. Our dear eldest sister will be fighting off my hungry suitors!"

Jude swatted at him and he hurriedly scooted out of her reach on the bench seat, fluttering his hand as if fanning the heat from his face.

His actions were at odds with his purely masculine, deep chuckle at his lark.

It only took a moment for her annoyance to fade and a smile to appear.

He jested with Jude constantly. She should feel honored to have their only brother's undivided attention so regularly when he rarely noticed Payton or Sam, but that also meant he kept better watch over her.

He loved his sisters, but Jude especially. Though he was a man about town, he never went long without visiting Craven House, no matter how often Marce insisted she did not need his concern over their well-being.

"You two will certainly send me to an early grave with your mischief," Marce declared, her voice thin with exhaustion.

The trio settled into a companionable silence as their carriage traversed the bustling morning streets. A footman followed with Garrett's mount. Each was lost to their own musings as the carriage found its way quickly home.

Mr. Curtis opened the carriage door with a flourish befitting a man half his age.

"M'lady." He bowed to Marce as she exited, his back creaking with his effort. "This missive came for ye when ye was out."

"Not another one," Jude heard Marce mumble. "This has to stop."

"You will rectify this shortly, will you not?" Garrett asked as he stepped down and turned to assist Jude. But she rebuffed his assistance and he turned back to Marce. "I do hope this is the last time."

"For all of our futures, I certainly hope so."

Jude hopped down from the carriage, snapping a quick glance at the letter before it disappeared into the folds of her sister's gown. The envelope was labeled as clearly as the others Jude had seen: *Notice: Delinquency— Funds Due!*

She couldn't help but feel she'd been privy to a conversation that was not meant for her ears.

In that instant, Jude regretted her decisions for the night, yet at the same time, knew the ends justified the means. She must remember she was, indeed, helping Marce and everyone who called Craven House their home. Though she needed to focus more on not getting caught if her great measures were to help and not hinder everything her family had worked so hard for.

Chapter Two

Simon Montgomery, the seventh Earl Cartwright—Cart to anyone who knew him personally—stepped through the front door of his London townhouse.

"Good morn, my lord," Squires, his butler, called deafeningly to him before closing the door with a slam louder than his greeting. "Your mother seeks your attendance in—"

"Simon!" Lady Anastasia Cartwright, his mother, screeched from her private salon before the poor man could finish. "Thank heavens you have returned."

Cart nodded to his elderly butler and quickly patted his shoulder. Squires had been employed by the Cartwright Earldom since Cart was in his mother's womb. His mother had sought to have the aging servant replaced on many occasions, but the funds were simply not available to hire another butler.

Thankfully, Cart's mother would rather have a new gown than a younger servant.

He squared his shoulders, preparing himself for the inquisition he feared was to come.

Lady Cartwright was as formidable as the great storm of 1703, but Cart would not allow her to drive him far off course. She was vexing, to say the least, but they did not have the coin to maintain another residence, either in town or the country.

Cart took a deep breath and pasted a smile on his face before entering his mother's salon. His morning had been a trying one, but there was no reason he could not put on a brave face.

The sight before him when he entered the room turned his smile into a most disagreeable frown.

"What is all this, Mother?"

Lady Cartwright had a large table moved to the center of her salon and upon it, in neat, orderly rows, were all her jewels—emerald necklaces, teardrop pearl earrings, a line of brooches, a diamond bracelet. The sheer number of gems with the morning sun gleaming off them from the open window was blinding.

The answer to all their prayers lay before him.

Jewels enough to line the Cartwright coffers anew.

"Mother," Cart sighed, attempting to hide his exasperation. "What are you doing?"

She turned a dour look to her only son, but quickly returned to her task. She held a pencil nub in one hand and a paper in the other.

Leaning in, he noticed the paper, and several more just like it, covered in notes.

"I am cataloguing all the Cartwright valuables." Her exasperation mirrored Cart's, as if any earl would know that when someone broke into your home, the first thing one should do is count the silverware and light sconces.

As if on cue, Mrs. Fryer entered with a tray piled high with the formal flatware.

"Do set it on the table, Ingrid dear." Lady Cartwright stood from where she sat in a straight-backed chair and looked over the pile. "Yes, there is no doubt. At least three pieces have gone missing."

"You cannot possibly know as much simply by looking at a heap of metal," Cart retorted. "It is highly unlikely."

His mother set aside her paper and nub to turn her stare on him—in his youth, that look would have sent him running. However, he stood his ground, refusing to cower no matter the hardness behind her look.

"Simon." She preferred using his given name only as it vexed him so. "I have been the lady of this house far longer than you have been in this world. I know every square inch of it and all it contains. I assure you, my assessment is correct."

He wanted to snort at her words. Even if a few forks went missing, no one would be the wiser or care as they hadn't entertained since before his father's passing—and his uncle's petition for guardianship of Cart until his majority. It was then everything had come crashing down on him. Not all at once, but a slow tidal wave of decay, his family title and estate going from once affluent to only a step above destitute.

It had taken his uncle, Mr. Julian Montgomery, a mere three years to empty the family coffers and abscond to The Colonies.

In the several years since Cart had reached the age of majority and returned from Eton to find his finances and estates in disrepair, he had worked tirelessly to recover all that his uncle had piddled away or sold. It was a tiring activity and frowned upon by polite society, but his drive had never waned, regardless of his mother's thoughts on the matter.

"Did you expect I would return to slumber?" his mother inquired. "And trust you to attain answers and justice for the violation of our property last night?"

Cart didn't expect anything from his mother—except the headache that was currently taking over.

Bloody hell, but she made it difficult to cherish her sometimes.

A man should adore his mother, as she should adore her son in return. Yet, his mother sought to undermine him at every turn.

"I did as I said I would do," Cart reassured her. "I followed up with the night watchman, who confirmed they had detained someone, but they found nothing on their person to warrant holding them or sending for a magistrate to take the matter further."

"And you did not insist on summoning the magistrate?"

"I was assured the night watchman likely plucked the wrong miscreant from the street." Cart had been disappointed as well with the assistance the night watchman had offered. Moreover, regardless of the inadequacy of the man, the thief was certainly long gone by the time the alarm was sounded. Cart had little to no confidence that anyone would be apprehended. "Alas, I will not see Theo worrying herself into a fit over this. I shan't allow this or anything similar to transpire again."

Lady Cartwright's brows pulled together, doubt clouding her expression. "You cannot say that with any certainty, Simon. Once you lock yourself away in that dreadful room or, heaven forbid, depart to see a *client*..." She said the word in a whisper as if it were a vulgarity not proper to cross her lips. "Your sister and I will be left to fend for ourselves once more."

The fact that their survival depended on Cart's *clients* as well as his need to earn a wage to sustain their way of living irked his mother to no end. As a matter of fact, it angered him, as well. However, they'd been left with no other option; anything not entailed to the Earldom had been sold—if it hadn't been pilfered by his scoundrel of an uncle first—and any servant who hadn't been with the family for over a decade had been helped to find another position elsewhere.

She'd gone so far as to demand he keep his disreputable activities from coming to light at social engagements. He'd readily agreed as he very seldom attended anything *ton* related, preferring to spend his unoccupied time searching through old tomes to increase his knowledge of antiquities or attending auction houses in pursuit of his own missing family heirlooms.

"I shall never leave you and Theo to care for yourselves," he promised, no matter how often his mind wandered to the notion of stealing off to the country in the dead of night with his sister in tow.

"Her name is Theodora, Simon. How many times must I correct you?" Lady Cartwright resumed her seat before the table containing every jewel on the property. "She is the daughter of an earl, not the bastard offspring of a sully maid. Such a nickname will tarnish her chances of finding a suitable match."

Cart longed to tell his mother a nickname was the least of Theo's worries pertaining to her future.

However, he wanted to hold on to hope that Theo would live a far less taxing life than Cart had thus far. He'd worked so hard to put aside money for her dowry—and to guarantee she would never gain worry that her family had been cast into ruin, as Cart had. He'd been overwhelmed and angry when Eton had discontinued his education due to non-payment from his uncle's solicitor. He'd been banished from his living quarters without benefit of any further explanation, his studies cut abruptly short just shy of his twenty-first birthday.

That was something Theo would never experience—he'd given her that vow years ago. He would move heaven and Earth to keep his promise.

Until their fortunes changed, Cart would continue to study and keep abreast of antiquities. As far as he figured, the market for making coin quickly dealing with rare objects was far superior to investing in shipping and business ventures, which required more funds upfront with little guarantee that any return on investment would be seen. And that the business allowed Cart to retrieve his own treasured family heirlooms in the process was a boon. A painting of the very first Earl Cartwright or a gilded, gold leaf chair constructed by his great uncle may not be of any significance to his mother, but his ancestors and their journeys were of great import to him.

He lowered himself into the chair directly across from his mother before responding. He immediately regretted his decision to sit because she huffed and went back to her work—her normal dismissive nature.

"Please, look at me," he requested. He needed to see her eyes when he spoke his next words; needed to see that she did not dismiss his meaning before she allowed the words to sink in. "You—and Theodora—are the most important people to me. Your well-being is my utmost priority, whether that means providing a financially secure future for you both or allowing you an ear for listening."

Her chin lifted ever so slightly in reproach.

He'd noticed her reactions to his sentiments for years, her guarded rejoinders and avoidance of their true situation. It was as if she had something more to say, some light she could shed on the situation. Instead, she reverted to silence or cutting remarks.

And Cart allowed it.

In a way, he felt like the wall she'd built between herself and her two children was warranted.

He'd let his mother down, disappointed his young sister—and never questioned the activities of a man he was supposed to trust. A man who had been as close to him as his own father. Cart had never thought his uncle capable of the dubious actions or the deceit he'd obviously been more than proficient at.

Cart continued to hold his mother's stare, softening his own expression to communicate his sincerity.

"You will care for us as you did with the night watchman?" she asked, looking back to her notes. "He said there was no need to further search for the person who broke into my home—who absconded through the room your dear, sweet sister resided in, no less. And what have you done about it?"

A sharp pain of hurt tore at him.

"Exactly nothing," she sighed. "As I expected. You took the man's word and, in turn, have left us vulnerable to thieves. What is to stop him from setting his sights on this house once more? What if word spreads in society about your lack of gumption? Who will do business with you then?" Lady Cartwright continued to fire questions Cart was unprepared to answer, though it was her way of things. If she overwhelmed her only son, then he would become speechless and do as she bid. "And think of Theodora! If anyone hears she was unchaperoned in a room alone with a man…"

He scrubbed his face with his hands, giving himself a moment to think. "Theo is only twelve years old. She is far from society's scrutiny—at least for the next several years."

"Then what about *your* prospects for the future?"

"Truly, Mother." Irritation inched into his words. It was a subject neither broached. His mother would not take kindly to becoming a Dowager Countess and Cart relished his many hours pursuing subjects that interested him. If he were to tie himself to a woman, it would mean the end of his pursuits for knowledge—a woman of an educated nature was a rarity. On this topic, he and his mother were aligned, a definite infrequent occurrence within their household. "You think I should divert my attentions to the fairer sex now?"

"I did not say it was what I wanted." His mother paused, staring out the open window. "Only something you should not banish from your mind."

Lady Cartwright, regal and domineering, would never allow her only son to marry a woman of his choosing, for that woman would not conform to his mother's wishes and demands—nor would Cart ever wish her to.

And so, Cart did not entertain the thought of marriage.

"What more do you plan to do to catch the person who violated *our* home?" She switched tactics rather seamlessly, using the term our, when normally it was "my" to refer to anything dealing with the Cartwright estate. "I fear that sitting back and doing nothing will only show other miscreants that my home is easily compromised and ripe for the taking."

He tired of the daily pressure to complete every task to his mother's specific instructions and wishes— no, demands. He'd thought that as their fortune turned around, she would loosen the noose about his neck, decrease the burden she heaped on his shoulders. Alas, she only became more challenging as the years passed.

Cart was not able to bring his father back, nor was he able to bring his uncle to justice for taking all he had from them. But he was doing his best to secure a favorable future for the three of them. One that included a proper education for Theo and allowing his mother a life full of society's frivolous living, as she'd been accustomed to her entire life. Surely Lady Cartwright understood it would be far less expensive for the trio to retire to the country, live a less grand lifestyle without need for extravagant wardrobes, carriage upkeep, and two homes with servants. However, his mother refused the move and demanded her lady's maid keep her position even though Cart had given up his valet, a man who'd served Cart's father faithfully for over fifteen years.

For his own selfish reasons, Cart partly agreed with his mother. If he were to remove himself from London, it would significantly reduce his meager income. There was only a small village surrounding his family's country home, with absolutely no other peers or collectors within a few hours' ride on horseback. Being in town provided Cart with the ability to visit bookstores and auction houses.

The stiff-backed chair afforded him no opportunity to slouch, much the same as his mother.

Standing, he looked down at the woman who'd given him life, wishing he could give her all she wanted, but knowing he—or any other man—would not be capable of living up to her high standards. "I will return to the night watchman after my appointment and request instructions for following the matter up with the magistrate."

"Very well," she said, looking up from her work. Her mouth was closed in a tight line. His words hadn't appeased her, but there was naught else she could say or do. "Please come to me when you return. I will be awaiting further resolution."

"Very well." He echoed her response as he issued a curt bow and departed, pulling his timepiece from his vest pocket as he closed the door.

The hour was later than he expected.

His meeting with Lord Gunther was scheduled for one hour hence and he was not a client Cart kept waiting, even though he had no new information about the lord's missing vase. It had appeared nowhere on the open antiquities market. There was no one seeking a quick and quiet exchange of coin for an unspecified ancient piece, nor any buzz about town of such a precious item being whisked out of the country. It was peculiar, to say the least. There were few collectors whose extensive collections were not public knowledge within their limited circle of antiquities enthusiasts.

It was possible a new collector was in their midst, working diligently to amass sizeable holdings before revealing himself.

Cart suspected in time the thief would be revealed or, if not the thief, at least a man who was not above buying stolen goods.

"Brother," a small voice called to him. "Are you going out once more?"

He searched the shadows under the foyer staircase. His younger sibling's preference for small, dark hiding spots was known to all who lived within their walls. Finally, he found her watching him from the deepest corner beneath the stairs, a book clutched in her hands.

"Come out of there, Theo," he called, holding his hand out. "You cannot actually be reading in such dim lighting."

She crawled from her spot, an unlit candle in one hand and her book tucked under her arm as she pushed to her feet. Once standing, her gown and pinafore fell to just below her knees, a light pastel pink with white stockings—now smudged with dust. Her hair, neither blonde nor brown in hue, was braided and pinned in normal fashion for a girl of her age.

Cart couldn't help but smile at her precocious ways.

"Why the unlit candle?" he asked.

"I heard you and Momma quarreling."

"We were not quarreling, Theo," he tried to reassure her. "We were discussing last night."

33

"You were quarreling," she said again with a shake of her head, as if she felt sorry that her elder brother did not have enough brains to realize they had, in fact, been having a tiff. "I heard the door close and did not want Momma to find me under the stairs—nor reading. You know how she wishes I would set my sights to more ladylike endeavors and apply my talents elsewhere."

He certainly did. His mother hadn't gained an education past learning to read and the basic arithmetic needed to keep track of household valuables. And, in turn, she did not think Theo needed any studies past this, either. However, Theo's continuing education had been Cart's compromise to remain in London proper.

Theo would have a full-time tutor until she voiced that she no longer needed her studies.

The shock of returning home after Eton to a sister who'd never learned her letters had saddened him greatly, but he'd remedied the situation quickly. Currently, Theo was mastering Latin and studying the Turkish Empire.

"Rest assured, I will not relegate you to the salon for needlepoint anytime soon. If—" he paused, pulling a serious expression.

"If what?" she demanded.

"If you promise to read with proper light. And no more staying up past midnight with your nose in a book. You need a proper night's rest to keep your mind primed for storing knowledge." He tapped her nose to emphasize his point. "Now, shall I have someone light that candle for you once more or will you be preparing for your morning lessons?"

She giggled, a light, airy sound that reminded Cart that there was a much less demanding life to live. A life with carefree mornings and afternoons spent learning, without rushing to and fro, meeting with clients.

"I think I can read another few pages before Mr. LeMaux arrives for my lessons."

"Very wise decision." Cart smiled to show his approval. "If you think you are in the correct mindset for lessons today."

He couldn't help voicing his concern for her after her encounter the night before.

"Oh, I was reading of pirates and treasure hunters," she gushed. "I was at the most exciting point in the story—that was the only reason I screeched at the sight of the intruder."

"Ah, well, you know I will not let any such thing take place again."

"Of course not, Cart," she said with a smile and wink. "But Momma may not be as certain."

"I do not need her to believe me as long as you trust me to keep you safe," he replied. He'd vowed to never allow anyone to take advantage of his family again—it was a promise he took seriously. "You believe me. Right, Theo?"

"Incontrovertibly."

"Word of the day?" he asked.

"Nope, it was my new word of the day yesterday." She handed him the candle and slipped her book from below her arm. "Now, if you will excuse me. I have only a short few minutes to read."

"And I must depart for a meeting." Cart leaned down and pecked her cheek in brotherly affection. "Scamper off now and enjoy your time before Mr. LeMaux arrives. Will you dine with me this evening, Lady Theodora?"

"Only if fish soup is not on the menu." She wrinkled her nose in disgust at their mother's favorite dish.

"I can assure you, I smelled pheasant cooking in the kitchen," he confided. "Maybe Mother will be having her dinner with friends this evening."

"I do hope we are ever so lucky."

"We will always be lucky as long as we stick together." He felt the truth of his words deep in his soul. "Now, do not let your stodgy, old brother keep you from your endeavors."

With a flip of her plaits, Theo took off to the stairs, her soft footfalls making no sound as she climbed.

Cart only hoped Lord Gunther was as silent at hearing the news of his still-missing vase.

Chapter Three

Jude looked over the expanse of the lawn before her, dotted with colored blankets spanning the entire rainbow. A light, warm breeze pulled at the edges of the coverings where they lay on the finely trimmed lawn. The same small gusts played with Jude's hair and the hem of her long skirt as she, Sam, and Lady Chastain stepped around picnic arrangements in search of Lady Haversham, their hostess for the day.

Women and gentlemen of varying social status blended and shifted between pairings, the jovial mood of the day reaching as far as the eye could see.

"Do hurry," Sam said, tugging on Jude's arm in an attempt to pull her closer to a grouping of finely dressed gentlemen. "There are many people I seek to make an acquaintance with."

Lady Chastain, Ellie to her close friends, shook her head at Sam's insistence. "Samantha, I was given strict instructions to keep a close watch on the pair of you."

37

"Then come with us." Sam turned her pleading stare on the younger woman, newly married only a short time before. "We cannot get into too much trouble under your watchful eye."

"Marce was very firm when she finally agreed to allow you both to attend Lady Haversham's garden party with me." The woman had matured much since marrying Lord Chastain, once a mere stable hand. No longer was she the girl with unruly, fiery red hair who favored a turn at pickpocketing strangers. Now, she wore her hair securely bound atop her head and wore dresses of the finest muslin and satin prints, compliments of her brother-in-law's shipping imports. "Besides, it is most improper to address a gentleman before the suitable introductions have been made."

Jude didn't mind wandering aimlessly through the crowd for the entire afternoon. She was lucky to be allowed out of Craven House at all. She'd expected her eldest sister to keep her locked away for a fortnight after Marce had collected Jude from the night watchman the morning before. However, when Ellie had arrived and begged for Jude and Sam to accompany her to the party, Marce had relented.

"Do you not know any of these men?" Sam implored.

Ellie eyed the group, most no older than Sam and Jude. "I think I may have met the tall one on occasion, but heavens, I do not know his name."

At that moment, one of the men looked in their direction, noticed them staring, and elbowed his friend. Both turned wide grins on the trio, but none ventured toward them.

"At least, someone has a bit of sense," Jude commented. "They know the height of indecorum it is and the gossip it would cause, to attend us without an introduction."

"I thought Lady Haversham favored casual gatherings and open conversations." Sam released Jude's arm and gave a quick wave to the men. "It cannot hurt overly much to stop and say hello. Or maybe I can discreetly drop my handkerchief and they will chivalrously rescue it from the ground and return it."

Ellie snorted and quickly covered her mouth at the unladylike sound.

"I enjoyed your company more before you turned all matronly," Sam prodded, hoping to draw out Ellie's fiery temper. "What next? You will be scolding young women for dancing too close at Almacks?"

Jude let out a laugh, its melodious sound echoing over the crowd, drawing a few stares.

"All I am asking is for you to await Alex's arrival," Ellie said. "He will be more than happy to make introductions to men of a proper caliber."

"Oh, poppycock." Sam lifted the hem of her gown off the ground and stepped around a couple enjoying tiny sandwiches on a lavender blanket. "Maybe we should have invited Payton along. At least she is still a sport from time to time. I suppose I will need to wander about until I meet a gentleman I've been properly introduced to before."

Jude followed Sam's gaze as she surveyed the gathering, lingering on a certain gentleman.

She narrowed her eyes to make out the man's features.

"Oh, there is my dear husband now," Ellie fairly sang. "Do excuse me for a moment. He is speaking with Lady Archiberry—I must rescue him. Do not go far, I will only be a moment, and then we will focus our efforts on introductions."

"Of course," Jude said as the woman moved to her husband's side.

Sam still stared at the older gentleman about thirty feet away, where he spoke with another man.

"I think that is Lord Asherton." Sam stood on her tiptoes as a pair of tall men blocked their view. "Do you see him?"

Jude had had quite enough of Lord Asherton—and any purported Bible leaves in his possession—after spending a night locked in a room due to being caught—both inside and outside his home. She'd never actually made the man's acquaintance, nor did she favor a meeting this day.

"Come, I have much to speak with him about."

"Sam, it is not safe," Jude said, not moving as her sister pulled her arm. "I was at his home not long ago. It was a fool's errand. He was likely toying with you. He owns no such valuables as he said."

"You know I want answers as much as you do," Sam encouraged.

"No." Jude shook her head, the ringlets framing her face bobbing with the movement. "I do not need, nor do I want answers. I want distance from the man. Let me remind you, a child within his home saw me."

"There—"

"Listen to what I am saying, Sam," Jude begged. "My cap fell to the floor; my auburn hair was exposed. The girl had a candle blazing, its glow reached me. She saw me. She was likely the one who described me to the butler, who called the night watchman. I will not venture forth. And in case you have forgotten, we are identical. Suspicion may be cast upon you, just as easily as me."

"I do not relish giving up," Sam said. "He is very clearly an unmarried man. He has been lavishing attention on me for weeks now. I am certain if a child were living in his home, he would have shared that information."

"Have you stopped to think he is not enamored with you?" Jude asked, striking the one area that Sam was most sensitive about. "Besides, he danced with several ladies the other night."

"I do not believe it." Sam's tone deepened as she spoke, her smoky voice catching the attention of the long-forgotten group of men. "He cares for me."

"Truly?" Jude whispered. "Do you care for him or only his valuables?"

"That is neither here nor there. Oh, look, he is coming this way."

Sam turned a triumphant smile her way as if to say she'd won, that Asherton was, indeed, attracted to her charms.

Jude wasn't so certain that was a prize her sister truthfully wanted to win.

They both smiled as Lord Asherton arrived, his cohort left behind to take up conversation with another man.

"Good day, Miss Samantha," he hailed, looking between the twins. His tentative smile told Jude he hoped one of the women before him would accept his greeting and end the awkward silence his unsure comments had started.

But both remained silent—a game Jude had once enjoyed, though now found tedious.

Jude had nothing to say, but Sam—for all her languishing over the man's affections—should have something to say in greeting.

Lord Asherton shifted his weight from foot to foot, waiting on Sam to out herself.

Finally, her twin put the man out of his misery. "My lord," she replied, giving him a quick curtsey. "It is a lovely day, is it not?"

The man grinned, showing off his slightly uneven teeth, no doubt something Sam would boast about finding endearing. "That it is, Miss Samantha. I do hope I find you…and your sister,"—he added as if in afterthought, though it was more likely he didn't remember Jude's name—"in good health."

"You do, my lord." Sam placed her palm at Jude's back. "May I introduce my dear sister, Miss Judith Pengarden."

Asherton bowed, certainly more than was deserving for two women lacking any substantial link to nobility. "It is a pleasure to make your acquaintance. Miss Samantha speaks fondly of you," he said conspiratorially as if Jude should be shocked.

"Odd that."

"Why, may I ask?" he asked.

"I fear my dear sister has never mentioned your name." For her snide words, Jude received a quick elbow to her ribs. "But, that is to be forgiven as she is overwhelmed by the grandness of her first London season."

"I am certain I have mentioned dear Lord Asherton on many occasions," Sam retorted with a smile of apology. "Maybe it is my youngest sibling who I've been regaling with stories of your dashing presence, my lord."

"It must be," Jude continued. "Or maybe it *was* I. Is Lord Asherton the man with the loving young child living with him?"

Sam forced a grin at her sister's cunning.

"Oh, certainly not," he huffed. "No children here. I have yet to take a woman as wife."

"No nieces or young cousins in residence?" Jude continued to prod.

"Only child, I am afraid," he confessed. "Though I am not opposed to a large family."

A puzzled expression crossed Sam's face at the man's words. Jude hadn't the faintest idea what had gone wrong. "Oh, then I must be mistaken."

"Maybe you are overcome by the season, as well, Miss Judith." The man tried to gloss over her previous words. "One meets many people while in society and even I, who've been about town for many years, find it hard to remember names, faces, and associations."

At his comment, Jude realized the man was, in reality, twice their age. Most men of his advanced years were settled with a family. However, Lord Asherton remained unwed. Curious, that.

"Oh, Samantha, Lady Chastain is waving for us," Jude said in distraction. "I believe she is ready for us to join her once more."

"Yes, I see that. Do excuse us, Lord Asherton."

"It was lovely to meet you," Jude said.

"Of course, Miss Samantha." He nodded. "Miss Judith. I do hope to see you about town soon. I would greatly enjoy a dance with both of you."

"You are too kind." Jude smiled reassuringly at the older man. "We shall both endeavor to save a place for you on our dance cards."

"Of course, my lord," Sam said with little remaining interest. "It was lovely to see you today. Have a fair afternoon."

After a quick curtsey, Sam and Jude started toward Ellie where she stood at her husband's side before veering off to an area unpopulated with partygoers.

"Did you send me into the wrong house?" Jude whispered vehemently. "Tell me you did not."

"I most undoubtedly did not do it on purpose."

"Nevertheless, somehow, you did," Jude seethed. "I should wring your neck."

"But you shall not," Sam smirked, knowing her sister would not risk embarrassing their hostess or Lady Chastain by acting in an unfashionable manner for all to witness. "You cannot be vexed with me. It was an innocent mistake."

It was certainly a mistake. But innocent? Jude wasn't so sure.

If things were not as dire as they were, Jude could have continued to rely on her eldest sister to provide for them, but something had changed in previous years. Marce continued to appear exhausted and strained. More women had sought out Craven House for help—and they never turned any person in need away. Mouths were multiplying faster than coin was made.

Marce had even gone so far as to sell her more fashionable dresses.

And then the letters of delinquency had started arriving. She'd tried to broach the subject with her family, but had been immediately silenced by her eldest sister each time. The bills and expenses of Craven House should not weigh on her, Sam, and Payton, Marce had insisted over and over.

And so, Jude and Sam had taken matters into their own hands, employing Jude's vast knowledge and passion for art and other rarities.

"I cannot believe I was in the wrong house the entire time," Jude sighed. "I could have been discovered the moment I entered. Then what would have become of me?"

Sam only stared, wisely keeping silent.

"No need to answer me. It does not take much pondering to know I would be thrown in the gaol, forgotten."

"Dear sister." Sam grasped her hands. "I will never allow such a fate to befall you—and if, heaven forbid, anything amiss were to happen, I would fight for you…I wouldn't let anything happen."

Jude wished that were true; that if they were ever caught, they could disentangle themselves from the troubles they'd put themselves in. She never wanted to put herself at risk again.

"Let us not speak of this further." Sam motioned over Jude's shoulder to where a pair of men made their way from the main house toward the garden party. "There will be many hours for us to figure where we went wrong."

With a closer look, Jude realized the man looked familiar to her, though she could not place from where she knew him. Possibly, they'd once danced at a ball or passed one another in the park. His brown hair fell over one eye, and he dressed as a workingman, certainly not a lord of any standing, though his steps were sure and confident. His hands were stuffed deeply in his trouser pockets as he and his associate discussed something of import, judging from the serious expression his face carried.

"Does that man look familiar?" she asked Sam. "Do not let them see you stare."

"I am unsure." Sam's brow furrowed pensively. "He is a bit older than I prefer—though possibly, he is a friend of an acquaintance…"

"Not the elderly man," Jude corrected. "His companion."

"Him?" Sam tilted her head and squinted. "I am fairly certain I have never seen the man before—or if we attended a function with him, I would not notice. He's dressed like a shopkeeper."

The men were within a few feet of them now, their conversation drifting on the breeze.

"…no. It is in bad form to assume a piece can be bought if enough money is proffered," the gentleman insisted to the older man. "I certainly can act on your behalf to make an offer for the piece, but aside from that, it is up to Mr. Honeycomb if he seeks to part with it."

The men grew closer still, as if their discussion was so intense that neither noticed Jude or her sister in their path. They walked slowly but with purpose, their heads slightly lowered.

Jude had certainly seen the man before; his brown hair, a bit too long for the standard, his dress not that of a lord but more a man of business…

"But you think he will look favorably upon my offer?" the older man asked.

Before Jude could stop her, Sam stepped from her side—directly into the men's paths and smiled, a sly upturn of the corner of her lips. Anyone who knew her sister—or other marriage-minded females—would see the devious bent in her stare.

"Samantha," Jude hissed in warning, but she was too late to deter her twin from whatever course she'd set out on.

"Oh, kind gentlemen," Sam gushed, coming to a stop mere inches from the men, stopping their progress toward the garden party. "I do apologize for nearly stumbling into you both. My sister and I"—she motioned to Jude standing a few feet away—"were on our way to…well, it's no matter where we were going."

Sam smiled coyly at the pair.

The brown-haired man seemed anxious to continue on their way—and with their discussion—however, the elderly man took Sam in from head to toe and back again, pausing briefly to admire the woman's snug-fitting bodice. He stood a bit taller at the sight of Jude and her sister. This was not an uncommon reaction when one—or both of them—were seen in public.

Identical in every way but their voice, Sam and Jude were taller than most women of their acquaintance with matching swanlike necks and long, auburn tresses. They sported green eyes that Marce said drew people to them, a mirror into a meadow after a rainstorm.

"My ladies," the older man said. "It is likely our fault our paths nearly collided. I am Lord Barton." He gave them a deep bow, bending at his portly waist with exaggerated action. "And this is Lord Cartwright, a dear friend."

Lord Cartwright turned an odd look at Barton as if he'd never met the man.

Jude took the time to take in the younger man's form; tall, with wide shoulders, but certainly not overly agile in the sense of a sportsman.

"I am Miss Samantha Pengarden," Sam said, dipping into a curtsey. "And this is my *dear* sister, Miss Judith." She used the same expression Barton had—and Jude was tempted to give her the same puzzled look Lord Cartwright had given the older man.

She'd been wrong about the man. He dressed the part of a man of business but held a title. He did not hold himself like many of the arrogant society men she'd met during her short time following her introduction to society. He more mirrored the image of her brother, Lord Garrett, and his set of friends—unpretentious, welcoming, and pleasant.

"It is a pleasure to make your acquaintance," Lord Cartwright offered reluctantly. It was as if Sam's charms and sultry tone went unnoticed by him. Nervously, he continued, "As Lord Barton stated, we offer our apologies for stumbling into your way. Rude, very rude, indeed. Do have a pleasant stroll."

Lord Cartwright looked to Barton, clearly expecting him to lower his head and continue with their discussion as they joined the garden party farther down the lawn, but the older man had yet to remove his watchful gaze from Sam.

Though he could hardly be blamed as Jude watched her twin preen before the man. She even went so far as to bat her lashes before turning her gaze to the ground as if a bout of shyness overtook her.

"Miss….Miss…Samantha." Barton's stare held at Sam's bosom for a moment longer than proper before he returned to his senses—realizing he stood not far from a garden party and his gaze was highly inappropriate. "May I offer to escort you for a turnabout the party?" He looked to Jude quickly, almost seeking her approval. "I shall return her to your care presently, Miss Judith."

Any gentleman worth his weight in salt should comprehend that requesting the presence of a lady, at the expense of leaving her sister without company, was in bad form, but the man was clearly smitten—as most men tended to be. From Sam's smile, he'd done exactly as she'd hoped.

"Do not fret," Jude attempted to reassure the man. "Lady Chastain, my dearest friend, is yonder. I shall seek her out."

"Allow Lord Cartwright to accompany you," Barton insisted, holding out his arm for Sam to take—to the other lord's extreme dismay. "See, now everything is solved. I will take Miss Samantha for a quick walk while Cart returns you safely to Lady Chastain, Miss Judith." The man seemed pleased with the plan he'd come up with, his toothy grin evidence of the fact. "What say you, Cart?"

Jude took in the man's panicked expression from the corner of her eye and wanted to laugh. Though she and Sam were identical, she knew she couldn't compare to her sister's allure, but neither was she atrocious. However, it seemed Lord Cartwright, Cart as Lord

Barton had called him, would rather be anywhere *but* where he currently stood.

"I do have much work—"

"Take a moment, my man," Barton chuckled, setting his free hand on Sam's where it rested on his arm. "It would be the height of boorishness to not enjoy Lady Haversham's party. There are many years ahead of you for work."

Jude knew the moment Lord Cartwright gave in; his shoulders slumped and he stepped closer to her.

"Of course, I would be honored to escort you to your friend's side."

His tone said he would be honored to do anything but spend one minute more in her company. Maybe he frequented Craven House and realized her relation to *the* Madame Marce; though she and her sisters were not permitted anywhere near the common rooms while her sister was hosting card games—to Payton's grave disappointment. She was not allowed to frequent the gaming hells or any card room, for that matter.

"I would not want to inconvenience you." Jude provided Lord Cartwright a means to escape the responsibility forced upon him by Barton. "I do understand you are busy—and likely have another you are eager to meet."

Jude wasn't sure why she made the comment. She surely did not care if Cartwright had escorted another lady. Her interest was only piqued as she searched her memories for when they'd met previously, though he gave no indication of a previous acquaintance.

Sam leaned in under the guise of a peck on the cheek and whispered, "I will learn more about what treasures Barton is hiding." Returning to Barton's side,

Sam gave a small wave and they started off. Her twin's throaty laughter carried on the breeze as the couple jested about something.

Lord Cartwright cleared his throat, drawing Jude's attention away from the departing pair, but he remained silent.

It was almost enough for her to feel sorry for the man, obviously uncomfortable with the task ahead of him—or possibly it was she who made him act in such an odd manner.

His avoidance of her stare gave her time to assess him once more. He was quite handsome, in an academic fashion. It appeared his skin rarely saw the heat of day. However, his hair was so light a brown, it was as if he were stained daily by the sun. He was tall, but not overly broad, leading Jude to believe his pursuits lie with business—or possibly education. She could not recollect where she'd seen the man before.

"Lord Cartwright—"

"Cart," he cut off her words. At her puzzled expression, he continued. "My friends call me Cart."

"Are we friends, my lord?" she asked, genuinely hoping the answer was yes.

"If we were not friends, then our continued presence in one another's company may be viewed as less than appropriate. Would you not agree?" His eyebrow lifted in question as he made eye contact with her for what felt like the first time. His words sounded like he was reciting them from a debutante's book of social decorum.

Chapter Four

Miss Judith's eyes rounded and her shoulders tensed in surprise at his mention of their precarious position, that of them being alone—many yards from the closest guests.

It had taken Cart only moments to realize when he'd seen the women before. Namely, where he'd seen her. At first, he was uncertain which twin he'd encountered outside the watchman's residence, but her airy voice gave her away. He prided himself on noticing the most subtle differences in items, which translated seamlessly to people. If Cart were able to ascertain the period in which a painting was commissioned and completed, then the lilt to a woman's voice should be all that much simpler.

It was what he'd dedicated his life to thus far. A profession that brought in coin to pay all the necessary notes coming in from the various vendors and shops his estate did business with.

Cart wanted nothing more than to know her reasoning for being at that house. He suspected she found him familiar, as well, though maybe she hadn't put all the pieces together as yet.

However, she quickly recovered with a timid smile. "Maybe we should venture back to the gathering?"

It was exactly what he should want, so why did his heart sink a notch at her suggestion?

He was here for business—namely, Lord Barton had sent a summons to attend him at Lady Haversham's garden party to discuss an upcoming acquisition the man hoped to purchase. A meeting at either man's townhouse would have been much preferred to a social gathering. However, Cart was in need of funds, and gaining a position as Barton's representative in the purchase of the piece meant a hefty payout for him.

After the recent debacle at his home, he would be lying if he didn't acknowledge it suited him well to be away from the residence—especially removed from his mother—for a few hours, even if he thought the time wasted on socializing when he could be reading in his study or strategizing his next move in locating his uncle and the possessions he'd removed from the Cartwright home. A stab of regret hit him at the thought. So much had gone on without him being any the wiser. A man who he'd trusted—who his father had held in the highest regard—had taken so much from the Cartwright estate.

Belatedly, Cart realized he hadn't answered Miss Judith's suggestion, nor had either of them moved since Barton fled with Miss Samantha. They stood before one another, strangers, yet unlike at the several other gatherings he'd attended since his return to town, it was not an awkward situation. Or, at least, not to Cart.

"May I escort you around the lake, Miss Judith?" he ventured. Her response meant much to him, though he told himself it was only to learn more about her presence at the watchman's residence than anything to do with the physical. She was a stunning creature, however. She was far more alluring than her twin, whose husky voice seemed a bit false to Cart.

"Jude."

"Pardon?"

"My family—and friends—call me Jude…short for Judith," she rushed. "I mean, when you have a house teeming with people, it is easier to—" she paused, taking in a deep breath. "Oh, I am certain you are unconcerned with such things."

Cart grinned. Something he didn't remember doing recently, except for possibly at Theo's antics. "Jude," he mumbled, trying the moniker out loud. "It is a lovely name, meaning praise."

And it filled him with a bit more confidence to know she was as edgy with this interaction as he.

The smile left his face as she eyed him closely. Why he always felt the need to fill conversations with fact and tidbits of knowledge, Cart would never know. It was just that he was far more comfortable conversing about all things academic and intellectual. His uncle used to tease if he hadn't been born to the Earldom, then he would have surely retired to a monastery to live the life of a studious hermit, confident in a vow of silence, which made casual discourse unnecessary.

"Are you agreeable to a stroll?" he asked again. His uncle had been gravely mistaken. Cart was immensely amenable to conversation, as long as it served a purpose. In this case, it communicated important information. Most specifically, she'd been at the home of a night watchman in the early morning hours. She'd been properly accompanied if he remembered correctly. A petite blonde and a gentleman not much older than Cart had ushered her into a waiting carriage.

He'd been a bit preoccupied at that moment. Therefore, Cart couldn't assess if the man were possibly her intended—or a relation.

Not that it mattered in the slightest.

It was only a short stroll, visible to the nearly one hundred guests milling about. Then she would be returned to her sister and friend, and Cart would forget about the entire encounter—his questions answered.

His interest in her did not signify any lasting impression on him or his life. Not that he was educated in this form of personal connection with another of the opposite sex.

With that realization, Cart lifted an eyebrow in query. "What say you, Miss Jude?"

The question seemed to sit well with her. She nodded before taking his arm. "Please, simply Jude, my lord." A splash of color crept up her cheeks as if she were not accustomed to requesting someone call her by such an informal name.

Her inviting smile sent a twinge of unease through him. Certainly she understood his offer of a stroll was just that—a proposal to spend a few moments in each other's company because it fell in line with society's expectations in this situation.

They began their walk, Cart taking immediate notice of Jude's long stride. He was not required to slow his pace for her to keep up with his footfalls. Understandably, this was one thing that irked him about women; they were either too short or their gown choice restricted their movements. Either way, this cost Cart precious moments that could be better spent in other ways.

However, at this moment, he wished they did walk a bit slower. Her hip grazed his every few steps and her long skirt moved about both their legs as they ambled. Her fingers held his arm more securely than was customary. He wondered how her hand, deprived of her soft satin glove, would feel against his skin—assuredly soft and warm—but would her fingers be stained by ink from letter writing or callused from hard work? It would be appropriate to her position that they be long and free of anything more damaging than the prick of a needle from her needlepoint.

He was tempted to request that she remove her glove to ascertain if his theory was correct. However, Cart kept his mouth shut. His lips were pressed into a firm line to keep from spouting facts of nonsense, focusing on identifying the shrubs that lined their path, many common varieties mixed with one another.

Conversely, her fragrance cut through his internal musings—it made him envision hot summer days and cold winter nights all at the same time. A cool glass of lemon water paired with a warm apple dessert. The duo should never be put together, logically; however, they worked well for her. Never would he combine the scents or flavors, though they would now be forever combined and ingrained in his mind.

Cart pondered leaning a fraction more in her direction to see if the scent grew stronger—maybe it clung to her hair, only becoming more pronounced as the slight wind tussled her red locks.

"My lord, are you well?"

Had she spoken to him while he'd been daydreaming of smelling her hair? Something was certainly amiss with him, but unwell, he was not.

"My apologies," he recovered. "Thought I spotted an acquaintance."

"If I am keeping you from something—or someone..." she added, pulling away to look at him. "My dear friend is not far. I can return to her."

Her stare seemed to challenge him, but to what purpose, Cart hadn't a clue. Maybe to admit there were more pressing matters that needed his attention, or that she wished him to call off on his invitation, enabling her to return to her own company.

Any gentleman worth his title would take her indication and allow the woman her freedom.

"Certainly not, Miss Jude. My presence here was at Lord Barton's behest. And currently"—he nodded toward the pond not far from where they stood where Miss Samantha and Lord Barton walked—"he is otherwise engaged. This is beneficial for both of us, as I can accompany you for a time and you will not be without company until your sister returns."

She laughed nervously, a light, musical sound. "I have said I am not without proper company, Lord Cartwright, neither am I a damsel in distress."

"I did not mean to insinuate that..." Cart was unsure he intended to imply anything at all, only pointing out that the pair found themselves alone at the same time. "I only meant that it must not be a coincidence we are both here and our companions have deserted us."

Out loud it did appear he could have insinuated something entirely different.

Jude began to walk again, leaving him uncertain if she understood his explanation or only sought to complete their stroll in a decorous manner befitting a debutante.

"What business do you have with Lord Barton?" She kept her gaze focused demurely on the ground before them. "Not that I mean to pry, my lord."

Could it be she was interested in him outside of a casual stroll?

"I am a collector." He peered out the side of his eye, gauging her reaction to his words. His questions for her were forgotten as a subject far more interesting to Cart arose. When she gave no response, he continued, "An amateur collector at best. I collect items of historical import."

Finally, she nodded and Cart was thankful she seemed a chit with some semblance of smarts about her. Too many evenings—when he'd been unable to come up with a compelling enough reason to call off—he was trapped by his mother and made to occupy her friends' daughters. Simpering, dull, and without knowledge of any current or historical references, though he surmised Jude would not be the same...although she'd said little to dissuade the thought that she'd been overly interested in his chosen profession.

"Often, I am called upon to give credit to a piece or locate an antiquity someone seeks to obtain." He ventured another sidelong look at her to confirm she wasn't tempted to doze off at their topic of conversation.

But to his astonishment, she asked, "By historical pieces, do you mean paintings, pottery, and ancient books?" Her hold on his arm tightened with each word, as if they thrilled her as much as they did him.

"Why, yes." His words came a little too eager to his own ears. "It is a worthwhile position that not many Londoners find curious." He was giving her another opportunity to withdraw from their acquaintance.

"There are many who would not know an antiquity's valuable if it grew a mouth and told them itself." Her interest was more than Cart could have asked for—and certainly more than he'd garnered from anyone outside other collectors and his younger sibling, Theo. Even his mother was highly skeptical. "What is your most prized acquisition?"

Cart pondered the thought as they reached the water's edge and started on the narrow path that would lead them full circle about the body of water and back to the far side of the garden party. "I would think my most prized piece is a rug said to have lain on the floor in a tenth-century Buddhist temple."

"Fascinating."

"Do you think so?" he asked, hard-pressed to believe any enthusiasm on her part. She was a woman of the *ton*, unaccustomed to seeing anything used and old as having any meaning or significance. If a dress were worn over a handful of occasions, it was to be cast out with the dishwater. "My mother would be happy to have the rug moved to the stables."

She laughed, not the nervous, singsong chuckle from before, but rather a sound that radiated from deep within her.

Belatedly, he realized he'd confessed to living with his mother.

Did sophisticated women frown upon men who resided in the same household as their female relatives? He hadn't the coin to search out a bachelor's residence, nor should that be necessary with his father having long since passed.

They continued in silence, walking along the hard-packed dirt path. The knee-high vegetation snagged at Jude's long skirt as shrieks of laughter came from behind them. The warm sun beat upon his face; a sensation he was unaccustomed to as he rarely sought outdoor physical activities.

Cart racked his mind for another thread of exchange, preferably one that did not include his mother. His conversation skills were indeed rusty—it might benefit him greatly to seek out Theo or her tutor for a lesson in idle chitchat. Surely, an afternoon's worth of instruction would do the trick. Unfortunately, it would not help him make it through this party without highly embarrassing himself.

Come now, he was an Eton educated man—though he'd been asked to leave his studies just shy of receiving his certificate due to non-payment of his tuition—he should be more than successful at entertaining a woman for the time it took to walk the circumference of a small pond.

By his calculations, using this stride length, it should take approximately—

"Lord Cartwright," she asked, turning a serious expression on him. "May I ask you a question?"

Cart nodded, pushing arithmetic from his thoughts.

"Have we met before?" She looked to him with questioning eyes. "It is only that when we happened upon you and Lord Barton, it was as if I had seen you before."

"Ah, well," he mumbled. "I am—"

Quick as lightning, Cart felt his boot snag on something and his balance shifted. He released Jude's arm, assessing his trajectory and speed of motion. His arms swung wildly in the air, attempting to regain his balance. However, Cart already knew it was pointless and would only serve to hurt his arm when he eventually hit the ground or worse, smashed into Jude.

Still, Cart was not prepared for the most humiliating moment of his life, to date.

One second he was trying to pull his hooked boot free and the next, water rushed over his head as he fell, submerging his entire upper body in the pond. His trouser-covered legs and boots betrayed him, refusing to follow the rest of him into the water, his knees landing in the mud bordering the once placid water.

"My lord!" Miss Jude frantically called, her words distorted to his ears. He felt a tug at his pant leg. The utter humiliation was enough to keep him below the water's surface until he perished, or everyone departed the party. "Cart, have you been injured overmuch?"

Cart moved to push himself up and above the water, his hands sinking in the muddy pond bottom. "Only my pride, Miss Jude," he answered, still praying the water's floor would open and swallow him whole.

Unfortunately, no such good luck was bestowed on him by the powers that be.

In fact, it sounded as if the powers that be were laughing hysterically at his major social faux pas. Turning his head toward the sound, Cart spied the gathering of people near the party, watching him with amusement as Lord Barton and Miss Samantha rushed to Jude's side.

"My poor dear," Lord Barton soothed a likely frazzled and mortified Jude. "I must apologize for Lord Cartwright's abysmal behavior."

Cart's abysmal behavior, he wanted to shout in annoyance.

And shouldn't the man be assisting Cart from the murky water instead of sidling up to Jude?

On principle alone, Cart felt the immense urge to turn away Lord Barton's request for representation and acquire the antiquity the old man sought for his own collection. If Cart had the funds required for the purchase, he would most certainly do just that—and burn the thing before Barton's eyes.

"No one fret," Cart said, pushing himself to his knees in the sludge and reaching behind him to untangle his boot. "I fear I have beaten all the odds and have survived."

"Cart—err, Lord Cartwright," Jude corrected quickly. "Do allow me to help you regain your feet."

He could hear Barton chuckle—and instantly wanted to unleash his fist on the man's bulbous nose. What had come over him? Cart was not by any nature a man inclined to violent outbursts, nor had he ever so much as attended a boxing club or witnessed a brawl.

"Do step back, Miss Judith," Cart called over his shoulder. "It would be highly *abysmal* of me to splash mud on your fine slippers or gown. I do not seek to offend you any further with my behavior."

"Very wise, Cartwright." Barton worked hard to suppress his mirth, but Cart could still hear his soft laughter. "I will attend the Misses Samantha and Judith to their relations while you disentangle yourself and depart."

Cart sighed, still kneeling in the mud. "That is ever so kind of you, Barton. Again, my sincere apologies, ladies."

He couldn't even bring himself to face Jude. His cheeks were likely tinted red with embarrassment. All that crossed his mind was how infuriated his mother would be when she learned of his blunder—and he would never expect Jude to align herself, even in friendship, with a man as inept as he.

Chapter Five

Jude silently signaled Sam and Lord Barton to return to the gathering without her. When Sam gave her a questioning glance, Jude cocked her head in the direction of the other partygoers once more. Neither she nor her twin was adept at taking direction—or hints—from others or each other. Many twins Jude had read about seemed to live in a constant state of awareness in regards to their womb mate, but unfortunately for Jude, that was not the case with her and Sam.

Except for their identical appearance, they could not be more different.

"Bloody fool, ignorant scalawag," Lord Cartwright mumbled as he lifted his leg and applied his hands to his bent knee to stand. "Inconceivable, blundering mug. You should refrain from polite society, for certain."

Jude wanted to laugh at the entire debacle but kept her gaiety to herself. Normally, social excursions fell into either the tedious category or utter boredom, but

Lord Cartwright was a bout of fresh air—though her amusement at this expense was not something she would ever share with him. She did not seek to wound his pride further than it already was.

His every movement was calculated and precise—something Jude was unfamiliar with as she was prone to hasty decisions. Obvious from her part in stealing the vase from Lord Gunther's home.

But Cart's stumble was nothing deliberate and Jude felt a measure of responsibility for his fall. She'd been distracting him, though if she were truthful, he had distracted her just as fully. His reluctant smiles and odd choice of topics had interested her greatly. That he looked the perfect gentleman next to her a boon. He did not speak of trivial things to appease her supposedly delicate sensibilities.

Lord Cartwright gained his feet and ran his hands down his trousers to remove some of the filth that clung to the material, his head hung in disgrace.

"If I traverse the edge of the pond and duck behind the trees bordering the property, I can escape without further incident," he continued to talk to himself, fully unaware of her presence on the shore. "But then how will I journey home? I arrived with Barton. Maybe a hackney? How does one gain the attention of one?"

Lord Cartwright continued to work through his dilemma audibly, something Jude had never witnessed thus. Nevertheless, she could certainly see the benefit to puzzling through one's problems aloud.

"Lord Cartwright?" Jude hated to disturb him or humiliate him further by alerting him to her presence. "My family carriage is in the drive. I can have my coachman deliver you home and then return for my sister and me."

"Jude." He turned to face her, heat creeping up his neck. "You should attend your sister…return to the gathering…enjoy your afternoon."

She should be doing all those things, yet, Jude could not abandon Lord Cartwright to sulk out of Lady Haversham's gardens. A quick glance over her shoulder told her the others had gone back to the festivities, Lord Cartwright's stumble into the pond forgotten for the moment—likely to be retold over evening meals in numerous households across London.

Instead of fleeing, Jude offered a warm smile and her arm—she only wished she was in the habit of carrying a towel with her. "I do not believe we are finished with our stroll, my lord." When he stared at her, his mouth gaping open, she continued, "Please allow me to accompany you to my carriage. My coachman will make sure you arrive home safely, without any further…" Her words trailed off, at a loss for what to say. "…incident."

"I am quite capable of securing transport home," he countered. "I am no damsel in distress."

Jude laughed at his twist of her previous words. "I think we have both established we are not helpless creatures." She hoped his wounded sensibility would improve with a bit of coaxing. "Same as we can agree that you requested my company for a stroll, not out of any obligation or male possessiveness, but because we might enjoy one another's companionship." He nodded. "This is much the same. I do not feel any obligation to assist you in departing Lady Haversham's gathering—I believe we have enjoyed our short stroll and wish it not to end on a sour note."

And Jude desperately wanted to learn more about his position as a collector—namely, if he or one of his associates would be interested in the vase. Her day had taken a grand turn by making his acquaintance; a new home for the vase was possibly on the near horizon, and money to add to the Craven House coffers. Lord Cartwright had made it clear that he was an amateur collector, which boded well for her and Sam. It was possible Cart had no previous knowledge of the vase's origins—or its current status as stolen.

"Are you certain you seek to be seen with me"—he gestured toward his soiled attire—"in this condition? I have it on good account that a woman's status in society is based on her every decision, both favorable and unfavorable. I would never wish a bad light to be cast on you or Miss Samantha."

Again with his verbiage mirroring a lady's guide to modesty.

"Do you always fret so much, my lord?" Jude didn't bother to dampen her grin. "I can compile a list of things far more worrisome than me being spotted in your company. Specifically, what your valet will say when he sees how you've fairly ruined your jacket and breeches. He will likely need hours to repair the damage done to your boots alone."

A startled expression covered Cartwright's face and he looked down at his once finely pressed linen shirt, his artfully tied neckcloth now limp about his neck.

Jude could only describe his look as utter and complete horror at the sight of himself. Water still dripped from his coattails and his hair stuck out in every direction.

"I jest with you, my lord," Jude teased. "But I do suggest we continue on our path, which will eventually lead to the front drive—and my family's carriage. I will make any excuses you wish as to your hurried departure."

"I am not usually such a wreck," he replied to her offer. "It is simply—"

"There is no need for you to explain yourself to me." Though Jude found herself wanting to know more about him, curious as he was with his odd behavior. "But if you wish, you may as we continue our walk." Jude set her hand on his wet coat arm and stepped back on the path, giving him little option but to follow her lead—or appear the ungentlemanly lord who refused her.

She didn't know much about the man next to her, but she did get the impression he would never insult someone so blatantly. And true to her assessment, he fell into step next to her. He did not, however, walk as closely as before, more than likely out of fear of soiling her skirt.

They strolled in silence until they reached the far side of the pond where they could continue a straight path and reach the front drive or continue along the water's edge and return to the gathering beyond. Jude held back and allowed Lord Cartwright the choice.

Would he feel obligated to return to the party, or accept Jude's offer of transport?

Ironically, he settled on neither as he stopped and faced her, taking a step closer to her and removing her hand from his moist sleeve. "It has been lovely making your acquaintance."

"And yours, my lord," she said with a tentative smile, unsure what was to happen next.

"I hope it is not too forward of me to ask, but..."

"Anything between friends can be overlooked." Her words were meant to encourage him to speak, but it only made him take a step back as he shifted nervously before her. "Cart?"

He moved his gaze from over her shoulder to meet Jude's stare. "Please tell me if you find this unacceptable." He paused again, gathering his thoughts—and possibly his bravado. "May I call on you at some future date?"

Future date... Jude wanted to ask exactly when that date would be.

Not only did she see potential for getting rid of that blasted vase and an end to her and Sam's outlandish notions, but—if she were completely honest—Jude had enjoyed their short acquaintance immensely. There was more to Lord Cartwright than anyone would ever assume. The method with which Lord Barton had dismissed him was unjust and insulting, to say the least. Though, inviting Cartwright into Craven House, her home and sanctuary, was a daunting prospect.

How did one tell a lord in good standing that she lived in a former bordello? That her mother, God rest her soul, had been the proprietor of London's finest gentlemen's house...and that many in the *ton* still believed the property housed all sorts of sordid activities, even though that hadn't been true in many years?

No, Jude desperately wanted to know more about Lord Cartwright, but at the expense of him learning her family's past transgressions... Jude was unsure. Many did not look favorably on Craven House's history.

He continued to stare, his brow furrowing and his mouth clenched tightly, awaiting her response.

"I would like that, my lord." She only hoped the "future date" was sometime very soon. There was little doubt that if he found out where she lived and whom she called family, he would certainly change his mind about calling on her. Even with Lady Haversham sponsoring her and Sam before all of society, their chances of finding suitable men to offer for their hands was not stellar. With no dowry to speak of and little to verify their acceptable lineage, they would be thankful to have younger sons or men of the upper merchant class for husbands.

"I will bid you good day, Miss Jude." Lord Cartwright bowed, his damp hair falling before his eyes. With a quick toss of his head, the wayward lock flew to the side, and again she sensed that they'd crossed paths before. "Thank you for your offer of transport, but I will procure my own conveyance home."

Without another word, he turned on his heels and marched across the rolling lawn toward the house, his feet squeaking softly in his saturated boots.

# # #

As soon as Lord Cartwright rounded the side of Lord Haversham's townhouse, Jude hurried across the lawn to where Sam sat with Lady Chastain. Both women were dressed in the height of London fashion, yet their look of boredom showed. Their feet were tucked beneath their skirts as they rolled a small ball back and forth—likely left by Neill, Lady Haversham's son.

Lady Chastain stood when Jude lowered herself to the blanket.

"I will return shortly." Lady Chastain—Ellie—hurried off to where her sister stood speaking with several older matrons. She *must* be overcome with boredom to seek out such a group.

"What did you learn from Lord Barton?" Jude asked in a hushed tone, spying the elderly man nowhere.

A dour look crossed her twin's face, creating creases at the corners of her mouth and above her brows. "Nothing of import."

"That is good to hear because I do not plan to be a part of any future misdeeds. Things were too close last time and I cannot place myself—or you—in that position again. We must hope to sell the vase."

"I am sorry for deserting you with Lord Cartwright."

Jude saw no sense in gaining Sam's curiosity with regards to Jude's opinion of Cart. "Lord Cartwright is a nice enough man. The few minutes we spent together were far more illuminating than your time with Barton, I would assume."

"How so?" Sam straightened her shoulders.

"He is a collector," Jude confided, allowing Sam's brain to work to the same conclusion hers had during her stroll with Cart. "Amateur collector and antiquities broker."

"And you think he will be interested in the vase?" Her twin's mind worked fast. "Lord Barton said he is an earl…seems unlikely a man of his status has extensive knowledge of historical artifacts. He may be the correct man to approach."

"I agree," Jude said, leaning in closer to make sure their conversation was not overheard. "I have not seen him about town, nor does he appear overly acquainted. We can only hope he does not know of the vase's theft—or make the connection to us."

"You did not tell him of the vase already, did you?" Sam asked.

"Certainly not." Jude should be insulted that her sister would think her so daft as to speak out of turn. Besides, there had not been enough time before he'd taken his tumble into the pond. "He did inquire about calling on me at a 'later date'."

"Oh, that sounds promising." Sam raised a brow. "I was certain you'd have fled with Barton and me when given the chance, but there was obviously a reason you stayed to assist the clumsy man."

It was on the tip of Jude's tongue to chastise her sister for speaking thusly about Lord Cartwright—her twin's unfair assessment was hurtful. And Jude hadn't stayed behind to learn more about his interest in antiquities, or at least not entirely.

Lord Cartwright intrigued her.

A man of the *ton*; however, he showed all the signs of a highly intellectual man—educated at the finest universities in England, no doubt. Not only in the common areas of financial and estate management but also in history, arithmetic, and the sciences. She'd met many men in her short time moving through London's elite who claimed cleverness. But Jude found most lacking except in their inflated esteem of themselves.

Oh, and their need to align others to their delusions of grandeur.

Lord Cartwright was different; she'd known it from the moment they met.

Jude's stare drifted across the crowd to avoid Sam noticing her ire at her sister's insensitive comment, or deducing that there was a far greater reason she'd stayed with him after Lord Barton and Sam had fled the unsavory scene.

"If Lord Cartwright calls," Jude said flippantly, "I will question him further in regards to his fascination with antiquities. He may be precisely who we have been searching for."

"And if he suits, you will do what is necessary?" Sam probed.

It irritated Jude to no end that her family saw her as the weak twin—the one who'd buckle under any pressure. Even Sam thought this of her. Apparently, stealing into two households hadn't changed her sister's opinion in the slightest. If Marce, Payton, and Garrett knew all she'd done of her own volition, they'd certainly think differently. And if Sam saw herself as the leader between the pair, she was greatly mistaken.

"Have no fear, I am dedicated to my family and will do all that is required to secure the money Marce needs." Every word she said was true. There was nothing more important to Jude than relieving what pressure she could from her eldest sister, even if that meant putting herself in jeopardy of discovery.

Chapter Six

Cart reclined against the fraying seat of his dated carriage as his mother lectured Theo on her decorum when visiting her first modiste. Unbeknownst to him, there was a proper protocol females used when attending their modistes. There were measurements to take, orders to be recorded, and fabrics to be chosen. All he saw was any advantage earned from Lord Barton's acquisition flying quickly from his hands to pay for ladies' finery; gloves, slippers, bonnets, and gowns. It was unimaginable how little his coin covered in the way of women's necessities—and Theo had yet to be presented to society. What then? Formal ball gowns and headpieces? A proper phaeton to take rides in the park?

Cart would do well to keep his options open. Business with men such as Barton was not enjoyable on a personal level, but provided the funds necessary to keep his mother happy with enough stashed away for Theo's grand presentation to the *ton*.

Expense, expense, expense.

Everything translated to a figure—a shilling here or a pound there.

There was no end in sight, certainly.

It would be best if he kept his eyes closed as if he dozed as the carriage delivered them to Bond Street with its fashionable modistes, mercantiles, booksellers, and even hat shops with exquisitely constructed—and preposterously adorned—headpieces displayed in large glass windows to lure in London's finest members.

It was a way of life Cart was uninterested in: the opera, the musicales, the dinner soirees, the balls. Not a single one drew his interest...until his encounter with Miss Judith Pengarden. Jude.

If she attended all social functions, it might very well change his opinion of them.

For now, he prayed for the midday traffic to lessen, allowing them to arrive quickly on Bond Street and for him to be rid of his mother, though he would enjoy a few uninterrupted hours with Theo to hear how her studies were progressing.

Curse his lack of a second proper carriage or suitable horse.

He'd been relegated to calling on Miss Jude only after delivering Lady Cartwright and Theo. And then he'd be beckoned to return within an hour's time to collect them.

As if he were a bloody nursemaid.

But there was little choice as he'd sold all but one of their family carriages shortly after arriving home from university. It meant fewer stables hands with salaries and upkeep on only one coach. As inconvenient as it was at this precise moment, it had saved Cart four hundred and twenty-six shillings in the last several years.

If his mother hadn't insisted the curtains be drawn tightly, Cart would have carried along his current periodical, *Silliman's Journal*, which offered fascinating theories on geology. The journal had arrived from the Americas only a fortnight before, and Cart was re-reading each scientific article with an eye for applying the information to his own studies.

An elbow nudged his side. "Simon," Theo whispered. "Are you sleeping?" For effect, he breathed in deeply, emitting a snore. Theo giggled and Cart cracked open one eye. "Oh, I knew you pretended."

"I am certain you did not," he huffed, closing his eyes once more.

"Either you bluff or you and Momma have far greater things in common than you admit."

Cart opened his eye a slit once more and took in Theo's smirk before giving in and sitting up straight.

He immediately wished he hadn't. Across from him, Lady Anastasia Cartwright had fallen into a slumber after her instructive tirade regarding proper manners when a lady arrived on Bond Street to spend her coin.

Unfortunately for Cart, and supporting Theo's claim, his mother reclined in the exact same position Cart had been in moments before, her arms even folded over the expanse of her bosom.

Theo giggled. "For a certainty, you look far more like Momma than I."

Cart wished he could deny Theo's words, but saw most of his best features mirrored in the woman directly across the carriage from him—that was, all except her tendency to ridicule. That was a quality he found highly distasteful and never sought to imitate.

"Oh, you think you are far removed from her?" he teased. When she nodded, he continued, "Let us hope you acquired Father's good sense and not hers." He laughed, startling Lady Cartwright where she dozed before she shifted and her breathing deepened once more. Part of him wanted to wake her and point out that she was wrinkling her dress—a gown he'd likely paid her maid an extra hour to press the night before.

He pushed the thought from his mind. He'd gone over this many times in his head—his chances of ridding himself of his mother's continued expenses were elevated if he were to allow her a significant allowance to attend society functions. His hope was that an aging lord would take notice of her and set his sights upon courting her, either improving his mother's sensibilities or taking her off Cart's hands entirely.

Several years now and his hopes had been dashed season after season.

No man took interest in his mother, or at least no man called on her.

He supposed there could be goings-on he was unaware of, but his ability to see all happening around him was strong. Certainly his mother was not able to slip away under his nose to meet with a suitor.

Theo elbowed him again. "Simon, I doubt you ever listen to me."

"What?" he asked to cover his inattention.

"Just so. I asked if you'd take me with you," she pleaded. "I do not see the need for new gloves or boots. I would much rather accompany you on your errand. It must be far more important than selecting the 'perfect shade of cream' for a new set of gloves that will likely be ink-stained before a fortnight passes, thus gaining me yet another scolding from Momma."

"You know I cannot liberate you from your fate this day." Normally, he'd have rescued Theo from his mother's clutches; however, today his errand was not of the ordinary sort. "But one day in the future, you will thank me for insisting you are properly educated in both your studies and…the less desirable daily female obligations." He was calling on Jude—at her home—and he was nervous beyond anything he'd ever felt. His palms perspired, his forehead was moist, and his pulse had elevated. No amount of breathing or calming arithmetic figuring helped. His unease had grown so intense that Cart contemplated joining his mother and Theo for their shopping excursion. However, that would draw far more attention than his accompanying them in the carriage as opposed to simply riding one of the aging stable stock.

He refused to arrive at Miss Judith's on a horse barely capable of carrying his weight. That was far more debasing than arriving in a carriage older than he. His financial situation was known far and wide within society, yet a part of him hoped that Miss Jude hadn't heard of his family's disgrace at the hands of his uncle.

He stiffened. Why should he care what she thought of him?

Cart was calling on her because he'd blurted his request before taking the appropriate time to thoroughly assess his words and the consequences that would follow his declaration. If he'd taken the time—and hadn't been drenched in murky, offensive-smelling pond scum—Cart would have seen the error of his request and adjusted the conversation, turning it in a more neutral direction.

Instead, he'd been made to offer as escort for his mother and sister on their excursion.

"If I must attend to Momma, your duty as my guardian and wise elder requires you to stay by my side." Between the pair, Cart was not convinced he was the wisest Montgomery offspring. Theo would one day be a worthy adversary in every endeavor she undertook, but for now, she was continually relegated to precocious girl by him, and bothersome child by their mother.

Her toothy grin told Cart she thought she had him bested.

"Aw, well…" Cart turned fully toward her on the bench seat. "My first priority as your guardian is to make certain you are properly cared for and all you require is available to you. Thanks to our scoundrel of an uncle, I must provide a service and collect my fee to maintain our home and provide you with an adequate education—and those delicate white gloves you so loathe shopping for."

Theo slouched in her seat, defeated.

"Do sit up straight, Theodora," her mother chastened. Neither had noticed she'd awakened, but from her dour expression, she'd likely overheard his comments about their uncle, her brother-in-law by marriage. "It would also suit you well to smile—young ladies who take to excessive frowning create horrid aging lines."

"Momma, I—"

"I do not need excuses, young lady, only action," Lady Cartwright continued, unfolding her arms, which had creased her gown. She pulled the curtain back, the late morning sun casting a bright trail down the seat between Cart and Theo. "We are almost there. Simon, I am happy to see you departing the townhouse—you'd do well to dispel your lone tendencies and mingle within society more. My friends fear you are turning into a recluse of the worst kind."

Theo sighed beside him and Cart wished he could give her what she wanted. One day, she'd thank him. He was certain of it.

"Simon," his mother called, still staring out the window. "Do return on time to collect us. I will not be wandering the streets of London like a vagabond awaiting your return."

"Of course, Mother." Cart would never leave Theo stranded, even during the busiest hours of the day in the most heavily populated thoroughfare in London. "I will not be long and will likely return long before you have completed your tasks."

The carriage slowed in front of the milliner's storefront and rolled to a jerky stop.

It reminded Cart that he'd planned to dash into Sir Everheart's Book Emporium very soon to select a book on the undersides of conveyances. With an adequate diagram, he and a servant should be more than qualified to repair the rigging and be rid of the continuous jostling of the carriage's occupants. As for now, that errand must wait.

The door swung open, and Cart disembarked to hand down his mother and sister with a farewell before entering once more to retake his seat.

Within moments, he was moving back through traffic toward the address Lord Barton had forwarded to him earlier that morning. Cart had written to the man to solidify their business dealings, but also inquired as to Miss Judith and Samantha's directions. His reasoning explained his need to send a letter with a formal apology for his boorish behavior at Lady Haversham's garden party.

Not that Cart, in any way, owed anyone an apology, but he did not want to run the risk of Barton holding back Jude's directions. There were certainly books on lineage he could consult. Though they were hardly the type he preferred to keep in his private collection—and asking his mother for her treasured copy would put the woman on alert to his activities.

Something Cart avoided at all costs.

# # #

"Good day, sir," Cart greeted an elderly man outside Miss Jude's home.

The man gave a barely audible grunt before returning to his work, wielding a large pair of clippers as he trimmed the shrubs bordering the walkway.

Cart paused to adjust his cravat—which he'd starched and tied far more elaborately than was his norm. He'd spent over an hour perfecting the Maharatta tie he'd seen featured on one of his mother's plates on current fashion for gentlemen. It depicted a dignified, astute-appearing lord, which was the exact impression he sought to make when visiting Jude today.

If astute men did not mind the immensely restrictive nature of current fashions, then far be it from Cart to dissuade them from their choices. Nonetheless, he had previously decided not to commit long-term to the trend. However, for this call, the necktie would stay.

The home before him was large, not anywhere near as grand as his own townhouse, but well-kept with a manicured landscape. It was no secret that the cover of anything could be in opposition to its interior. Take Cart's own townhouse with its bare walls, his family's paintings having been stolen and sold by his uncle. Or his sparse staff, many long-standing, hardworking servants seeking employment in other London residences that could afford their wages.

Certainly, from the outside, the Cartwright townhouse gave the impression that its occupants were as they'd been for over five generations—wealthy, titled, and elite. When in actuality, Cart worked night and day brokering antiquities deals and searching for his own family heirlooms.

Then again, Craven House—as the sign out front dubbed the manor before him—could be inside as it was outside. Not every façade hid secrets within.

Cart stepped to the door and knocked.

A young girl pulled the door wide, her smile growing as she looked him up and down—in similar fashion to how Lord Barton had taken in Miss Samantha. Was this a socially acceptable manner of greeting? If so, it made Cart highly uncomfortable. He mentally added this to his list of less than desirable things he would never become contented with. Right below the Maharatta knot, that is.

When she kept silent, Cart shifted his feet and squared his shoulders, the tightness of his necktie very apparent in the moment. "I am here to call on Miss Judith."

"I'm certain you are."

"Is she about?" he inquired when the woman made no move to invite him in.

"Possibly." Either the woman was newly appointed or had dreadful manners; Cart couldn't decide which it was.

"Is she receiving callers?"

"Do you have a card, my lord?"

Immediately, he realized it was he who was not following formal guidelines when calling on a lady. With efficient fingers, Cart found his calling card in his front pocket and presented it to her. "Lord Cartwright—err, an earl." He had no reasoning for adding his title; however, the need to legitimize his visit was daunting.

"You are here to pay Jude a visit," the girl mused. "But you bring no flowers or other gifts?"

Flowers? Should he have arrived with bouquet in hand? Cart's smile fell, and with it, his confidence.

"Who is at the door, Payton?" a deep, commanding voice called from somewhere within. "I am expecting no one. If it is a delivery, instruct them round to the kitchen."

The girl—Payton—glanced over her shoulder. "Not a delivery...a gentleman caller."

"Well, then do step aside." A woman, certainly older than Jude but far more petite—and fair-haired—stepped forward. Her smile was welcoming, if not a bit dubious. "May I help you, my lord?"

If he'd been made nervous by the appraisal of the younger woman, this woman was a force far greater and more serious in nature than that of the other. He only vaguely remembered her as the woman who'd attended Jude at the night watchman's residence. "I am here to call on Miss Judith." Cart cleared this throat. "We met at

Lady Haversham's garden party and she agreed to my calling on her at a future date—this is that future date." He was rambling again, offering far more information than was warranted.

"That it is," she agreed. "An entire eighteen hours, in fact."

She stepped back, opening the door wider and motioning him to enter.

"I do hope she is receiving visitors." Neither female had confirmed that Jude was even in attendance. "I apologize for my lack of flowers, err—"

"I am Marce Davenport, Jude's eldest sister." The woman was all business. Cart was torn between shaking her hand and bowing. "And this is Payton, our youngest sibling."

"How many of you are there?" he asked without thinking, regretting the rude implications of his question. "My apolo—"

"Not necessary, my lord. There are five of us: Jude and Sam, Payton, myself...and Garrett, our lone, outnumbered brother."

"It is nice to meet you, Lord Cartwright," Payton said as she closed the front door, officially cutting off his means of escape. "Shall I show him to the parlor, Marce?"

In short order, Cart was deposited in the parlor—a sunny, feminine room covered completely in pastel blue. The door soundly shut behind Miss Payton and Marce.

Did one sit whilst making social calls, or remain standing until their hostess arrived?

Eyeing the delicate settee and lounges dominating the room, Cart decided to stand. By his calculations, the thin pegs that served as legs for each of the pieces would likely buckle under his weight, average as it was by current standards. The things were constructed for women of modest size. Cart was not willing to risk another embarrassing situation after having tumbled into the pond.

A shelf held a stack of books befitting a household of women—a fashion journal, an older tome of poetry, and several books on etiquette. All likely to be found in his mother's sitting room.

Cart was tempted to remove the book of poetry, but he refrained from touching anything. It all seemed as any other home would; paintings adorning the walls, acceptable lighting down the hall, a woman's needlepoint sitting by the window, and even a cape lying discarded over a chair. It was a normal house. Far more elaborately decorated than his home at the moment.

Not at all what he'd expected.

Why was that? Simply because it did not lead him to any answers as to why he'd seen Jude leaving the night watchman's home. Neither her eldest sister nor Jude recognized him from that morning. Could it be as his sister always accused, that Cart was overly aware of things that others noticed not?

A soft click sounded behind him and Cart turned to see both twins enter the room. For two women who'd shared such a tight spot during development, they could not be more dissimilar—with the exception of their identical looks.

"Miss Jude, Miss Samantha." He issued a quick bow to each in order. "Thank you for receiving me without notice."

"You did say you would be calling on me at a future date," the twin who he suspected was Jude responded, confirming his knowledge. "Our conversation was halted ever so abruptly."

The mention of his fall to disgrace caused his neck to heat and his cravat to add pressure to his airways. "Yes, I sincerely offer my apologies for my gaucheness." He kept his stare on Jude to assess her willingness to forgive him and he was rewarded with a smile, her lips parting to reveal straight white teeth, a slight overbite noticeable. Though that did not detract from her allure.

"Lord Cartwright, do have a seat—and call me Sam," the woman so much like Jude requested, motioning to a chair he hadn't noticed during his first perusal of the room. It was certainly more adequately constructed. "I will see about tea."

Cart noticed the knowing wink Sam gave Jude before hurrying from the parlor, leaving the door cracked open only slightly.

Jude took the seat closest to his chair, arranging her skirt to cover her crossed feet. However, Cart had gained a quick look. Her boots ended at her ankle, with cream stockings continuing up to disappear and encase her shapely calves—not that he knew the shape of her calf, but he'd seen many images depicted in medical journals.

"How can you tell us apart?"

Her hesitant question surprised him and he took a moment to think. How could he *not* tell them apart? "Your voice is the obvious difference, certainly," he started. "But at the gathering, I noticed your penchant for pastels as opposed to Miss Saman—Sam's— tendency toward bolder colors. I did not think much of it then, but the case is the same today. And you have a slight overbite."

She lifted her delicate hand to cover her mouth, her eyes rounded in shock.

"Oh, do not take offense," he gushed. "Not another soul would notice. Only I. And then there is the way you look to the side when you are pondering a question or your response." He hadn't expected to add that last difference, planning to keep it to himself, but he wanted to distract her from worrying over her overbite.

"You are an astute man, Lord Cartwright," Jude grinned, returning her hands to her lap.

Chapter Seven

Lord Cartwright was clearly the most incisive man she'd met to date. On most occasions, she and her twin were still able to fool their siblings into thinking one was the other, as long as they didn't speak. However, he'd noticed something that Jude hadn't even thought of as a *tell*, as Payton would refer to it. That little tick or subtle gesture that allowed an opponent to know if his adversary was bluffing.

She wondered if he were too smart for the ruse she and Sam were playing. Namely, the fire they'd been juggling since stealing that bloody vase. It was almost as risky keeping the antiquity under their roof as it was to get rid of the thing. Jude had insisted the piece be disposed of properly, to a home where it would be treasured—no harm coming to it. Sam had insisted it wasn't a dog or a child, but a piece of clay. Jude knew it as art. Something she'd studied and taken great pleasure in for most of her life.

"Tea should arrive shortly," Jude ventured, breaking the silence.

"I am not parched, but thank you."

Jude couldn't quite understand Cart's odd behaviors. It was as if he were completely unaware of social niceties one moment and spouted random etiquette passages the next. Though not of the upper crust, Marce had instructed her siblings in all aspects of proper society—Lord Cartwright, as an earl, should be well versed in social decorum.

"What I mean to say," he said, "is a cup of tea would be much appreciated."

"May I ask you a question, my lord?" She'd always been of the mindset that if one wanted answers, one needed to ask questions. When he nodded, she took a deep breath and asked, "Are you new to London—and society?"

His brow furrowed in thought. "No, I have lived in London most of my life, with only a short spell away at university, and some time at my country estate when I was younger."

"And your title, is it newly acquired?" She'd started her line of questioning, so she might as well ask all she wanted before Sam returned with their tea.

"No, my father passed many years ago, before I reached my majority." He leaned forward as if the change in topic were a comfortable one and not one of loss and sorrow. When her own mother passed, Jude had been young, as well—unprepared for a life without parental guidance. "I went away for schooling and then university, only returning once I'd fin—"His eyes squinted nervously. "Once I'd completed the allotted coursework allowed. I returned to my family's home in London thereafter."

"Very interesting." In fact, it was not all that interesting, rather quite the norm. "I have resided in London my entire life."

"Pity," he sighed. "There is much beautiful countryside in England."

"So I have heard." Jude thought quickly, trying to steer the conversation back to his expertise. "When did your curiosity in art and antiquities start?"

Jude felt the question subtle and coaxing—undoubtedly the direction the conversation needed to go for this visit to be deemed a success.

"I cannot say for certain," he said, his voice growing deeper with comfort at the subject. "I have always admired history and the sciences—and with that came an interest in those things important to those topics, namely, artifacts, books, and the like. And you? If memory serves, you expressed a strong liking to antiquities, as well."

The conversation, while immensely agreeable to Lord Cartwright, was now unsettling to her. Jude meant to prod him about his collection; specifically, what pieces interested him most, not discuss her views on the subject. Though they could likely converse for hours about the many works of art Jude admired. "I am fairly uneducated on the matter in truth, but find I enjoy inspecting objects of a certain age and quality." The only thing untrue in her statement was the part about being uneducated. Her room housed over fifty books pertaining to art, historical items, and museum collections—so many, that Sam often complained about Jude's tendency for clutter. "I am only a lady who finds herself with spare time and chooses to amuse herself with pursuits of a historical nature."

"Oh, come now," he said, swatting his knee as if what she'd said were hilarious. "One either has the gift for collecting or they do not. It is a passion I find great pleasure in and…" He paused, searching for the right words, possibly losing his train of thought. "If you find the same, then there is no need to diminish your aptitude for the matter, especially with me."

"Very well put, my lord." And the opposite of what she'd expected a man of privilege to say about an educated woman. "I do find myself lacking a counterpart who enjoys speaking on the subject of antiquities. What do you find yourself more enamored with, books, vases, or possibly…paintings?"

He grinned, the corner of his mouth turning up as he relaxed into his chair. "I cannot select one."

"No? Even I find I prefer certain items over others," she pushed.

"If I had to select one…" His eyes sparkled in merriment, obviously enjoying their discussion, and Jude told herself to also be at ease. Lord Cartwright had thus far been a kind man. Besides, she'd met many men who could not hold a conversation past what their last meal had included. "I do enjoy books, but my true interest is in items of great historical relevance; a chalice from the great Knights Templar, or a rug that once adorned a great palace far away."

Their conversation should improve Jude's spirits, yet she paused at taking advantage of Lord Cartwright— as unsuspecting as he was.

"You must come to my townhouse and see my collection," he offered. His eyes grew round as he realized what his request insinuated. "What I mean to say—"

"My lord." Jude held up her hand, cutting another apology short. "I know you do not mean anything untoward by your invitation." Though a part of her wondered what the man would be like without his overly starched necktie and tendency to converse only about intellectual matters. Without his crutch—take away what made him comfortable, maybe his linen shirt for instance—what would he say? Or better yet, do?

His hands would likely be tender when they touched her, so used to holding delicate things.

Jude looked away, her cheeks burning with her scandalous thoughts.

With a quick shake of her head, she refocused on Cart, who stared at her intently, awaiting her response while she undressed him in her mind. And in all the time they'd been alone, the door all but closed, he hadn't once looked away from her face.

If her face wasn't suitably reddened already, then it surely was now.

"My lord." Jude concentrated, not allowing her eyes to wander once more. "I would much enjoy seeing all you've collected."

She'd never been the young woman to entertain inappropriate thoughts about men she'd only recently been acquainted with. Or men she'd known longer, for that matter. It was always Sam who had a wandering eye worse than any rakehell. If this was how much Sam had to fight against her natural instincts every time she laid eyes on a pretty face, then heaven help Jude because Cart cut a dashing figure—and had an intellect to match.

"Ah, that is very well." Abruptly, Lord Cartwright stood. "I will bid you farewell, Miss Jude. Until next we meet again."

Jude popped to her feet, shocked by his sudden rush to depart. "At a future date."

"Well, yes." He looked at her as if she'd said the most obvious thing. "I am certain it is not proper for you to call on me the very same day I visited you."

It was a jest, a play on his words from the gathering at Lady Haversham's. She wanted to tell him exactly that, however, he bowed and was already moving toward the door.

"Allow me to show you out," Jude called, catching up to him as he crossed the room.

She almost collided with him when he stopped in his tracks and turned back toward her.

"I was only just shown in by Miss Payton. Your home has no winding corridors, nor hidden doorways. I can find my way out without fear of getting lost. Do not fret."

Jude hadn't feared any such thing and lacked any idea of how to respond.

And so, she moved around him and pulled the door open for him to depart.

"Thank you, Miss Jude." She thought him on the verge of bowing again—which was entirely unnecessary. She should curtsey to him, not the other way around. "I have had a lovely visit. Unfortunately, I must fetch my mother and dear sister from the modiste's shop. I mustn't be late. I will send word with my directions and an agreeable date presently."

He fled the room and headed straight toward the foyer, taking a left turn when necessary, easily retracing his steps, leaving Jude with more questions than answers about the man. She hoped "a future date" coincided with "an agreeable date", not that she had any other choice.

His demeanor had been off balance most of their visit, except when they'd spoken of his precious antiquities. It had been much the same as the garden party. When he discussed things of import to him, he was a man at ease, confident and strong. However, when things strayed to other subjects, he was not as composed.

The echo of the front door closing had reached her only moments before Sam rushed into the room, no tea service in sight.

"So?" she asked, throwing her hands to her hips.

"So, what?" Jude was not ready for her sister's knowing stare—a blush likely still stained her cheeks. All she wanted was time to think through her response—and her scandalous musings—in regards to Lord Cartwright. The last thing Jude wanted was to discuss it all with her twin.

Sam's expectant look turned to one of confusion. Just as quickly, she seemed to work something out in her own mind, but pushed it aside before continuing, "Do you think he will be willing to purchase the vase? How deep are his pockets? We must fetch a handsome price if you insist on sticking to your declaration of no more thievery."

The vase…of course, Sam was making reference to the vase and nothing more.

Her twin had no idea of the disgraceful fantasy that had played through Jude's mind during Lord Cartwright's short visit—nor did Jude plan to tell her. It was one thing that belonged to her and her alone. Not like their shared room or their shared pearl-handled brush and comb set or their combined dressing closet.

No, Cart was Jude's—and only hers.

Though no one need know that she'd labeled him thus.

Confident Sam hadn't any notion of her uncouth feelings, they set about planning Jude's visit to Lord Cartwright's townhouse.

"He has invited me to his home to view his collection." She should feel proud of the progress she'd made, considering not long ago she was sitting in a dank room facing exposure for her misdeeds, only to be rescued by her siblings. And shortly, with any luck, she would give Marce enough coin to satisfy any debt her sister owed.

Jude and Sam sat close together with their voices lowered, afraid to garner the attention of Payton.

A loud bang brought both women back to their surroundings as the front door slammed shut and the bolt was thrown.

Jude and Sam were on their feet and rushing to the entry before either exchanged a word. Their home was peaceful and serene during the daylight hours, for the most part, so an unexpected arrival sent all the siblings into action at a moment's notice.

Entering the foyer, Mr. Curtis stood with his back to the front door and a small woman recoiling from the elder man's reach, her hands covering most of her face.

"Mr. Curtis," Sam called quietly as Jude rushed to the woman. "Jude and I can handle this."

"It be only proper to send for Lord Garrett with Madame Marce gone on errands."

"That is not necessary," Jude argued. She wrapped her arm lightly around the woman's shoulders and steered her toward the kitchens in search of a bite to eat and a cool drink. "Were you followed?" Jude asked as they walked slowly down the corridor.

"I do not think so." She removed her hands from her face and Jude took in the cruel realities of her situation. One eye was already bruising a deep purple and her lip was split, the blood now dried. "I am sorry for all of this…it is only that I had no other place to go."

"You came to the right place." Sam followed closely behind them.

"What is your name?" When the woman seemed apprehensive about sharing the information, her eyes darting around as if she were cornered, Jude continued, "Only a first name, so we know what to call you."

"Kathleen."

"It is nice to meet you, Kathleen," Jude said as they entered the kitchen. "I am Miss Judith Pengarden. My sister, Marce, runs Craven House. Please, have a seat, and we will get you a clean cloth to wash your face and some refreshments."

Sam pulled out a stool that sat at the long, rough table used by Cook to prepare the meals. "Sit here." Jude's twin busied herself by retrieving a cloth and dipping it in a basin of warm water sitting on the stove.

"Kathleen." Jude pulled out the stool next to the woman and sat, staring her directly in the eyes—one already swelling shut. "Who did this to you?"

Marce had spent many hours lecturing her younger siblings on the proper questions to ask when women arrived at Craven House. Who did this? Do you have any place to go? What can Craven House do to help you? Most women came with a plan in mind, but lacked the monetary means to put their plan in motion.

"Take this." Sam held the cloth out to Kathleen and set a plate of bread and cheese at her elbow before retreating to the far side of the kitchen. They'd also been taught not to overwhelm anyone who came for help—and Jude was by far the friendlier sister.

Kathleen pressed the wet material to her eye. Jude sensed she'd been struck before and knew the pressure would reduce the swelling. Her other hand, already stained by dried blood, swiped at her busted lip.

"My maid," she mumbled. "She told me you could help me."

"Of course, Kathleen." Jude felt the familiar heartbreak cast a shadow over the room. No matter how many women and children she saw physically or emotionally abused and mistreated, it never failed to pull at her heartstrings and reinforce how fortunate she was. "Do you need a place to stay? A post with a good home?"

"Neither of those things." She shook her head and hissed at the pain it caused. "I need to be away from London as soon as possible."

"Do you have a place to go?" Marce had immeasurable connections within and outside of London proper. If Kathleen were fearful of someone or something, then Jude had a list of people she could contact—places the woman would never be found until she was ready. Even Lady Haversham, Jude's and Sam's patroness, allowed women and children to stay at her orphanage when the need was urgent. "If not, I can find a suitable place for you."

"No, that will not be necessary." Kathleen's voice was low and she spoke slowly to avoid splitting her lip open once more. "My sister has a home with her husband and children near Windsor. It is only…I do not have the funds to pay for transport."

"We can help with that," Sam said from her place across the room. "We can even replace your tattered dress and get you a warm woolen coat before you go."

Jude and Kathleen glanced down at the woman's attire as if noticing the blood that marred the front and her ripped sleeve for the first time.

Kathleen's chin bent down and her shoulders sagged. The woman clearly felt discomfort at her situation.

"Sam," Jude called to redirect everyone's attention. "Please check the mail coach's schedule for today. I will allow Kathleen some space to bathe and don a new dress for her journey." Next, Jude turned to their newest ward. "Does your sister know to expect you?"

"I have written to her of my need to be away from Father…" She'd said too much, allowing her words to fade.

"Very good," Jude said. "Our housekeeper will take you to change while I collect enough coin for your passage to Windsor."

Darla appeared in the doorway to the kitchen, likely having been notified by Mr. Curtis of the woman's arrival. "This way," Darla motioned.

Kathleen slid from her seat, hugged Jude tentatively, and fled the room behind the housekeeper.

"Jude." She looked up to see the concern in Sam's eyes. "You have a call to make. I can handle this."

"No." It was important that Jude see this through. It was her lot in life—to help Marce in any way she could. "I only need collect the money from Marce's office and you can take her to the station while I continued on to Lord Cartwright's townhouse."

Sam wrinkled her nose as she tapped her finger against her lips in thought.

"Everything will be as it should, I promise," Jude said, attempting to convince Sam. "Please, find the coach schedule while I get the money."

"Fine." Sufficiently convinced, Sam departed the kitchen after Darla and Kathleen, with Jude close behind.

Sam hurried to the front of the house while Jude headed for Marce's office—and the chest where she kept money in case of emergencies. She also used the stash for the butcher, the candle maker, and the daily market purchases.

The box sat behind Marce's small white desk on a shelf, surrounded by books on fashion and decorum. A book on peerage was even present. The chest itself was adorned with gaudy sea-green adornments pasted to the wooden frame. Anyone entering the room would think it housed nothing more than female knickknacks and useless novelties. Jude and her sisters knew better.

Popping the lid, Jude peered inside—a gasp leaving her lips. Barely enough coin to pay Kathleen's fare with some left over for a meal at an inn along the way sat in the bottom of the box. Things were far more dire than even Jude had realized. Their card nights at Craven House were less and less popular as the years passed. The gentlemen of the *ton* discovered the Craven House of Madame Sasha's time was not returning—no more women of loose morals, endless spirits, or other depravity under Marce's roof.

It made Jude's decision to push the vase on Lord Cartwright all the more important and exceedingly imperative. The notion of replacing the money—with much to spare—before Marce's return from her upcoming trip filled Jude with a sense of usefulness. She just hoped that Marce would not look in the chest before departing.

The day would surely come when her family was charged with helping more women and they needed to be prepared for that responsibility. It was a task she and her siblings took very seriously since their mother's passing—to help those in need, something their mother, Sasha, hadn't been prepared to do.

Chapter Eight

Cart repositioned the inkpot once more, moving it a hair to the left, then aligned the stack of correspondence he'd brushed out of place when adjusting the ink. He sat up a bit straighter in his chair and put on his spectacles, but just as quickly removed them. Again, something with him was off. Today should be no different than any previous day. While Cart was partial to things in their place, he'd never been one to fuss over the exact settlement of items on his desk—as long as they were all there and not removed, it suited him.

Looking around the room, he noticed more objects out of place or missing altogether, which should be hard to spot in his sparsely furnished study that doubled as his library and housed many of his most prized antiquities. He pushed back in his chair and stood, moving across the room to a deceiving landscape painting hanging nearest the door and farthest from any source of natural light so as not to compromise the oil's integrity.

It was one of his first acquisitions and meant nothing in the grand scheme of collectibles. The small painting had cost him little but had been commissioned by his father around the time of Cart's birth—it depicted his family's country estate, a true manor home, known to him before his life had been ruined. His father's passing was only the start of things. Now, Cart was unable to journey to the place that held so many fond memories for him; a place that had been filled with love and contentment. A wonderful mother, who had ceased to exist in her former state, and only the vague remembrance of a man who'd taken him about the land, tending decaying roofs alongside his tenants and hearing grievances, were all that remained.

Cart's biggest regret was having never located the other painting his father had commissioned at the same time—another landscape, but of the opposite view of his ancestral estate. He'd gone so far as to spread falsehoods about the painting's worth, longing for someone to find it and contact him as a buyer for the piece—alas, no one had come forth with the other painting and Cart continued to speak of it when meeting with other collectors.

Currently, the country house was filled with the keepsakes and belongings of another family. Cart had been forced to allow another lord and his relatives to live in the home he'd cherished, only collecting enough rent to keep the property from total deterioration.

The opportunity to enjoy a carefree existence in the country surrounded by people who'd served the

Cartwright Earldom for decades had been stripped from Theo—something that Cart would one day rectify.

Cart looked to the large chair pushed close to the window for light where Theo sat, curled under a blanket, reading yet another novel. If it were a book about the formation of the British colonies or a tale of pirates and treasure, he didn't care. She was happy, made evident by the smile that played about her face, reaching all the way to her eyes. He was determined to give his younger sibling far more than had been taken from his family.

The coin stolen was returning, bit by bit, with Cart's hard work.

The heirlooms and other family treasures were being located slowly but surely, though Cart lacked the funds to acquire them all.

One day, he would journey to his childhood home and reclaim what was theirs—for himself, but mostly for Theo.

He watched as she brushed one long plait from her shoulder and gazed out the window in thought. They were so much alike—their mannerisms, their looks, and especially their love of knowledge. It was his hope that soon he'd have the funds to send her to a proper school, giving her the education she craved. No more tutors, no more living under their mother's thumb, no more suppressing who she wanted to be. Theo would have the chance to accomplish all she dreamed of—and it would not be cut short, as had happened to him. There would be no snake in the grass, pulling the metaphorical rug out from under her feet. If she chose to be a female doctor, or a barrister—or even a captain of a ship, setting out to explore the wild oceans—he would give her that, with no conditions, no drawbacks, and no worries.

"Simon?"

He blinked several times to clear the haze from his sight, wishing he hadn't removed his glasses.

"Is something troubling you?" Theo closed her book and wedged it between her leg and the arm of the chair. "You look pensive, as usual, but also a sheen has appeared across your forehead."

It was not proper to burden his younger sibling with his worries, so Cart smiled and laughed. The sound was brittle to his ears. He was certain if it went on another second it would crack and turn into a sigh. "I am grand. Promise," he answered. "I am awaiting a guest."

"Oh, who is coming?" Theo uncurled her legs, her stare following Cart as he made his way back to his desk—attempting to appear normal. "Are you meeting about another treasure? May I see it? Is it the scepter you spoke of a few days ago?"

This time, Cart did laugh. The tension in his shoulders was temporarily released.

As much as he viewed her as an educated young woman, she was little more than a child. A child, he knew, who specifically loved shiny things—seeing them, holding them, and researching them.

"Not to disappoint you, but my guest has nothing to do with work." He'd expected her to lose interest when she heard this, yet he'd underestimated where her actual attention lay. Not in his business ventures or the many antiquities that passed through their home, but rather in her brother's activities. "I am afraid my meeting today—more of a visit, actually—is nothing of grand import."

"Nothing of grand import, dear brother?" she queried. "You have organized your desk three times, put on and removed your spectacles more times than that, and you are now seeking to defuse my interest in the matter. It can only be one thing…"

Cart did not like how her voice trailed off as if she'd come to some foregone conclusion that any right-minded person would.

It was best he remain silent—and by no means realign his collection of pens on his desk.

"A woman is calling."

Cart looked up from where he stared at the smooth surface of his desk to meet her look. He found nothing but certainty there.

"Why would you think that?" he asked.

"At first, I suspected it was a man of a certain age—mother's specific age—who was coming to meet with you—"

"Why is that?" Cart prided himself on being discreet or, at least, not completely readable. He was much more guarded since his return from Eton.

"The way you pushed Momma out of the house, even sending her on an errand for you." Theo paused, rising from the chair. She paced to the door slowly, her forefinger tapping her chin as she did. "But then, you remained on edge, checking the clock several times and even moving to the looking glass hung in the hall."

"I did no such thing." At least, Cart hadn't meant to pause before the large mirror to take stock of his cravat, less elaborate today but still finely pressed and tied. Nor had he suspected he'd disturbed her reading.

"I seek to verify all is well, that is all. And I do apologize if my movements disturbed you in any way."

"So, you do have a woman calling." She bounced in excitement, clasping her hands to her chest. "This is wonderful news."

He in no way understood how Theo equated a woman calling on him as wonderful news—or even newsworthy information. "She is coming to see some of my antiquities, that is all. She is a collector of sorts, as am I."

"This is far better than I previously thought," Theo said, moving to his desk and motioning him to stand. She looked from his hair, brushed as was proper, to his necktie and the lines of his coat. She couldn't see past that because he still stood behind his desk, but he felt ridiculous to have his twelve-year-old sister appraising his appearance. It was absurd, but what worried him further was that Cart desperately wanted to ask if he looked satisfactory. "I had wondered why you'd taken an enhanced liking to cravat knots. I'd thought it only another thing you'd set out to master, but now, yes, you've done a fine job learning."

The hall clock in the foyer struck once, and he stiffened, placing his hands flat on the desk before him as he breathed deeply.

He could not reconcile why Miss Jude made him feel so…so…tense and anxious.

She was no more than any other woman of his acquaintance. It did not signify that she was as beautiful as the great Helen of Troy, who he'd seen in an ancient text—if she allowed her light auburn hair to flow freely. Nor should it matter that she found interest in many of the things Cart did.

She was merely a woman.

As he was simply a man.

And they were meeting today not to speak of men and women, or any attraction that one may feel for the other, fairer sex.

A loud knock echoed down the hall and made its way to his study.

Effectively stopping his train of thought before it strayed to something very improper—and made it impossible for him to leave the safety of his desk chair for fear all would take notice of where his mind lay.

"Theo, is it not near time for you to start your afternoon studies?" He knew she couldn't refute his words. After all, he'd planned Jude's arrival to coincide with his mother's charity meeting and Theo's afternoon tutoring session. His only mistake was thinking that anything ever went as planned. Not even the smallest of things—a social call—could go as planned. "You cannot expect to attain the position of barrister if you do not study well."

"I am not studying to be a barrister," she retorted. He knew his words would vex her. She had little interest in the law. "But Mr. LeMaux should be awaiting me. I will leave you to your guest, but I cannot promise I will not discuss this with Momma." A twinkle lit her eyes with her thinly veiled threat.

The little minx was blackmailing him. "What do you seek, Theo?" He gave in to his sister, knowing anything she could ask for was far less demanding than his mother would be if she heard.

"The scepter—I want to hold it." She crossed her arms over her chest.

It was an impossible request, especially since Cart hadn't located the item as yet.

"No," Cart said, hearing the front door close. "Anything else?"

Theo grinned and Cart knew he'd been taken once more. She'd never thought he would allow her to hold a scepter fabled to be over a thousand years old, but she'd used the ploy to attain what she truly desired.

"I'd like to meet her."

"Another impossibility." Cart feared he'd be so tongue-tied he'd start rambling off mathematical equations or the scientific method for freezing water.

"Come now, Brother," she whined, setting her hands on her hips. "You must promise me something for keeping your escapades from Momma."

Escapades? A female caller during the height of visiting hours could hardly be classified as an *escapade*.

"I will compromise with you," he gave in. "You hide in the shadows of the hall, behind the large potted fern, and you can sneak a glimpse of Miss Jude from there." Theo began to bounce up and down once more. "But, you are not to say a word. She is not to know you are watching."

"Yes, yes." Theo could barely contain her joy. "I promise—not a peep from me."

"And when we enter the study, you will continue on to your tutoring?"

"Of course," she squealed.

"I must say, your interest in this baffles me," he confided. "But let us get this over with. Gain your position and I will go to receive Miss Jude properly."

Chapter Nine

Jude understood the grave mistake she'd made the minute she stepped over the threshold and into Lord Cartwright's home. Her hesitancy had nothing to do with her being an unchaperoned female of worth arriving at a gentleman's home without proper companionship. In fact, Sam had fairly begged to come with her. Languishing on and on about the usefulness of a man such as Lord Cartwright. Jude hadn't liked her sister's tone or her insinuation when she'd spoken of Cart—namely, the chances of him having a collection so vast he wouldn't notice an item or two missing.

Even the sparsely decorated and meagerly furnished home before her wasn't what put her on high alert as to her surroundings and the critical error she'd made by accepting the butler's request for her to enter. Certainly, the paltry adornment of the foyer with its brass sconces, lack of portrait where one had clearly once hung, and the bare floor should have sent her running—giving her sincerest apologies and fleeing the house at once.

It had nothing to do with her improper appearance at a gentleman's home or the fact that Lord Cartwright was anything but wealthy.

No, Jude wanted to—*needed* to—depart with all haste because she currently stood in the home she'd almost been caught trespassing in. That she hadn't noticed the neighborhood when her carriage had delivered her, spoke to her severely compromised thinking where Cart was concerned. She wished she had brought Sam with her now. At least she would have had one person with the common sense to extricate her from this delicate—and dangerous—situation.

"Miss Jude," Cart called to her from down the hall, the direction of the only locked door she'd encountered during her first trip here—ending in her choice to depart the house with all haste. It was only fitting that it held all his treasures. "I am pleased you could come."

"My lord," Jude said in greeting. It was almost as if he were surprised at her appearance. Made odder by the note and directions she'd received with her morning meal, requesting her presence at this exact time and place. "We spoke of your collection. I thank you for the invitation to view it."

Jude clutched her handbag until Cart stood before her, smiling.

He clearly didn't notice her fretting, nor had the butler sounded the alarm at her arrival. Was it possible the little girl who'd discovered her hadn't shared any further information about Jude's appearance? The young woman who Jude now suspected was Cart's sister. He *had* mentioned a sibling; she was sure of it.

"Please, come this way." Cart turned back the way he'd come and Jude followed slowly behind him. She peered down one hall, expecting the girl to jump out and expose Jude for the thief she was, but the house was eerily quiet. As it had been the night she'd entered through that unlocked window.

"Ah," she said tentatively. "You have a sister, do you not?"

"I do." He kept his eyes straight ahead as they walked.

"Mine are always underfoot," Jude continued. "How do you keep yours from doing the same?"

"She is in the school room at his hour, dedicated to her studies."

Jude breathed a sigh of relief, quickly continuing to mask her slip. "That is an admirable quality. Learning, especially for women, is very important."

"My sister is far from being considered a woman," he snapped, a bit too harshly.

"I did not mean to—"

"No, no," he mused, glancing at her quickly before focusing once more on their path. "It is not your comment but my sister's insistence she be treated as an adult."

"My youngest sister, Payton, is much the same." Jude's tension eased as they moved farther into the house, knowing the girl was not lurking around any corner. "I believe you garnered a rather good example of her antics when you visited the other day."

"That I did." The room he led her to was the one she'd been unable to gain entrance to, but today, it stood unlocked and open—almost invitingly so.

Lord Cartwright paused outside the room, turning his focus down the hall. Jude glanced in the direction but saw nothing but a potted plant with a small table nearby. He allowed Jude to pass, entering the room before him. He lingered outside the door. A look of perplexity crossed his face before he shook his head and entered the room behind her, leaving the door ajar.

She couldn't help but suspect that he searched for something but did not find it where it belonged.

"Shall I ring for tea?" He always seemed uncertain with social norms and decorum, though today, he seemed in command of his person—a new confidence taking over. Much like the other occasions they'd discussed topics surrounding antiquities and collecting.

"Yes, thank you," Jude replied, though she'd come for things that didn't include food or drink. "Unless you do not find yourself parched, my lord."

This was the man Jude found she liked most; self-assured and in control, though his timid and uneasy side was just as prevalent. It interested her greatly how quickly Lord Cartwright shifted dispositions.

Her brother—the only man she was routinely near—seemed consistent with his nature.

The room was exactly as Jude had pictured it. Most collectors were known for their cluttered rooms, teeming with objects, books, and the like, but not Lord Cartwright. He favored a more thinly furnished and orderly study, free from the chaos Jude had a tendency to favor. Every item had its place. It suited him well—however, she was unable to reconcile which personality this structured life came from.

Did it fall in line with his obsessive nature of things, or did it show his confidence?

Or possibly, there was an entire third option she'd yet to witness.

Jude took a seat in a tall-backed chair and surveyed the room at greater length when Lord Cartwright hurried around the room, gathering pieces to show her—after all, that's what she had visited for. Bordering a large bank of windows, a plush chair sat pushed against the wall with a book lying forgotten on the seat. She envisioned curling up in the chair with the tome open on her lap, the windows overlooking a back garden or the stables below. Maybe a fire would be roaring in the hearth with Cart inspecting a new acquisition, or reading a book close by. It would only be an hour's time before the butler would summon them for supper and prepare for their evening at the playhouse or maybe a soiree. They would laugh and exclaim how they'd both been lost in their individual musings. She blinked several times to banish the image and thoughts from her mind—she barely knew the man sitting opposite her. Any future she conjured was one based on false impressions and misleading truths.

"Lord Cartwright, may I ask you a question?" Jude needed to remind herself why she was here; specifically, to assess the possibility that Cart would be willing to purchase the vase—or better yet, find a buyer for her. But that all hinged on his knowledge and if Jude could overlook the trouble Cart would be in if he were found in possession of the stolen artifact.

He looked up from where he'd stooped to grab an obscure-looking pipe. "Certainly. I expected nothing less. We are both cultured minds seeking to expand our horizons."

Jude averted her stare, finding it hard to look him in the eye, knowing she'd come to deceive him. Or maybe it was hard to meet his gaze because she hoped he'd see through her ruse and call her on her deceitful plan. Either way, he was a kind—if not unsuspecting man—who didn't deserve what she and Sam had planned for him.

But there were things more important than her own integrity—her family and their home. Jude remembered Marce's empty chest in her office. Candles to keep Craven House lit. Food to keep the hunger away. And a bit of coin for the butcher and baker was welcome, too.

But that would not be possible for much longer if she didn't sell the vase.

In all likelihood, Lord Cartwright would never know her deception. He would acquire the vase and keep it hidden here in his study—or broker a buyer who would see the item's worth and keep it secreted away for fear it would be taken and returned to Lord Gunther.

"Jude...errrr. Miss Jude." Cart returned, sitting in the chair next to her, the pipe in hand. "You had a question for me."

Jude kept her hesitation at bay long enough to ask her question, made all the worse by the open smile he gave her. "You say you are not only a collector but also research and locate pieces of worth for others similar to *us*." She was unsure if she emphasized us for his benefit or hers—as if she were anything like him. She did not deserve to be in such a man's company. "I have a vase, gifted by a friend from an old estate in Manchester. It was buried in a stable. It is quite old, but not what I tend to gravitate toward."

His brow rose in interest and Jude knew she'd captured his attention with the mystique around the piece.

"I was wondering if it is something you'd be fascinated with." Jude paused, her ability to lie to someone she'd come to respect hampering her. If Cart weren't so adept at deciphering between her and her twin, Jude would have agreed to let Sam come in her place. "I only want it to belong to someone who will appreciate its beauty and rarity."

"What do you know of it?" Enthralled, Cart scooted forward to the edge of his seat—so far that Jude worried he'd tumble to the floor at her feet. "I admit I am very taken by pieces of obscure history."

"It is certainly obscure. I have been unable to find out much about it—though it seems to adhere to the traits of the Greek Geometric period. The way the vase is shaped and the painting technique match exactly what I've researched. But it is in excellent condition." His eyes widened at her use of the correct terminology. She'd allow him to think she'd obtained it through reputable means, all the better if Cart were to discover it was stolen—very recently. She would claim ignorance. And pray he showed her mercy. "I will have to check with my sister to inquire if she, indeed, would like to be rid of the vase, but—"

"Do not take my silence as reluctance," he said, his head nodding. "I would very much like to see it. Maybe I can help you date the piece—not that I am overly learned in vases, but I have the appropriate knowledge to research further and a connection at the British Museum."

Her first reaction was horror at the mention of having the piece assessed by someone at the British Museum—for that would surely call to question her possession of the vase. "Oh, there is no need to bother someone as important as an expert at the museum, but possibly I can bring it for your appraisal?" She in no way wanted him to *research* the vase too heavily. It was her wish that he'd purchase the vase—or send her in the direction of another collector who'd be interested. It was a delicate matter; one she was already regretting drawing Cart into.

"Certainly."

Jude knew she'd crossed another line. Much like the last several lines she'd crossed, she did it with her eyes closed. It had been a shock to be apprehended, spending the entire night locked in that dank room. That alone should have been enough to send Jude on a straight path, one that did not include her and Sam risking their respective freedom.

"And what have you here?" Jude nodded to the forgotten pipe in his hands, changing the subject away from anything having to do with the British Museum. "Is it a musical instrument?"

His responding smile told her she'd guessed correctly, though she'd never seen or read about such antiquities.

Cart held the piece out for her to take.

"It is very light," Jude said, holding it at arm's length. She turned the pipe this way and that, unsure how it was used—or what sound it would make. It was comprised of about eight wooden tubes harnessed together with a thin piece of twine and another long, narrow wooden strip. "How old is it?"

"It is a Greek panpipe or syrinx, commonly used by shepherds during a time of great lore," he whispered. "Many say it was crafted by the Greek god Hermes."

"This exact panpipe?" she asked in disbelief. "It does not appear any older than a hundred years—at most." She handed it back, terrified she'd drop it or worse...

"I have only recently acquired it." He gently set the pipe on the desk before them. "But I can assure you, though the seller boasted of the piece's age, it is likely no more than five hundred years old."

Jude gulped. Five hundred years? It was difficult to imagine anything being that old, though the vase was centuries older.

A clock chimed somewhere outside the study they sat in, startling them both.

Jude pushed the feeling of unease away, but Cart seemed unable to uncoil his stiffened shoulders.

"Miss Jude, What plans have you tomorrow?" He stood as he asked the question, moving to return the pipe to its cabinet.

His continued peculiar behavior had her scrambling to keep up with his topic changes.

She searched her memory for what tomorrow would consist of for her. Jude was fairly certain she hadn't agreed to attend any functions with Ellie, nor had she received word from Lady Haversham about routs. "I believe I will be taking a turn in the park with my sisters."

"Lovely," he said. "I shall meet you there. Which park and at what time?"

"Ummm…" If this were his strange way of asking her if she'd accompany him to the park, then it was certainly an odd one. "Hyde Park—"

"Of course," he interrupted her. "My mother and sister often take in the fresh air at Hyde Park."

"I suspect around half past five, my lord."

"That is agreeable to me." He moved toward the door, signaling their visit was at an end. "I will promptly arrive at Hyde Park at the predetermined time of half past five. I will be on foot—I do hope you will accompany me for a stroll."

"As long as it doesn't end in a like manner as our last stroll," Jude teased. When his face blanched, she regretted her words. "I am jesting with you—and if it puts you at ease, we shall take a path far from any water."

"The odds are not in favor of such an occurrence happening again," he replied. "Also, I will endeavor to keep watch of my footing in the future."

He leaned precariously close to her and, for a split second, Jude thought he meant to kiss her. Her eyes fluttered shut…and she waited.

But nothing came.

Creaking open one eye, she noticed he brushed at the sleeve of her gown.

"A piece of dirt, likely from the pipe, fell to your gown." She looked down to see nothing there. "But it is gone now."

"Why, thank you, my lord." Her breathing returned to normal as she continued to look down, unable to meet his stare. She truly must gain her wits when around him.

"Do you know the way out?" When she raised her eyes from the floor to answer, she noted he stared at her lips—maybe they'd had the same thought moments ago.

His dismissal was direct, a quality Jude normally preferred in others. But with Lord Cartwright, their connection was unclear. She'd certainly pictured his lips on hers. Every so often, she caught him staring at her longingly. But in times like this, he appeared cold and disinterested.

She could not blame him, as neither had made any move to clarify what was currently transpiring between them. Were they two individuals who shared a common interest, or a couple finding a reason to spend time with one another?

Jude thought over that exact question as she stood to depart Lord Cartwright's townhouse.

The only thing she knew for certain was that she was playing with fire—for all Lord Cartwright's unassuming manner, he was an astute man, and unlikely to overlook Jude's transgressions if discovered.

Chapter Ten

Cart breathed a sigh of relief as soon as he heard the door shut behind Jude. It had been his plan to show her all type of antiquities in his possession—an intellectual wooing, if you will. The pair of them finding a mutual affection based on common interests...that would lead to more. More of what? Cart hadn't thought that far, which was evident in his almost disastrous visit. The hour had passed so quickly, he'd lost track of time.

If he were lucky—not that Cart took much stock in luck—but if he were, Jude was not currently being accosted by Lady Cartwright as she left Cart's townhouse.

Overall, his time with Jude had gone as well as could be expected.

Returning to his desk, Cart sank into his chair and placed his spectacles on the bridge of his nose, flipping the ends over his ears. A stroll in the park...tomorrow at half past five. He opened his appointment log to see that he had a meeting at two in the afternoon. He was free after that.

Very good, he thought.

It was not often he ventured out for any fresh air or exercise beyond what was necessary to meet with someone, such as the garden party with Lord Barton. Even during his time at Eton, Cart did not take to archery or riding as most of the students did. It was far more beneficial to his future that he use the library and other educational services offered. Years after his requested departure from the university, Cart still longed for the quiet hours surrounded by books of learning with access to scholars in any given field of study.

Cart was resigned to spending an increased amount of time outdoors if it was something Jude partook in regularly.

"Simon Montgomery!" Lady Cartwright swept into the room, snapping Cart from his daydreaming of Miss Jude—an irrational waste of time, to be sure. His mother, dressed in the height of fashion, or at least what had been fashionable five years prior, discarded her wrap and handbag on the seat Jude had vacated not long ago. "A carriage was departing as I arrived home. Did I have a caller?"

He remained silent, deciding whether he should deny any knowledge of a caller.

"Oh, you were locked in here and didn't hear a thing," she said, answering her own question and providing Cart with a way out of correcting her. No one corrected Lady Anastasia Cartwright, especially her own children. "It is not healthy, all this stale air and musty books."

Cart removed his glasses and massaged the bridge of his nose, a headache taking hold at her shrill proclamation. Nothing his mother hadn't said before. Though, somehow, her words rang truer than before. Maybe it had been unwise of him to dedicate so my years to his studies, the search for his family heirlooms, and his quest to collect. Could it be his overwhelming need to hunt and gather was due to everything he held dear being stripped from him without any type of warning?

It was only in his nature, a personal correlation between his identity and his need to possess, which drove him to crave the tangible. It was something about himself he'd never felt the need to question.

And Cart still hadn't the time to question why he felt the way he did…it simply was.

Especially when his mother had him pinned by her unrelenting stare.

"I will need an increase in my allowance," she said, obviously irritated to have to repeat herself and beg her son for coin. "I have incurred unforeseen expenses that I simply cannot neglect."

"Another new dress—or possibly a hat much like the many you currently have sitting unworn in your dressing chamber?" The ache behind his eyes intensified. Cart had no clue why he argued with her over expenditures. He would give her the coin regardless of the frivolous nature of her desires. It was the ruin they'd settled into. She badgered him about his ineptitude, blaming him for his uncle's deceptions. And he pretended to be the penny-pinching, ungrateful son, who would cast his aging mother out of his home if he could pull himself away from his studies long enough.

It was exhausting—and Cart yearned to be rid of the charade.

If not only to relieve himself of undue pressure but also to put Theo at ease. She didn't deserve a mother and brother who were constantly at war over trivial things. Purchasing a new dress and parting with coin that could buy an entire meal was not as monumental as Cart and his mother made it out to be.

"Mother." Cart gave in. The time it would take arguing over the increase in allowance was better spent working. "My apologies for my insensitive comment. How much will you be needing? I will have it delivered to your chambers when I return after my appointment—or, if you prefer, I can send the funds directly to settle your account."

"Handle my affairs as if you are my keeper?" She was affronted by his offer, further maddened by his gall—when in truth, he only sought to help her. "Do have it delivered to my rooms. Besides, I find myself longing for travels. I have been in this crowded town too long. It is time I see a bit of what lies beyond London."

At that moment, Cart would have agreed to deliver it to St. James' or Buckingham Palace to end this. He would do anything to not see the accusing stare or hear the accusation of his negligence that led to her throwing herself at his feet for funds in the first place, though traveling—especially outside London—had been something she'd been vehemently against for many years. "How much will you need?"

Her chin notched up, showing her disdain for her place in society. "I am confident twenty-five should be enough."

It was almost her entire monthly allowance. "I will collect twenty-five shillings." Cart would not admit he did not possess that amount lying about his study.

"Pounds."

Cart's eyes narrowed and his throat constricted. "Pardon?"

He wondered if his hearing were worsening along with his eyes, for he'd most definitely heard her incorrectly.

"I am requesting twenty-five pounds." She pronounced the words slowly, as if he were an infant still working to grasp the English language.

His butler didn't make that amount per year. "Have you lost your mind?"

With that amount of coin, she could travel to the Orient—or farther—and live for years without wanting for anything.

Her face reddened and she stomped her foot, much like Theo had done when she was younger—before growing out of such childish ways of self-expression. "It is my money," she shrieked. "Your father promised—"

"It belongs to the Cartwright Earldom," Cart corrected.

"Which I am as Lady Cartwright," she countered.

"Mother." Cart massaged the back of his neck to lessen the gathered tension. "Most days, I find it difficult to scrape together twenty-five shillings. Where do you suggest I find twenty-five pounds?"

"Sell something." It was always her answer. She never offered anything of value belonging to her to sell, however.

"If you still have your jewels close, I can select a few pieces and have your funds by day's end."

"You shall *not* sell my things," she huffed, waving her arms wildly about his study. "Since you are responsible for the financial crisis we are in; why not be rid of all the useless things I see you toting in here daily?"

How she could blame an eighteen-year-old boy for their family ruin was incomprehensible. He'd spent more years than he cared to admit knowing he was responsible for his family's financial woes—countless nights assessing what he could have done differently to foil his uncle's plans and innumerous days spent trying to gain back all of what his family deserved. Yes, his mother blamed him for all their troubles, but it was nothing compared to the culpability he laid at his own feet.

Cart hadn't yet reached his majority when his father passed. His uncle was appointed as his guardian until Cart finished his studies. His mother had been the one present while Julian Montgomery, his father's only sibling, pilfered every penny from the estate—and his treachery ran far deeper than that.

"I have worked tirelessly—for years—to restore our family's wealth and possessions." Cart slammed the palm of his hand on the desk, rattling his neatly organized quills. His mother's eyes widened and she gasped at his uncharacteristic display of emotion. "And every day, you find joy in telling me how it will never be enough for you—never be restored to what we once had."

Lady Cartwright crossed her arms and glared at him, as if challenging him to prove he could ever be enough for the Cartwright title.

"Have it your way." He wasn't giving in, only seeking to use the situation to his advantage. "I agree to dispose of one of my antiques, however..." He let the words trail off, not wanting to jump straight into his compromise with her as she'd likely spot his manipulation. "In exchange for the twenty-five pounds, you will not take Theo with you but allow her to attend a school of my choosing—away from London."

And you, he added silently.

"I have told you repeatedly, I forbid her to attend a school away from this townhouse and if she were to travel with me, her education would continue to be seen to." Cart knew the possibility of her agreeing to his demand was slim. She was a fairly rational thinker and disregarding his offer so readily did not suit her character. "However..." She sighed as if seriously considering his proposal. "When would she leave?"

"As soon as I've located and interviewed a school—and found it appropriate."

"Thirty pounds." Lady Cartwright was nothing if not insightfully clever with her bargaining skills. "And she does not depart until after the season ends and I've settled on my own travel plans."

"You understand that as Lord Cartwright—and Theo's legal guardian—I do not have to obtain your permission?" he asked. "I only seek to keep the peace in this household by extending to you my plans for her future, no matter if they impede yours."

"You will ruin any prospects she has of a proper match," Lady Cartwright accused. "No man will seek

126

the hand of an overly educated, free-minded young woman."

"I think you misjudge what gentlemen find appealing in the fairer sex."

"It most certainly is not a woman who seeks a career as a doctor—or heaven help us both—studies the law."

She could not understand why any woman would seek to study more than needlepoint and the harpsichord. However, times were changing. The roles of men and women were blurring—and Cart would not allow his only sibling to enter her adult life without the skills and knowledge to care for herself and her family. It mattered naught that Theodora was a woman and, therefore, deemed less than a man.

Cart shuddered to think what would have happened if he'd been a woman, arriving home to find out someone had taken all that should have belonged to him and should have supported many generations to come. Theo would never know that fate.

"School for Theodora—and thirty pounds for you to do with as you wish," he offered. "In exchange for you not fighting me on this decision."

It was the best agreement Cart could hope for. It would definitely be worth the many pieces he would be forced to sell in order to scrape together the funds he'd promised her.

"Momma." Theo's voice came from the open doorway.

Cart replaced his peeved expression with a welcoming smile for his sibling, hoping his mother saw fit to do the same.

"Yes, my dear." The words were strained.

"Cook is looking for you to discuss the menu for supper." Thankfully, Theo appeared oblivious to the debate regarding her future that had only moments before heated hotter than ever. "She awaits you in the drawing room."

Lady Cartwright swung back around, a generous smile playing across her lips as if to show him she were still in control—at least where the staff was concerned. "I agree with your proposition, Simon. Do fulfill your obligations quickly. I have much to prepare for."

She turned on slippered feet and marched toward the door, pausing briefly to peck Theo on the cheek before departing the room with her skirt billowing in her wake.

"What have you been quarreling over this hour?" Theo asked, entering the room further.

"You know us too well, Sprite," he replied, hoping to distract her from the question. When she refused to rise to the bait of her hated nickname and only stared, awaiting an answer, Cart continued, "It is of no import—only adult matters."

"I am not far from being an adult, Cart."

He took a moment to look her from crown to toes, shocked by how true her statement was, but never would he admit it. At her age, there were many young women already promised to their husbands. "I assure you, the thread of our discussion was as uninspiring as the unseasoned duck soup Cook makes every Christmastide."

Her nose wrinkled. "Yuck!"

"Exactly so." Cart relaxed into his chair. "Now, where did you run off to when my visitor arrived? You were very serious in your negotiations to see her."

Theo's face paled. "Oh, I realized neglecting my studies only to gain a peek of your caller was not my wisest decision."

"You seemed very convinced of it before," he said. "Why the quick change?"

"I am almost of an age to be rid of these plaits and short dresses. It would not be in my best interest to gain a reputation by spying on others." Theo had been taking note of their mother's strict lectures on decorum. "Besides, whoever she was cannot be all too interesting. She was here to visit you, after all."

Cart chuckled. "Yes, yes, I know. You find your older brother highly tedious and dreary."

A bit of coloring returned to her cheeks with his laughter. "I will let you return to your dull routine."

She dropped into an exaggerated curtsey, one their mother would in no way approve of, her hands lifting her skirt high enough to expose her stockings where they ended just below her knees.

"You are allowed to pester me any time," Cart said, settling his glasses on the bridge of his nose once more. "And I think you shall be meeting my visitor at some point."

Theo's smiled wobbled slightly and he filled with concern.

"Is all as it should be?"

"It is just that your mention of routine reminded me that I must practice my piano before Gustavo arrives for my lesson."

"Very well." Cart nodded in dismissal, though he felt her words were forced.

But there was much he need ponder before his afternoon in Hyde Park on the morrow. None of it having to do with his mother or her travel plans and all to do with Jude; namely, how he would hide his lack of a proper open-air carriage—or rideable horse.

Chapter Eleven

"I have confirmed several times, Marce." Garrett was at his wits end, Jude could tell. He'd untied and discarded his cravat over an hour before, his empty tumbler sat unattended on the table in Marce's gold and red receiving room, and he currently lay prone on her low-slung lounge, his free hand toying with the hanging golden tassels. His pose was in direct opposition to the exasperation in his tone. "We go through this every year. I promise to keep watch on the girls, manage Craven House as best I can, and keep the card room steady and the clients happy."

His words did nothing to alleviate Marce's furrowed brow and hectic movements behind her desk.

"Sister, things will go as they do every year," Jude said, attempting to help her brother. The grimace he gave her told Jude she needed to work harder. "Come now, Marce. You've taken this journey each year since Mother passed. This year will be no different. You will depart from four siblings and will return to four siblings."

"This year is very much different." Marce pulled open a drawer and removed a stack of thick stationery embossed with her initials MD, placing it in her travel case. Next, she made sure her ink was closed tightly and would not leak. It followed the paper into the case, along with several quill pens and Craven House's household ledger. "Everything is out of control."

"Do you not mean *everyone*?" Payton had the good sense to mumble behind her hand to Jude and Sam.

The three women sat on the settee across from Garrett, their bodies wedged close together on a seat meant for two. Each with their own reason for staying silent when Garrett and Marce discussed back and forth about the upcoming week.

Jude hadn't any idea why Payton or Garrett sought to push Marce along on her trip, but her twin and she knew a few days without Marce's hawk-like watch over them would benefit them greatly...namely, giving them the opportunity to be rid of the vase.

In the foyer, Marce's traveling chest awaited her exit.

In her private salon, her siblings awaited her departure.

Not a thing was out of order.

Part of Marce's unrest was normal—something each of them noticed as her time away from Craven House approached each season. In the days leading up to this time of year, Marce was even more domineering than usual. She'd made the journey like clockwork since their mother's passing, the same as Madame Sasha had before her. Marce never spoke of where she traveled to or who sent the carriage to collect her. When they'd been younger, Jude, Sam, and Payton had dreamed that a prince sent for Marce—that the well-sprung, ornately adorned traveling carriage with the deep green velvet seats arrived each year to whisk their eldest sister away to a far-off castle where she was actually a princess.

Their assumptions were never met with agreement or denial. When Marce returned home after her time away, she was once again the jovial and even spirited—though commanding—family leader they loved.

Marce was correct in thinking everything was out of control—more so than Jude hoped she realized. It was not many nights ago that Jude spent time locked away and if Marce hadn't been in town, there was no telling what might have happened to her.

They'd never imagined that Lady Haversham—with Ellie's help—would take the trio under her wing and present them properly to society, but that was the reality. No longer could Marce lock them away in their schoolroom, forcing them to master their studies.

Each knew that Marce could not support them forever. At some point, they need marry or find a means to help support themselves and Craven House.

Their home had undergone many changes in recent years. No longer was the name synonymous with ill repute. Gone were the many rooms used to entertain gentlemen of the aristocracy, as well as the women who survived by serving them. Yes, remnants of olden days remained, specifically, the card games Marce hosted several evenings per week to help support the women who sought out Craven House for aid. The same women that Madame Sasha, their dear mother, would have helped by allowing them to sell their bodies under this very roof. But Marce had found a way around that—given those same abused and abandoned women hope for a future that did not include further abuse, no matter the coin they made.

Though it had come at a huge financial strain and was affecting their entire family.

Jude respected Marce's decisions, even though they meant many sacrifices for them all. They had no lady's maids to attend them, no fancy gowns ordered regularly, and sometimes, meals were little more than what Cook could put together from the small garden behind Craven House.

There were hardly enough funds from the gaming hell for their barest necessities.

Marce insisted the sacrifice would be worth it for them all.

As it already had.

Marce—and her siblings—were permitted a life on the fringes of society. It was not much, but it would guarantee them all some sort of match. In turn, her sister was wise enough to use her connections within the *ton* to secure honest work for the women who came to Craven House for help.

That meant much secrecy and avoidance when peers asked of their relations. The perceptions of Craven House among the *beau monde* were not favorable in any way. Surely, men had enjoyed the entertainments provided by Sasha, their mother, but many thought that meant Jude and her sisters were women of loose morals, available for the taking. This was only overshadowed by the wives and female relations of men who'd frequented her home in the past. They assumed all measure of debauchery still existed within its walls—which created fallacious perceptions of Jude and her sisters.

The one thing Marce did for herself was this journey each year.

A soft knock sounded at the door.

"Come in." Marce sighed, standing from her seat behind her desk as Craven House's only full-time servant entered.

"Your carriage has arrived, m'lady." Mr. Curtis bowed his head. "Should I gather your belongings?"

They all held their breath, fearing Marce would cancel or postpone her departure until her siblings came to heel and things returned to a more orderly state.

The silence dragged on, when finally, Garrett pushed to his feet. "Marce, you know you must go."

Must? Jude stared at the pair—some silent message and answer traveling between them. For the first time in many years, Jude questioned her closeness with Garrett. She knew he favored her, their personalities closely mirroring one another, and that she served as his confidante, but there was obviously something he kept from her. Though Jude was guilty of doing the same of late.

Marce reached into her drawer once more to retrieve a stack of correspondence, slipped it into her bag, secured the flap on her travel case, and stepped around her desk. She stopped before Jude and her sisters where they all sat, quiet yet watchful.

"Will I regret this decision?" Marce asked, turning a hard stare on each of them in turn. She stopped when she got to Jude. "Can you remain out of the watchman's residence?" She didn't wait for a response but moved back to Sam. "Can you refrain from starting a scandal that will cast a dim light on Lady Haversham?" She was a full head shorter than Sam and Jude, but her stance and glare made her appear taller than Garrett's near six feet. "And do not let me hear that you snuck into the card room while I was away."

Payton moaned. "That is unfair."

"Would you like to know what is unfair?" Marce's hands went to her hips, her lips pursed and her voice stern. "Me being woken from my bed in the middle of the night to collect Jude. Me working all day to make sure the three of you have a meal to eat. Me having to settle your gaming debts, Payton."

Jude turned sharply to her twin, who gave her the same puzzled expression. Could the notices her sister had been receiving all be due to their youngest sibling? But no, they had always been cautioned against overspending or requesting frivolous things. Since their mother's passing and Marce taking charge of Craven House, things had changed and the normal funds they were used to receiving had all but dried up.

"What debts?" Garrett voiced Jude's question. "I have heard nothing of this—and who would take seriously a wager against a child?"

"I am not a child—"

"Who is not important, as I have handled the situation with no one the wiser—even the lot of you. I had agreed never to bring it up again, but..." Marce cut off Payton's protest before pausing and breathing deeply, her bosom heaving, straining against her tight bodice. She picked up her case once more. "I think it is imperative each of you knows that there will be serious repercussions if I return to find any of you have gotten into trouble. Do I make myself clear?"

Garrett threw his chin up, motioning for them to stand.

They popped up from the chaise lounge so suddenly that their movement pushed it back a few inches, its feet scraping against the hardwood floor.

"Of course," Sam inclined her head.

"Very well," Payton sighed.

"You will not regret taking your yearly holiday." Jude stepped forward and embraced her sister. Payton's gambling debts were not the worst of the family problems—it could not be the only thing that weighed so heavily on her sister's shoulders, the delinquency notices pointed to far deeper troubles for Craven House. "We shall endeavor to not embarrass you—or Lady Haversham in your absence."

Marce wrapped her arms around Jude and returned the hug, her small stature holding the strength of a woman twice her size. "You better hope you do not. I would have no regret locking the trio of you in your rooms for the next decade."

When Jude released Marce, Payton and Sam gave her quick hugs, and the three stepped back.

Marce turned to Garrett. "Are you certain you can spare the time to keep watch at the card tables?"

"Have I let you down?" he asked. When Marce said nothing, he added, "Recently?"

It broke the tension that had clouded the room since Marce had summoned them all not long after the noonday repast.

Curtis, their manservant, cleared his throat from the doorway. "My lady, the driver says if ye are to arrive before nightfall, ye must depart now."

She nodded to the elderly man and with one last lingering look to her siblings, Marce walked toward the door. "I shall be gone a week, at most."

And only a three or four-hour carriage ride from London, if she were to arrive by nightfall as Mr. Curtis hinted. She certainly wasn't traveling all the way to Bath in such a short amount of time.

"Godspeed, dear sister," Garrett called, retaking his place on the lounge.

"Do keep everyone from the gallows while I'm away."

"I can't do any worse than you, I fear," Garrett answered with a chuckle.

"I am serious."

Jude, Payton, and Sam kept silent, content to watch the encounter between their eldest siblings.

It was only imperative that Marce be gone shortly, Sam and Jude had a ride in Hyde Park to prepare for—and neither wanted any questions from their sister.

Marce handed her traveling case to Mr. Curtis before walking through the open door. Her footfalls could be heard as she made her way to the foyer, the elderly man in her wake.

# # #

"I thought she'd never leave!" Sam fell across her bed, the ropes holding the straw-filled bedding in place creaked at the sudden weight. They'd quickly made their excuses and departed for their bedchambers after the front door closed behind Marce. "How are we supposed to get rid of that blasted vase with Garrett so close at hand?"

Jude had been worried about the same thing. It was her hope that Payton kept him occupied while she and Sam did what they needed to do. Namely, be rid of that cursed item and, with a bit of luck, put their thieving ways behind them for good. Or at least that was Jude's expectation. Unfortunately, their only option at the moment was Lord Cartwright. Even though Jude despised misleading him.

She was torn, even though it was a necessary evil—helping her family keep their home meant lying to and misleading a man who'd captured her interest beyond a handsome smile.

Intellect was a rare thing to find in London. Most men were concerned with the cut of their suit, their next night at their gentlemen's club, or finding a way under the skirt of an unsuspecting woman. Cart was different. Certainly, she'd noticed the way he'd taken in her charms, but he did not limit their visits—as odd as they were—to matters of the weather or talk of insignificant gossip.

Jude did not consider herself of high intellect, though she knew her tastes ran deeper than most men of the *ton* were willing to embrace. A woman who was learned in history, culture, and the arts was not something the *beau monde* normally found appealing.

The lords of her acquaintance favored debutantes whose interests lie in current fashion trends, needlepoint, and other household matters—all things that would make a suitable wife.

Or men—certainly many that Sam had turned her eye to—were looking for women interested in the darker side of London living. An improper night at Vauxhall Gardens, strolling down the unlit paths where many turned a blind eye to unchaperoned women and the men who accompanied them. Jude had even witnessed men arriving at Craven House with scantily clad women, who certainly weren't their wives, dressed in attire not befitting anyplace outside the bedchambers. The women would sit on the men's laps as they played hand after hand, drinking themselves into a stupor. The females would giggle and fuss when the men's hands roamed over their bodies, lifting their skirts to touch the secrets hidden below, but Marce would quickly shoo them from the house when they took things too far and crossed the line of decency.

Sam and Jude had spied activities such as this at a tender age. Jude had found the touching uncomfortable to watch, while Sam had been captivated by the scenes before them. Another difference between them—matters of the flesh enthralled Sam, while Jude took more of a cautious stance on them.

Their nightly escapades down the servants' stairs to spy on the nightly carousing ended not long after it had begun when Marce had stumbled upon them. They'd been punished and sent to their room, forbidden from leaving the upstairs of their home for nigh over a month's time. When their sister threatened to lock them in their room for the next decade, it was no empty promise.

"Jude?" Sam called, craning her neck to see her twin. Jude stood a few paces inside their room, stuck in the many thoughts going through her mind. "You know Garrett best. How can we keep from his notice?"

Jude shook her head, dispelling her worries and bringing her thoughts back to their current situation. "I think the vase is safe where it is and we must continue as we've been. Marce is convinced we are making a successful splash in society. We are attending gatherings, acting the proper, demure misses. We shall continue in that vein."

Sam pursed her lips.

"Today we will prepare for our ride in Hyde Park. Lady Chastain was kind enough to allow us use of her open carriage. We will mingle, be the proper young misses, and if Lord Cartwright shows up, I will do what I can to help solve our dilemma."

Sam's eyes widened in surprise as Jude heard the door behind her swing open.

"I would favor a ride in Hyde Park," Payton gushed entering the room. "Why was I not told?"

"You are not tagging along," Sam and Jude said in unison.

Payton set her hands on her hips and glared at her sisters. "We will see what Garrett has to say about that—and that pretty vase that appeared in Marce's private salon. I am certain you have both noticed it, that quiet, ugly thing. My, but it looks old. Far too old for Marce's tastes—and the colors are all wrong. I thought to ask her if she wanted me to dispose of the obnoxious thing while she was gone, but—"

"You are not to touch it!" Jude said, raising her voice and exposing their secret.

Payton smirked.

"What do you know of that vase?" Sam asked.

"Oh, only that I saw you sneaking in late one night with it tucked under your arm. And then Garrett summoned Marce early one morning and they departed in haste, returning later with Jude in tow—but I guess our dear sister knows nothing of the vase, am I correct?" Their youngest sister was known for her watchful eye, which suited her best at the card tables, though obviously not as good as Jude had thought, judging from Marce's earlier comment to the contrary. "You think your activities have gone unnoticed, which may be the case with Marce, but not me."

"You know nothing," Sam accused.

"I suppose that is possible, but I may also know far more than the pair of you think."

"What do you want, Pay?" Jude's mouth suddenly went dry.

"I shall continue to cover for you, but sometime in the future, I will need the pair of you to cover for me—no matter the situation." A gleam entered Payton's eyes, knowing she had her sisters exactly where she wanted them.

"We cannot allow you to put yourself in peril and not say anything." Jude loved the girl, but her antics were far more treacherous than theirs—if Marce's comments of gaming debts were to be believed.

"At this point in time, I do not see that either of you have any choice but to surrender to my demands." She remained silent until both twins nodded. "Oh, and I shall accompany you to the park today."

Sam moaned, burying her face in her pillow.

"Come now, Sam," Jude prodded. "It is a little ride in the park. She cannot annoy you overly much in such a short period of time."

It was advantageous for Jude to have their youngest sibling along for the ride. It would allow her a bit of time with Cart, without Sam keeping too close of a watch on them—if the man showed up, that was.

"Now that that is all settled, Garrett sent me to inform you that Lady Chastain's carriage has arrived to collect us." Payton turned to leave the room, throwing a glance over her shoulder. "I will meet you in the carriage, do not keep me waiting…there is never any guarantee what I might say or do when I am bored."

"Meddlesome imp." Sam pushed from the bed, smoothing her skirt and glancing into the mirror above her dressing table. "I was hoping to re-pin my hair, but time will not allow it."

Jude took in her own appearance. She was not one to don a morning dress only to have to wiggle out of it two hours later in favor of a walking dress. In that vein, Jude had dressed for their ride in the park before taking her morning repast—and now, she was happy she had.

She hoped Lord Cartwright favored the paisley print she'd selected for the day.

Chapter Twelve

Cart resisted the urge to fan his heated face or remove his overcoat. He'd never understood the need for ladies to carry hand fans with them at all times, but the insufferable afternoon heat was enough to have him hoping that a fashion trend started, allowing gentlemen to tote them, as well.

Not a breeze moved through the trees as the sun beat down on him. Unlike the garden party, where gusts of wind had rolled across the open areas lifting the pockets of muggy air above the crowd, no such weather pattern was evident today. Cart moved between the hordes of finely dressed women with elaborate headpieces and men dressed as if they were peacocks with their feathers on display. The scene before him was shockingly absurd. The sheer amount of fabric adorning the thousands of *ton* members milling about on foot, on horseback, or in carriages, would take several large merchant ships to import.

He'd dedicated his time and energy to antiquities, but the far safer—and more lucrative—venture may very well be imports. Textiles in particular. The utter vanity Cart witnessed made him question his desire to be a part of it all. By birth, he was an earl, one of London's elite, but by nature, he would not allow that to define him and his future.

The crowd surrounding him moved at a snail's pace, no one being in any hurry. His mother had spoken of the benefits of daily walks in Hyde Park, gaining a turn of exercise, but not a single person moved fast enough to increase their heart rhythm. In fact, many stood slightly off the paths, socializing in groups.

Clearly, Cart had been misinformed about the *ton*'s reasoning for visiting the park.

Not that any of that mattered to him—he was here for one reason.

To see Jude.

Miss Judith Pengarden.

It was odd to call a woman by her given name. Their acquaintance had moved so quickly and had turned to a sort of friendship where one was given permission to address another so informally. He'd convinced himself that their relationship was founded on nothing more than a mutual interest and possible future dealings. That was where her interest in him ended—and his as well if he were smart.

He must remember to address her properly before her sisters, so as not to cast any doubt on the nature of their association.

If he were ever to locate Jude—the park was far grander than he imagined.

It had been years since he'd scoured the terrain with his father, bringing his archery bow and taking to the less populated areas to hone his skills. That had been over fifteen years ago, and his bow had been long forgotten—likely stolen by his uncle.

Surely the foliage-covered area hadn't grown in size. He scanned the park once more, his eyes settling on no one in particular, lest they recognize him and insist on conversing.

He reminded himself yet again that he was not against idle conversation. But he was here for a purpose, which was not empty discourse.

Jude had mentioned arriving by carriage, so he'd found a path—a large loop—where many open-air conveyances traveled at a slow pace, allowing their inhabitants to talk to friends and acquaintances in other vehicles as they drove past. Several were stopped, their occupants in conversation, others pulled to the side to allow men and women to depart and continue on foot.

At this rate, Cart had a slim chance of spotting the one carriage he searched for, especially from his low vantage point on foot.

He hadn't any idea the color of her horses or carriage. For a man who prided himself on being well informed, Cart was lacking exponentially today.

Veering off the path, Cart moved to a small rise that would enable him to reach a higher lookout point. The short climb left him short of breath and wishing it were acceptable to remove one's coat and shirt during times of overexertion.

The view was unquestionably better than from the base of the parkland.

Once again, he scanned the crowd, his eyes passing quickly over blonde and brunette heads, also uninteresting were the women who wore extravagant headpieces with plumage and frills, for Jude was not a woman to don such frivolous attire.

He stopped short at the thought.

Cart did not know her well enough to put stock in his reasoning. True, they'd spent time together on three separate occasions and not once had Jude donned a silly hat, but that was in no way proof that she would not on a trip to the park.

Thoughts of Jude were clearly muddling his mind…he only hoped they didn't cloud his judgment in the same manner.

The idea of returning home and sending Jude a note of apology was tempting, removing his coat and untying his neckcloth.

A spot of auburn with the barest hint of gold laced through it caught his eye.

A closer look showed not one but two women with matching hair, a brunette between them.

Cart issued a wave, feeling foolish for attracting the stares of so many people as he attempted to flag down Jude's carriage. The open carriage was directly before his elevated position on the rise when the occupants finally took notice. The woman closest to him leaned forward—likely issuing a command to stop the carriage—and they pulled to the side, allowing others to continue on.

Smiling, Cart traversed back down to the path where he saw all three of the women departing the conveyance. His stomach clinched. It was only proper he entertain the trio of sisters. Why hadn't he thought of this before? It was trying enough to gain the nerve to speak with Miss Jude, but her sisters, too?

His only meeting with Miss Payton had gone dreadfully. The young woman had seemed uninterested in his presence at Craven House and had gone so far as to mock him while he awaited entry. Jude's eldest sister had scolded the girl and sent her away, but Payton's rationale for her harsh jests were blurred to him.

"Lord Cartwright!" Jude called as he arrived before the party.

"Miss Judith. Miss Samantha." Cart nodded to the pair and finally turned to their younger sister. "Miss Payton. It is lovely to see you all. Such a clear, bright, inviting day. Is it not?" He suspected the women noticed his discomfort—with both the weather and all their presences.

"It is a fine day, my lord," Miss Samantha greeted him. "Jude was starting to worry you hadn't come."

Miss Samantha's sly smile and Payton's snicker told him the pair was making light of their sister, which irked him for reasons unknown. Another thing he might want to scrutinize more in his leisurely time.

"Miss Jude has nothing to fear on that score," Cart attempted to rebuff Miss Samantha's comment. "I am an honorable, punctual gentleman. If I give my word, I will always follow through."

Miss Payton gave her sister a peculiar look before slipping her arm through Miss Samantha's. "Ah, well, I am desiring a stroll around the water—and since Lord Cartwright likely seeks to remain dry, we will meet you back here after our walk." Payton chuckled once more at her jest as the pair smiled to Jude and gave a small hand wave before starting on their way. Apparently, the twins had told their younger sister of his debacle in the pond.

Cart eyed the pair as they retreated, their heads bent together in conversation, Miss Samantha's strides much longer than Miss Payton's short ones. "Have I offended Miss Payton?" he inquired.

"Why would you think such a thing?" Jude set her hand on his arm and they started toward a path that kept them far enough from the pond Jude's sisters were now heading toward.

"She was not"—he paused, fearful of insulting Jude's sister—"the most welcoming when I arrived at Craven House for our visit."

Jude laughed—a light, airy chuckle much the same as she had at the garden party—and patted his arm with her free hand. She continued to stare ahead at the path before them.

"Did I say something humorous?" He'd feared insulting her kin. She had laughed instead of being offended. "I apologize—"

"Lord Cartwright—Cart," she corrected. "Do stop apologizing for any little affront you perceive and worry over." She smiled at him and his worries, indeed, melted away, much as he feared his body was from the heat. "Pay thinks you are grand—never fear."

Pay—short for Payton—Cart found he enjoyed their shortened names, much as he and Theo had pet names for one another. "I would never seek to slight or cause insult to your family, Miss Judith."

They continued in a comfortable silence as they meandered down a shady path, out of the late afternoon sun. Jude nodded to acquaintances as they passed, but at no time stopped to engage people further.

As the silence lengthened, Cart couldn't help but wonder if he'd ruined something, destroyed their companionable association with his tendency to continually fret and evaluate his surroundings.

He concentrated on placing one foot in front of the other as they ventured down a path less traveled—keeping his eyes from straying to the way Jude's gown lay delicately across her breasts—many would say a fraction too constricting. As before, their strides aligned as if they spent every day walking side by side.

The crowd of ramblers trickled down until they'd trekked for several minutes without encountering another soul. The branches from the low-hanging trees and the overgrown shrubs began to narrow their path, causing Jude to walk closer to his side to avoid snagging her hair or dress on the encroaching plant life. The soft fabric of her gown pressed to his arm and he tried to convince himself he hadn't drawn her closer, allowing the side of her bosom to touch him, but rather that she'd moved ever closer of her own volition.

She slanted her head to avoid a branch and one hanging curl brushed his face.

"My lord?" she said on an exhale, returning to their formal address.

"Yes, Miss Jude?"

"Have you had more time to think about the vase?" She kept her voice soft and low as if fearful someone would overhear their discussion. Her whispered words had foreshadowed a request of great import. However, her inquiry took him off guard. Had he wished for her to ask something of a far more intimate nature?

Cart was certainly interested in the piece, if not for his own collection, then as an item for a client who favored the time period and crafting details.

Though he did not seek to give her the impression that his interest in her began and ended with antiquities. The odd somersaults of his stomach and tingling at the spot her hand rested on his arm pointed to his interest in her being much deeper than mere relics of historical value.

"I have thought about it a great deal." Lie. Truth: he'd thought of *her* a great deal. "Is it possible for me to see the vase? It would be far simpler for me to ascertain its origins and provide you with an accurate assessment of its value if I were to examine it."

Finally, she looked away from the path before them, smiling at his attentiveness. "I pondered bringing the vase today, but did not want to risk any bump in the trail jolting the piece. It is very delicate."

Cart concentrated on his mother's calendar of events and when she'd be away from home next—when Jude could bring the vase and they'd have a spot of privacy. After their stroll, he'd be tasked with meeting a local curator to assess selling several items to collect the funds requested by his mother.

"Please let me know when you are available. I have a sizable catalogue of research materials at my home—"

"Would you mind meeting at Sir Edwin's Circulating Library?" she asked.

Cart hadn't thought of the possibility of her being agreeable to meeting in public. Nonetheless, Sir Edwin's was highly preferable to anywhere his mother's prying eyes could be. "I haven't visited the library in several years."

"He has amassed a rather extensive collection of antiquity registers with hand-drawn inserts." Her words sped up with excitement, something he well understood. "It has been my home away from home for some time now."

"If you think the establishment will suit our needs then far be it for me to dissuade you, Miss Jude," he conceded. Even if the library lacked the proper ledgers to identify the time period and origin of the vase, at least he would have another afternoon in Jude's company—hidden amongst a large number of books—his previous favorite pastime, joining with his newly discovered one. "Is your family agreeable to us spending time together?"

She stopped at his question, turning to him. Facing one another, their eyes met on almost the same level, Jude only a couple of inches shorter than Cart. "They do not disagree, my lord."

On some level, Cart realized that agreeing to their association and not disagreeing meant two utterly different things. But the way she stared at him, her rounded green eyes an open book and her lips in the slightest pout with a peek of her straight, white teeth visible, with one long, curling strand of rosewood red hair teasing the side of her face, had him disregarding his instincts on the matter.

With only a slight bit of reluctance, Cart reached forward, allowing her hair to curl around his finger. It was as silky smooth as he'd expected—teasing his senses with a hint of lavender.

"Miss Judith," he mumbled on an exhale. "I find everything about you to my liking."

She stood frozen before him, both of them forgetting to breathe. Scared to make any movement and break the bond forming between them, encompassing the space around them.

Cart could not be the only one feeling the pull to be close. "Can you feel that?" he asked. He'd heard of certain electromagnetic forces at work. He'd read the words recently in a science pamphlet, but had doubts about the believability of invisible fields of force surrounding objects—and especially their ability to draw things together.

Some unknown force—magnetic or otherwise—was pulling him and Jude together.

He could not move away if he wanted to.

And Cart certainly did not want to step away from Jude.

In fact, he yearned to have her nearer. He slid his free hand around her waist, drawing her ever closer, his fingers lightly running across her gown. The stays hidden by her overskirt could be felt underneath. It was a liberty he'd never taken with a woman.

The few inches separating their heights was apparent with Jude so close he could feel her warm breath on his neck as she raised her eyes to his.

Cart expected to see questions in her gaze—or uncertainty—but she continued to stare, her tongue darting out to wet her lips before retreating, her lips remaining slightly parted.

Tightening his hold, Cart brought Jude up against his body, her bosom pressed securely to his chest and her hands secured to his shoulders. Even their thighs rested against each other's. A connection, both emotional and physical, that he'd never allowed himself—nor sensed that he wanted. Letting another so close was not something he was against, but it was not something necessary to his objectives in life.

But now, after this, how would he want anything less? This joining of not only bodies but also minds in a way that captivated him completely.

Her fingers gripped his shoulders and he knew she felt the connection, too.

Cart released her curl, his fingers grazing her cheek to settle at her exposed neck.

The next moment passed quickly, but also lasted what seemed like centuries.

He breathed in the scent of her lavender hair and the sweetness of her exhale—as if she'd enjoyed marmalade with toast at her last repast. Their lips met and Cart was lost.

Lost in the sensation of such an intimate touching, Jude's soft, plump lips pressed to his far stiffer mouth. The light brushing of their mouths turned to something deeper, more sensual, when Jude's hands moved from his shoulders to tangle in his hair just above his collar. There was not time for Cart to examine his lack of knowledge on the physical act of kissing. Certainly, he was unversed in the emotional aspect of the act, as well. But as the pace quickened and their lips found their own rhythm, any timidity on Cart's part was forgotten.

The distant sounds of laughter, carriage wheels, and horse hooves faded completely as all his senses focused on Jude and her fingers grasping his hair, tugging slightly. Even the smell of her receded, replaced by only the feel of her: her soft gown, her hair brushing his face as their mouths moved, the feel of her quickened pulse at her neck where his fingers rested.

And her lips against his, which suddenly faded when he felt her pull back slightly and something foreign grazed his bottom lip. It startled him to realize it was her tongue. He'd never read of such a thing being done during a kiss. It shocked him, yet at the same time, it also lent an air of exhilaration to the moment.

His hand stroked her back while hers continued to caress his head.

Sensation after sensation swept over and through him.

It was no wonder great men were brought to their knees by pleasures of the flesh—any longer, and Cart would fall heavier than most, but he found everything about Jude intoxicating.

Suddenly, Jude stiffened in his arms, her hands falling to her sides and her lips freezing against his.

"Did you hear that?" she mumbled against his lips, still pressed close.

"No, I —" Cart started before he heard something coming from the shrubs not far away.

"It is a rustling." Jude stepped fully from his arms, glancing both ways down the path. "Maybe it is time we return."

Cart wanted to scream his disagreement, pull her back to him, and finishing what they had started—whatever that may be. Instead, he nodded.

He noticed her face was a lovely shade of rose when she brought her hands to her cheeks before quickly running them down the front for her gown, looking in any direction but at him.

Another new experience; what should one say or do after a particularly pleasurable kiss? A kiss that left a person mentally fuzzy with no track of how much time had passed. It was certainly not the first time he'd felt this way in her presence, but it seemed to worsen with each meeting.

He ran his fingers through his hair in an attempt to tame any wayward pieces that were out of place from her wandering hands. Thankfully, he'd left his spectacles at home or they'd have likely been knocked from his face.

"Miss Judith—"

Laughter, followed by footsteps, sounded from the path they'd traveled down.

With regret, their moment alone had come to an end—to his extreme disappointment.

Jude finally gazed at him, an unreadable expression on her face—pensive, but at the same time, weary—as if she, too, had experienced something new and pleasurable and was sad to see it end.

"There you two are," Sam's throaty voice deepened with suggestion. "I thought we'd need venture off the path to find the pair of you."

"My apologies if I kept you waiting long," Cart rushed to offer explanation for their extended absence. "We were making our way back to your carriage just now. Allow me to escort you all back to the main trail."

Cart glanced at Jude, offering his arm. She gladly set her hand on it, moving once more to his side. Her blush had lessened and both of their breathing had returned to normal, though he noted her lips were a bit fuller than usual.

Something he'd do well to remember in the future—kissing was a dangerous thing, leaving its mark for the world to see if one weren't careful.

# # #

Cart paused, looking up at the swinging wooden sign proudly proclaiming *Lewis Stanford Auctioneers*. The place—its smells, noises, and patrons—was all too familiar to him. It was the place Cart had spent countless hours combing through written documents and searching room after room for his family heirlooms. He'd found quite a few for all his efforts.

But today was different.

He was not here to locate a precious treasure or to bid on a newly discovered one.

Cart sucked in a deep breath, hefted the large box he'd lugged from his home—loaded on a hackney and unloaded here—into his arms and pushed through the door. A bell chimed, announcing his arrival.

"Good morn, my lord," Mr. Stanford greeted warmly. "I was not expecting you until the end of next week. What have you here?" The shopkeeper came around the shelf of books he was organizing as Cart set the chest on the floor.

It was something Cart had hoped never to have to do, but with his mother's demand for increased funds, he had no other option. So, he'd spent his evening the night before collecting anything of significant worth that he could part with. They were all objects of little to no sentimental value—but that did not lessen the loss he was feeling even before handing them over to Mr. Stanford.

"I brought a few neglected pieces to sell, things I am sure others will appreciate far more than myself," Cart lied. He'd rarely met another collector who treasured a piece of art of historical worth better than he, but now was neither the time nor the place to anguish over the difficult decision he'd had to make. "I thought you might be interested in some or all of the pieces—several paintings, a few statues, and even a ring fabled to belong to an Egyptian queen."

The man eyed Cart suspiciously before scurrying close for a look, unable to resist the lure of anything that could turn a profit.

Cart flipped the latch on the chest and opened it wide to reveal the treasures within.

He averted his gaze, focusing on objects around the cluttered room as if interested in a purchase. "Have a look. There is much you'll find to your liking."

Stepping away, Cart lifted a ceramic statue of a Greek sea goddess, Amphitrite, and inspected the fine sculpting skills needed to craft such an exquisite sculpture. The piece was not particularly old, but kept his attention so as to avoid watching the man paw through his things in search of anything that caught his eye.

Stanford mumbled exclamations of excitement several times as he rummaged through the chest.

"Thirty-five pounds for the entire lot." The entirety of its holding was far closer to forty-five pounds by Cart's estimates, but he needed the money now—not tomorrow or in a fortnight. He did not possess the liberty to haggle with the man.

"Twenty-five—not a shilling more," Stanford retorted.

"Absolutely not," Cart refuted. "I am insulted that you would balk at my asking price."

"My lord." Stanford shrugged his shoulders. "I am but a lowly businessman seeking to support his family."

"That is poppycock!" Cart couldn't believe the nerve of the man. "You are unwed and I know you recently purchased a farm outside London—do not try to fool me, Stanford."

"Thirty pounds," he gave in, throwing his hands up in disgust. "A man cannot make an honest living at such rates."

It was the price Cart had hoped to garner from the chest's contents, but it stung to part with them all the same. "Agreed," he said through gritted teeth.

He sincerely hoped his mother appreciated all that he'd done to rectify their current predicament. This had to be the last time she requested such a large allowance or they'd be forced to be rid of necessities next.

"On another matter," Cart said, his irritation at the man dissipating quickly. "Have you heard any word on the painting I've been searching for?"

Stanford cocked a brow at Cart's interest. Cart knew if the man did, indeed, find his father's painting, the price would be steep. Most days, Stanford was an honest shop keep and auctioneer of collectibles. But on those other days, he dabbled in business of the more illicit kind, either dealing in stolen, lost, or long-forgotten items. He was Cart's main source of information when he'd been hired to find an antiquity—and a large majority of the time, the man could either locate the piece or direct Cart in the right direction.

"Not a word, my lord." Stanford shook his head, disappointed he'd been unsuccessful in his search. "I do not believe the painting is in London—or even in England. I have done as you said and offered a reward for the painting or any information on its whereabouts...but nothing."

Not every assignment Cart undertook was a success, but this one was personal. His family's painting, commissioned by his father—the last of such things.

It meant a great deal to him and the need to locate it would never diminish. "Please, ask around again and let me know if you learn anything."

"Of course, Lord Cartwright. This way." Stanford led Cart to the back of his shop that housed his coin case, where the man counted out the appropriate pounds and handed them to Cart. "While I appreciate your business, I do understand the sorrow in letting these pieces go." The man seemed satisfied that the transaction was complete and he could now boast at his great acquisition. "I will make sure the pieces are sold to deserving individuals."

"See to it, Stanford." Cart turned to leave, tucking the funds into his coat pocket for safe-keeping—until he was required to hand them over to his mother.

"Will I see you next week?"

"I'm afraid not. I will be otherwise engaged." Cart tried his best to look downcast at missing this month's auction. "Do send word if anything I may be interested in comes available."

With a nod of agreement, Cart left the shop, destined for home—and his mother, Lady Cartwright.

Chapter Thirteen

Jude sat, a book open in her lap, waiting for her sisters to take their leave. Payton's tutor would arrive shortly, and Samantha was departing for the Haversham townhouse for tea with Lady Haversham and Mrs. Jakeston. It was the perfect opportunity for Jude to grab the vase and slip from Craven House without her elder brother noticing. He'd been told she would be visiting Lady Haversham with Sam. It would allow Jude several hours of time for her and Lord Cartwright to research the vase—which Jude didn't need. She knew all there was to know about the item, especially that she couldn't risk being seen with it in such a public venue.

But she'd had little choice but to suggest the library for their meeting—it was either that or risk being recognized at Lord Cartwright's townhouse. Her luck of going unnoticed could not last long—and the child could not be kept in her schoolroom indefinitely.

It had been agreed upon that Jude would gain whatever coin Cart was willing to spare for the piece and that they'd wipe their hands of it—allow him to suffer the punishment for being in possession of the stolen artifact.

Sam had no regrets about their plan, concocted before they'd found a suitable collector to purchases the piece and certainly long before she'd met Cart.

Jude had nothing but regrets at the moment.

It hurt most to realize her largest pang of guilt was meeting Lord Cartwright, stumbling upon him at Lady Haversham's garden party—and then fooling him into befriending her.

And her greatest remorse?

Allowing him to kiss her.

A lie she'd been telling herself for the past few days since their walk in Hyde Park.

She hadn't allowed him to kiss her—she'd initiated the kiss. She'd taken advantage of him by stepping close in that wooded area and pressing her lips to his.

Jude's first kiss.

And it had been a sham. It was a kiss given under false pretenses.

But she knew time was running out for Craven House, if the notices were to be believed. Marce owed someone money—and selling the vase was the only way Jude could help with the situation. Her eldest sister wouldn't speak of the dangers awaiting them if the note was not satisfied, but it did not take much for Jude and Sam to piece together the consequences. They'd be thrown from their home and would have no place to go.

That left her a mere few days to get rid of the vase and collect the coin—which made Cart her only opinion.

More shameful was that she hoped their lips met again—as soon as possible.

And that had nothing to do with the vase or rescuing their home.

She felt her cheeks heat at her indecent thoughts. Glancing around the room, she confirmed that neither of her sisters paid her any mind. Sam flipped through the gossip rags as she did each week and Payton sat idle, staring out the window at nothing more than the shrubs lining the drive. Her youngest sibling—and her affinity to retreat into her own thoughts—worried Jude, but lately, she hadn't the time to explore her sister's melancholy ways. Marce and Sam were happy she'd dispelled her youthful, petty whining. Jude was not convinced a withdrawn Payton was favorable over a whimpering, selfish miss.

Maybe it would take a special someone to pull her from her musings—and introduce her to…

Jude stopped herself, pushing the thought from her mind. However, it struggled its way back in. There was nothing left to do but close her eyes and allow her mind to wander—it did not hurt anyone if her thoughts explored the longings newly aroused in her.

First, she remembered the feel of his lips—so unlike she'd imagined. They were possessive in the most inspiring sort of way, firm and commanding. And at complete odds with the man who possessed them. Cart had taken an imposing role during their embrace, yet he'd been unsure of his actions and retreated when her tongue grazed his lip.

It was with wise thinking that he'd wrapped his arms around her or Jude would have likely collapsed when her legs turned to mush, betraying her.

Would he be so daring at Sir Edwin's Circulating Library?

She imagined a tryst hidden within the many narrow shelves of books or a stolen kiss in an alcove bordering the main reading room. Her chest tightened and her breathing increased, thinking about the possible opportunities to be in his arms.

No one would know her there—she'd lied when she'd claimed the library was like a second home to her. Jude had visited the archive only twice, and both times were in the early morning hours before most of her household had departed their chambers. Yes, she'd explored the many sections—science, history, newspapers—but she'd hesitated being seen in the place for fear if items began to disappear around London, someone would remember her scouring the ancient volumes on similar matters. Her interest in history and artifacts should not be compromised by her decision to steal the vase. Their illicit activities had to end, before it was too late and her family was connected to any wrongdoing.

And so, Jude had kept away from a place she knew she'd love if given greater opportunity to explore its treasures.

Exploring treasures—oh, how she'd take great pleasure in exploring a certain man who was soon to be arriving at the library.

"Miss Samantha, Miss Judith," Darla, their housekeeper, called. Jude opened her eyes to see Darla in the open doorway. "Your carriage is waiting in the drive."

Jude acted disinterested as Sam stood, her fashion plates forgotten at the prospect of visiting Lady Haversham's home during prime calling hours.

"I am not feeling quite the thing," Jude exclaimed. "I think I will remain home, but do give my sincere apologies to Lady Haversham and Mrs. Jakeston."

"You cannot desert me," Sam said halfheartedly. There was nothing more her sister enjoyed than being the only twin.

"I am certain you will manage without me this once." Jude had found herself exhausted from Sam's incessant wonderings over the vase—when it would be gone, when they'd have the money for it, and why Jude hadn't pushed her acquaintance with Lord Cartwright. What her sister was unaware of was that her *acquaintance* with Cart had surpassed what was proper and if Jude had anything to say about it, would venture into scandalous territory. It was for many reasons that Jude wasn't telling Sam her plans for the day. "I will await you here so you can regale me with news of how your afternoon went."

Jude was hedging her bets on Sam's need to feel important and it worked.

"Very well." Sam smiled, her light green dress complementing her hair coiled tightly at her crown.

"I can accompany you," Payton called from her place at the window. "I am in my last year of studies anyways. One missed lesson will hurt me naught."

"That is not necessary." Of course, Sam did not wish her sister to tag along, usurping the lavish attention heaped on a newly introduced debutante. "You are far too young—and inexperienced—for Lady Haversham's salon. Imagine if you embarrassed Marce. She would be very upset."

"Good afternoon, dear sisters. Who are you three upsetting now?" Garrett strode into the room, bending slightly to place a quick kiss on the housekeeper's cheek. Highly inappropriate, though it was Garrett's inclination to push boundaries and shock people whenever possible. "Must I lock you all away until Marce returns? That would mean more work for me—and you know I abhor labor of any sort."

Sam crossed her arms, turning a scathing look on him.

Payton laughed, an unrestrained sound of merriment—a rare occurrence.

"Why you always think we are up to no good, I will never know," Sam exclaimed, affronted, before pushing past him to follow Darla from the room.

"She does always know how to make a dramatic exit." Garrett moved into the room and slung himself on the lounge, much the same as he'd done the day Marce had departed for her trip. "For a previous bordello, this house is certainly the most boring and tedious residence in all of England. Is this all you ladies do all day?"

"Brother, you brought the dreary shadow of boredom with you," Jude teased. "Alas, it will not be by our hand that you see any type of excitement while Marce is away. We are taking her warning to heart and keeping ourselves out of trouble."

"And what will occupy your day, my dear, favorite sister?"

His words rankled Payton, as he'd intended. There was nothing that annoyed their youngest sibling more than feeling the odd one out. Marce and Garrett were linked by the many years they'd spent together before their father passed away and their mother moved on to have other children. Sam and she were close, for obvious reasons, but with Marce and Sam gone, Payton desperately longed to be the favored sibling to their only brother.

True to form, Payton stood with a loud huff and followed Sam from the room.

"You certainly know how to clear a room of females," Jude said with a chuckle. "How do you expect to gain the notice of a proper lady and con her into wedding a rakehell?"

"I am not lacking in female companionship, never you fear."

"I said *proper* female."

"Proper women of the *ton* are lying in wait at every corner,"—he sighed throwing his arm across his face—"and those types of women will never be conned, as you put it, by a mere younger son with no title or money. Besides, if you and Sam are any indication of what constitutes acceptable behavior for young debutantes, then I am ecstatic to stay far from your drab kind."

"My drab kind?" Jude laughed.

"You heard me correctly." He moved to sit, tossing a golden pillow her way. "You were much more entertaining before you set your sights on being accepted by society—even Payton could be counted on for a laugh every once in a while, but now…"

Jude longed to share with her brother exactly how unladylike and nonconformist she and Sam had been of late. Part of her knew he'd find a way out for them—fix everything before it went awry—and keep Lord Cartwright from learning that she was a complete fraud.

Alas, she'd sworn to her twin to keep everything between them, never to tell any of their siblings the lengths they'd gone to help Marce—and keep their home.

"I am sorry you find your family so entirely unappealing, dear brother." Jude stood, eyeing the vase nestled unwittingly on the table behind the lounge Garrett occupied. "What are your plans for today?"

"I thought I might visit my fencing club." He closed his eyes and pushed out an exaggerated breath. "Or maybe attend Tattersall's. I am unsure, but I must return to prepare and organize for this evening."

Jude needed to retrieve the vase and leave immediately if she wanted to be on time to meet Cart. It would be disastrous if he thought she'd called off on their plans.

"I think I will retire to my chambers." Jude stood, navigating her way toward the table. Garrett's position made it impossible for him to keep his watch on her. She gathered Sam's fashion plates for guise and grasped the vase before turning toward the door. "Please send for me if you need assistance with anything."

"Certainly," he said, waving his hand in dismissal. "Enjoy your afternoon."

"I intend to." Jude knew her mistake the second the words left her mouth—it wasn't the words but the way she'd said them.

Garrett lifted his head from the chaise and followed her progression toward the door. "What have you there?"

Jude raised her hand that held the plates. "Sam forgot her things. I will return them to our bedchamber." Slyly, she tucked the vase to her side, praying her skirt hid it from his view.

She slipped from the room and took the stairs quickly to their bedchambers. Once safely inside, she pulled a satchel from under her bed and sat it on her dressing table, propped open. It would be necessary to wrap the delicate antiquity in something soft and nonabrasive for her walk to the circulating library. She grabbed Sam's forgotten wrap that hung limply from the foot of her bed. It would offer enough padding and protection for her short trip—and with any luck, Jude would not return with the piece—but a tote full of banknotes.

A tendril of regret burrowed deep, taking hold as she placed the vase in the satchel.

But Jude couldn't allow herself to feel guilty over using Cart. Her family needed the money and he would be overjoyed to possess the vase.

She must think of it as a fair trade, anything to relieve the immense regret that plagued her as she hurried from Craven House. It would not be wise to explore the reasoning behind her guilt over duping Lord Cartwright. One thing was for certain, it was not because she longed to kiss him again. Her chances of fulfilling that wish if he ever found out her duplicity would be nil.

Chapter Fourteen

Cart wandered down an aisle housing what the library called their *Ancient Section*, which was certainly a jest, for the row only boasted approximately eighty-two books of varying sizes. By Cart's calculations, that was the most a bookcase of these dimensions and construction could support before the shelves gave way due to the weight.

It was not worth pondering the ridiculous notion that these eighty-two books held all the knowledge recorded about *Ancient* anything. In his own library, Cart had double this amount on the history of weather patterns across the known world alone.

Why had he allowed Jude to convince him that Sir Edwin's Circulating Library would offer all that was needed to date and record the origins of her vase?

For certain because it eliminated the possibility of Jude and Lady Cartwright coming face-to-face. The last time Jude had visited his home had been too close for comfort. Not that he wished to hide his budding friendship with Jude. He only hoped to spare her the barbed tongue of his mother.

The place was inviting enough; housing a large room filled with tables, chairs, and settees for visitors to sit and read—or visit with acquaintances. The temperature was not stifling, nor chilly, but somewhere in the middle, which would enhance the energy needed to retain any book read within. It was a favorable environment for learning—if only there were not so many people and voices to contend with.

He reached the end of the aisle he'd been browsing—going between nervous anticipation of when Jude would arrive and utter dread if she had a change of heart and called off—and searched the main room for Theo, who'd tagged along in delight at visiting a true circulating library. Cart had regularly sought out the small areas at White's Gentlemen's Club that offered minimal volumes but afforded much space for one to hide if one wished to get away from an overly loud household.

There was no such silence to be had here—it suited Theo grandly, but left many things to be desired for Cart. The only positive was that due to the public nature of the establishment, Jude need not bring a chaperone—or so she'd said a few days past at the park.

The park.

Cart shook his head to rid the thoughts swirling on the fringes of his subconscious.

Images replaying over and over…some very real, while others were more of the imaginary nature.

But even with the thoughts gone, he could still feel the warmth of her lips on his and the softness of the skin above her gloves when he'd truly stepped over the boundaries and caressed her upper arm just below her sleeve. The moment had taken him by surprise—so much so that he'd run the moment he returned Jude to her sisters. His mind shouted that it needed time to reconcile what the kiss had meant—for both of them. He certainly hadn't instigated the intimacy, but neither had he stopped her when he realized her intent. And, undoubtedly, he had not been the first to pull back.

To think that anyone could have wandered upon them… Jude would have been ruined, caught in the embrace of a man. He shuddered to think what would have been necessary on his part if they had been discovered. A confession about subjects he never sought to tell her; a side of him he hoped to keep from her.

He was a pauper.

He had been swindled out of most of his inheritance by a trusted relative.

He was a proven dullard. A family disgrace.

He was *earning a living* to keep his family fed and clothed.

And, debatably, the worst, he lived with his shrew of a mother, who reminded him of all of those facts each time they both frequented a room at the same time.

Finally, he located Theo across the large room doing much the same as he, wandering a section far less grand and organized than it should be. Though a great distance from him, Cart made out the signage about the row: *Novels (Adventure, mystery, and thrills).*

He smiled, knowing she'd located the perfect area for her tastes, which would make for a far more enjoyable afternoon, out from under their mother's watchful eye. She'd likely find a book filled with tales of swashbuckling pirates or a maiden princess. Fabricated stories that lent no true learning, but rather taught the young that belief in the imaginary was a worthwhile pastime.

For him, that time had passed when he'd learned his time at university would be cut short, his return to London demanded immediately. He hadn't even the funds then to hire a proper carriage, nor had his mother sent one for him. He'd begged enough coin from a professor to gain transport on a mail coach that had left Eton before dawn one morning, traversing the twenty-four miles from Windsor to London in cramped quarters.

He gave a small wave when Theo looked his way and ducked back into the row, not wanting her to stumble upon him and Jude…if she ever arrived.

The tall clock in the main room chimed once.

Jude wasn't late at all. It was he that was early, being unsure how long the walk would take.

Cart concentrated on calming himself. It would not do to have her arrive with him so nervous his forehead perspired and his palms became moist.

His physical response to her didn't make sense in the slightest and he feared it was mainly due to his emotional reaction to her person—or just the thought of her. Her silky auburn hair. Or her height—tall in comparison to most petite debutantes. Though he found her slender form pleasing to the eye and comfortable to walk next to. It could also surely be her way of laughing when he spoke out loud instead of analyzing something in his mind.

Her mind…his body most definitely had a positive reaction to her mind. They hadn't spoken of the weather or other mundane topics since their first acquaintance.

It was both refreshing and terrifying at the same time.

"Lord Cartwright?"

Suddenly, she stood before him, appearing out of nowhere—or maybe manifesting from his thoughts. She'd slipped into the library unnoticed, even though Cart had glanced toward the doors often.

They hadn't seen one another since the park and the images locked in his mind did not do her justice. She was truly breathtaking, especially with her long, dark coat buttoned to her throat and her hair partly freed to hang about her shoulders.

"I hope I did not keep you waiting overly long," she said, her eyes avoiding his gaze.

He wanted to tell her he'd wait an eternity if it meant she would eventually come to him. Instead, he replied, "No, not at all. I was able to survey the selection while I waited."

They stood a few feet apart in silence.

"Shall we sit?" He gestured to a small table with two chairs set apart from the main room. "Do allow me to take your coat and bag. It must be heavy."

She released the satchel with no fuss and followed him to the table where he pulled a chair out for her to sit—only hoping it was the proper thing to do. She inclined her head as she quickly unbuttoned her coat and handed it to him.

"I hope your journey here was uneventful," he said, his attempt at idle talk while he took his seat across from her.

"The walk was brisk and refreshing, though without incident."

"You walked," he stammered. "Alone?"

"It is daylight hours and the streets are populated. I assure you, it was quite proper."

He was startled to realize it was not propriety he worried over but her safety. "I was not calling into question your respectability."

"That is good to hear because someone would certainly see our time together at the park highly indecent."

She regretted their kiss—wished it had never occurred.

He'd known this possibility existed and shouldn't be shocked that she was voicing her concern over their actions on that day.

Her hand landed on his where it rested on the table between them and she grinned.

She was being nice, yet firmly communicating to him that another kiss was not in their future. The pit of his stomach dropped at the thought, for what else could her words and gesture mean?

She pitied him. At least, she was kind enough to continue their friendship.

Cart cleared his throat, determined to show her he could also overlook what they'd done and continue a suitable relationship. "May I see the vase?"

It stung that she obviously hadn't been impacted the same as he by the kiss. Or that she had, but had since changed her mind.

Cart eyed her as she tugged the satchel toward her and pulled a wrapped bundle from inside. Jude had taken great care with packaging the precious vase before leaving her residence. It was something to be admired, for there were so many who abused antiquities, causing them irreversible harm, but not Jude. She'd swaddled the vase in a crocheted shawl of some sort.

"Would you like to unwrap it?" she asked, holding the object out to him.

He desperately wanted to remove the cloth and behold what secrets lay beneath—his heart pounded and his breathing became shallow at the anticipation of it. It was much the same with any new piece he beheld. It was a rush and, currently, the only thing that could lighten his disappointment in Jude's reaction—or lack thereof—to their kiss.

Taking the bundle, Cart slowly unwound the material guarding the vase.

The piece was light, almost weightless in his hands as the last of the material fell away. Cart couldn't stop from gasping.

He wanted to hand the vase back to Jude, act as if he hadn't seen it, and allow their relationship to take a step back—a mutual fondness for antiquities, a thirst for historical knowledge, enjoyment in academia—but he knew he had to inspect the vase. Make sure his suspicions were correct, leaving no doubt in his mind that the woman before him was a fraud.

Flipping the piece on its side, Cart identified the subtle orange undertones created by the artist, the rough base, and the nick Lord Gunther had caused himself.

He kept his gaze trained on the vase, for he was certain his eyes would give away his anger, his shock, and his total disbelief.

"Where did you get this?" he questioned in a whisper.

"It is beautiful, is it not?"

For a moment, Cart felt sympathy for her. Certainly she did not know the vase was stolen or that Cart had been retained to find the piece and get it back at any cost to its owner. She could not be the heartless woman he saw before him, a woman playing off his emotions and using him for her own gain.

"I asked where you obtained it." His voice was deep, almost a growl as he slowly pronounced each word.

"I told you—I…"

Her words were lost to the severe pounding in his head. "When did you get it?"

"Some time ago."

"How long ago?" he prodded. "Precisely."

"Several months, I would guess," she answered. "I have kept it safe and away from natural light until I brought it here. To you."

"I will purchase it," he said. Everything began to make sense—their chance meeting at Lady Haversham's, her claimed interest in him and her untrue obsession with antiquities. Her presence outside the night watchman's house was enough to convince him that trouble with the authorities was likely not a new thing for her. Cart had been a fool once more. "How much do you want for the vase?"

In his hands, he held the item that Lord Gunther had commissioned him to locate almost three months ago—a vase that had seemingly disappeared from view, not a single collector having been approached to purchase the stolen piece.

He couldn't look at her, for if he did, he'd see the woman who'd been hidden from him since their forced meeting. Not the beautiful, enchanting, intelligent woman he'd grown to care for, who he looked forward to seeing, but a conniving, scheming... a charlatan.

"Is that not why we are here?" she asked. "We must research the piece and discover an appropriate price."

"I will pay anything. Please, name your rate."

He couldn't handle looking at her as he reluctantly handed the vase back to her. His stomach rolled at the thought of allowing her to walk from the circulating library with the vase in her possession, but he had no other choice.

"Fifty pounds," Jude said confidently. "I believe that is a fair price."

A fair price to pay a thief? Cart wanted to inquire. He should alert the proper authorities immediately and allow them to handle the situation and return the vase to its rightful owner.

Instead, he heard himself answer, "That is an agreeable price."

Cart wanted away from this woman, out of this airless room, and to put distance between him and her. After all he'd been through, he was still as gullible as he'd been as a young lord, newly titled. He was the prey with ample predators to hunt him.

He was unsure what wounded him deeper, that he'd been taken advantage of again or that it had been by *her*.

The vase could fall to the floor and shatter into a billion pieces and Cart couldn't care less. He'd still be overwhelmed by the enormity of her betrayal.

He stood abruptly, his chair scraping the floor, causing others to look his way at the noise.

Nodding and waving them away, he turned to finally meet her stare—her unknowing, innocent stare.

Fifty pounds. The measly amount of coin was nowhere near what the piece was worth. In Cart's mind, the vase was priceless, something of such rare and ancient origins that no other treasure compared.

And she'd asked a paltry fifty pounds.

He wanted to laugh but kept the sound within. And to think, he'd possessed half that amount not long ago before he'd given it to his mother.

If she were playing him, then she was the greater fool, for the vase could fetch close to ten times that amount at Stanford's auction.

"I will send word when I have arranged the funds you request," he said with a curt bow. Not that she deserved such respect, but Cart needed to keep his anger hidden well or she and the artifact would likely disappear. "It will not be long, a few days at most."

"You can keep the piece," she insisted with a reassuring smile, pushing the vase back toward him as she too stood.

"That is not how such things are done, Miss Judith."

The smile dropped from her face as she scrutinized him, noticing his suddenly guarded nature. "Oh, I trust you, Cart." She attempted once more to hand him the piece, but when he took a step back, Jude quickly wrapped it back in the shawl and stowed it in her tote, holding the bag close to her body.

Cart held her jacket out for her to slip her arms in, pulling it onto her shoulders with more force than was necessary. His meaning was clear.

She turned back to him, her lashes lowered as she inspected his demeanor.

Their afternoon at the library was over—never to be repeated. The furthest thing from his mind suddenly was the only thing that'd been on his mind all day. He wanted to walk out of the library and never set eyes on Jude again, but he had to collect Theo first, which meant he needed to stay long enough for Jude to depart before locating his sister.

And within a few days, he'd need to face Jude again—the thief. "Good day, Miss Jude."

"It was a lovely time," she said cautiously, trying to lure him into further conversation. "I would much enjoy doing it again."

He'd conveyed himself more bluntly than he ever had previously. However, she stood before him…making no move to depart and making her intentions known that she planned to continue her scheme. She was more versed in the art of deception than Cart had suspected. If he hadn't discovered her misdeeds, he wouldn't hesitate to agree to her request for another afternoon together.

The seconds passed, making Cart nervous. He adjusted his coat and reached for his artfully tied cravat, tugging at the corners. She expected him to answer. Cart was afraid if he opened his mouth, nothing good would come forth and attention would be drawn to them.

With one last look, she slung the satchel over her shoulder and turned to leave, her brow furrowed in concern.

Cart sagged in relief when she took her first step toward the crowded main room.

Chapter Fifteen

Jude's afternoon with Lord Cartwright hadn't gone as planned—at all. Certainly, she was overjoyed at the prospect of ridding herself of the vase and gaining the pounds to pay Craven House's debts before Marce returned home.

It stood to reason the only emotion Jude should be feeling was relief. Instead, a measure of unease and concern had overtaken her at the dark shadow that settled over Cart during their time together. Sam had insisted that men were of a different breed when it came to conducting business, but Cart's severe mood change was something more than a singular focus on the transaction at hand.

He'd become withdrawn and abrupt—even more so than usual.

It made little sense. Even when she'd been so bold as to express her agreement at meeting again for another afternoon together, he'd said nothing. Showed not even a spark of interest at her suggestion.

She'd fretted that he possibly knew of the vase and that it had been stolen a few months before, but she'd seen no signs of recognition on his face. Normally, his emotions were clearly conveyed through his mannerisms and facial expressions. But at the library, he'd donned a mask of expressionless disinterest.

Not disinterest in the vase, but in her.

It had been unwise to be so daring as to step into his arms at Hyde Park. Clearly, he hadn't wanted to kiss her. What other explanation was there for his cold treatment?

His labored breathing when Payton and Sam had stumbled upon them on the path had mirrored her own. She hadn't imagined his reaction to their intimacy.

Jude sat between an elderly widow and a youthful—though very hard of hearing—baron. She awaited an opportunity to slip away from the gathering, providing ample time for her to repeatedly go over what had transpired between her and Cart.

If anyone wondered where her sister was, they hadn't asked, though few in attendance were acquainted with her. While her twin sister would have spent her evening tittering senselessly over a jest made by one of her dinner companions, Jude had been forced to fairly scream every word to the deaf baron or hold her breath as the elderly widow leaned her way to continually share on dit after on dit of useless information about other party attendees. All the while, Sam hid in the ladies' retiring room, wearing a gown that matched Jude's exactly.

There was nothing for her to do but smile, nod, and act as if the evening were the most enthralling time she'd had in her entire life. At least, that had been

Marce's sole advice to her sisters on their debut into society. The only way to *make friends* and secure a favorable position was to make every person they entertained think they were royalty.

And so her evening had progressed from socializing in the salon with women and men of varying ages and statuses, to a seated dinner of pheasant and duck soup with a lavish vegetable spread that could only be grown in a hothouse far from London. With only the musical portion of the event left, Jude was counting the moments until she'd be free to disappear into the darker, unoccupied areas of the house.

With the time passing quickly until Marce's return and Jude's less than successful sale of the vase—thus far—they'd been forced to steal another piece of art. This time, it was a painting. It would be far easier to collect coin for. And that was what Jude needed. She'd witnessed Mr. Curtis collecting yet another missive regarding their ruinous financial status. When she'd asked about it, he'd deflected her comments of concern and told her that Lady Marce had given him strict instructions to collect any correspondence and deliver it directly to her private bedchambers.

Jude glared at the head of the table, willing their meal to come to an end.

Her task of blending in and going unnoticed was working, even Lady Haversham hadn't glanced in Jude's direction since they'd sat down to dine—six full courses ago.

"Miss Judith," Sir Glassglow shouted, a mere two inches from her ear. "May I request your company during the musical portion of the evening?"

Jude did her best to hide her cringe at his loudly proclaimed request. On the other side of her, the Widow Jenkins smiled like a cat who'd stolen the dinner meats.

"In my day," the widow leaned in to whisper conspiratorially, her foul breath making more of a statement than her words. "I would do far more than be his companion while a silly, young girl decimated her harp solo."

Jude looked sharply at the older lady, for once hoping she'd continue. But she only winked as if Jude should know what she would have done forty years ago.

All the ways Jude could punish her twin began to run through her mind: black dye in her hair treatment, tacks in her slippers, crushed onions in her face powder... More than likely, all three; however, an evening of musical treats promised to Sir Glassglow was fitting retribution.

It was past time that Jude not be the one to sacrifice herself in every scheme, all while Sam waltzed and enjoyed her time immensely. There would be no distinguished marquis or rakishly handsome duke for Sam this evening—no, a hard-of-hearing baron it was for her.

Jude looked down at her plate, her dour mood settling firmly around her. It had been several days since she'd heard from Cart after he'd abruptly ended their visit at the library. Certainly, he'd departed all of their visits as abruptly, but this time had felt different—his demeanor unlike anything she'd ever seen him exhibit previously. His shoulders had been tense and he'd refused to meet her gaze.

Not that she had a soft shell, but his treatment—and further avoidance—of her stung.

She'd thought they'd been growing close. She even dared to call them friends.

Especially after their kiss at the park.

Maybe she shouldn't have endeavored to push the vase on him and found another unsuspecting gentleman instead, one she had no connection to. Her asking price was far less than what the man at the auctioneer's shop had told her a similar piece would be worth.

She'd acted unbecoming in the park. That must be the reason for Cart's drastic change in manner. After she'd stolen the vase, Jude had lived for weeks dreading every knock on Craven House's door, thinking someone had spotted her leaving Lord Gunther's townhouse or suspected her in the theft. But no one had come and her paranoia over being caught had faded so much so that she hadn't immediately considered Cart suspecting that she'd stolen the vase.

Jude had vowed to wait another day before sending him correspondence. Maybe he was finding it difficult to gather the pounds or he'd found a collector who was interested but needed time to do the same.

"Miss Judith?" the baron asked at her elbow.

The man looked at her expectantly.

He was likely a very kind, attentive man—one that would make the perfect husband for any woman who'd give him a moment of undivided attention, but that was not Jude. Or, at least, that was not Jude this night. She had something important to attain—something she'd be far safer forgetting.

"I would be honored to be escorted into the musical portion of our evening," Jude said with a bright

185

smile. "You will collect me after you enjoy a drink with the men?"

Sir Glassglow leaned precariously forward, his cravat skimming his soup, to glare at the head of the table. Could it be they both wished for the meal to end swiftly? "As long as you promise to remember my request."

"I am most convinced our paths were meant to meet this evening, sir," Jude said with a faint smile. It was enough to pacify the man, for he smiled in return and turned to the young lady on his right. "Miss Orellana, such a wonderful meal this has been."

Why did it bother her so that the baron was so quick to turn his attention to another eligible female?

Unquestionably because Lord Cartwright only had eyes for her when they were together. He knew the expressions and mannerisms unique to only her. He ventured to discuss topics unlikely to be favored by other men of the *ton*. He'd never once asked about her stock—her lineage. Therefore, he had never discovered that she was the illegitimate product of an illicit love affair between her late mother, the proprietor of Craven House, and her father, a peer in high standing.

Every other man she'd met hadn't been as steadfast as Cart—they seemed of the opinion that she and Sam were interchangeable. A pair...though no better than a single being.

Jude needed to remember that she was not in attendance to socialize—or make any sort of lasting impression. She was the twin who could blend into the background and go unnoticed when the need arose. Until the time came, she was to smile, appear charming and demure, and under no circumstances draw undue attention to herself. This meant hours of discussing the inclement weather patterns of the season, fawning over Lady Ferguson's newest fabric choice, and nodding like a hen, without a speck of sense in her head.

It was exhausting.

She'd thought acting the unassuming, reserved debutante would be simple—though it took much effort to appear empty-minded and meek. The only thing that could make the night worse was if someone asked her to apply her female talents to the pianoforte. That would be the one request doomed to mortify Jude—and Sam.

The baron cleared his voice and nudged her.

Jude focused on the table to see that all the dishes had been cleared while she'd daydreamed, hers included, and everyone was standing in preparation of the men retiring to the study for tumblers filled to the brim with spirits while the ladies rejoined in the parlor for games and musical entertainments.

Looking over her shoulder, Jude nodded to the servant waiting to pull her chair back and then stood with the rest of the party as she set her cloth napkin on the bare table before her.

It was her cue to slip from the group as soon as possible, confident that Sam would take her place in the drawing room until the music started.

Lady Haversham sent a smile her way, likely noticing Jude's discomfort. She returned their patroness' grin.

They'd accepted the duchess' invitation to this dinner party only that morning. Lord Cartwright hadn't made contract with her about exchanging the vase for money and Marce would return to London before the week was through, which meant their eldest sister would be forced to reconcile their debts. If she and Sam had any hope of disposing of the cursed vase and slipping the banknotes into Marce's private chambers without notice, they needed to work fast. Or find another—far simpler—way to obtain the coin they required.

That led to Jude graciously accepting Lady Haversham's kind invitation to meet her at the Duke of Chamberlain's annual dinner party. It helped that the duke boasted his riches far surpassed those of the royal family.

Jude fell in line with the other guests departing the room but kept from gaining the notice of any unaccompanied men in the group. The grouping split, with the men continuing on to the duke's study and Jude trailing behind the women as they approached the duchess' drawing room. Gradually, so as not to garner any suspicion, Jude began to slow her pace, pausing every few feet to inspect a hall table or painting on the wall. Even the wall sconces didn't escape her scrutiny— fine silver candleholders had never been as enthralling and appealing to her eye as they were this night. She went so far as to run her finger along the frame of a large landscape hanging slightly askew in the hall.

From a room farther within the townhouse, a door shut, confirming that the men were safely within the study. They would not to emerge for the appropriate time allotted for them to enjoy a moment of peace away from the nagging feminine voices of their wives, sisters, and mothers. Even the draw of unattached, alluring debutantes was not enough to make a man forgo a strong drink and a cigar.

Jude fully halted before a large, gilt-frame oil painting depicting a man—probably the duke's long-deceased ancestor—with a bulbous, scarlet nose, and blotchy, sagging jowls. If the artist had sought to show favor on the lord, then Jude shuddered to imagine the honest look of the man.

She raised a brow as she pondered the life circumstances of the man. His red tinted nose and swollen face were surely due to an overindulgence of fine spirits and an unhealthy food regimen. In similar fashion, he probably spent many nights away from his wife and when in residence, sought to avoid his own offspring. That was the way of the privileged class.

To think she was stealing from a wealthy and depraved lord to give to the less fortunate and downtrodden allowed her to sleep at night. Yet her nightly slumber had not been peaceful of late. The cause of her discord was not one she relished contemplating. She'd spent weeks telling herself it was that blasted vase—and the risk its possession would cost her—that plagued her every night, but she'd only begun to lose sleep after meeting a very specific earl. And she refused to speculate over his latest mood change. Her eyelids lowered as if of their own accord and she imagined her and Cart's embrace along the path at Hyde Park—his arms securely around her but still gentle enough to allow her escape if it was her wish.

Feminine laughter drifted down the hall and snapped Jude from her thoughts.

She had only a brief time to locate the canvas and remove it to her waiting carriage while Sam slipped in to take her place with the partygoers. They'd convinced Lady Haversham to allow them to meet her at the dinner party instead of traveling together for the sole purpose of keeping the duchess far from their nefarious activities. She was a smart, perceptive woman, who'd not tarry in alerting Jude and Sam's sister to any transgressions on her watch. Lady Haversham hadn't found anything suspicious about Sam remaining home due to a dreadful headache.

They'd seen fit to ask Mr. Curtis to keep the carriage close if Jude found herself needing to leave early. If the elderly man noticed their late-night comings and goings and odd requests, he kept it to himself.

With one final look toward the partially open door to the drawing room, Jude walked leisurely back toward the formal dining room they'd departed. She discovered it did not house what they sought. No, the painted canvas would be kept in a far grander chamber where more guests could admire the artist's mastery. As it hadn't been hung in the dining area, Jude's next thought was the grand ballroom—a part of the house left unused for the small gathering being thrown that evening.

Jude knew the risk was great, but the ballroom's double doors stood at the top of the grand staircase—the main stairs were the simplest path.

The foyer was deserted, all servants tasked with accommodating all attending guests in the salon and study; even the butler was hard at work away from his post by the front door. This allowed Jude a moment to cast her gaze to the landing above—and the firmly closed double doors. She hoped she wasn't wrong in assuming the canvas could be found within, for Jude's luck was running out quickly.

She need only climb the stairs, grab the painted canvas, and make it out the front door without being seen—far simpler than breaking into a house through an unbarred window and fleeing after being caught.

"Can I help ye, miss?" a quiet voice asked behind her, causing Jude to fairly jump out of her skin as she yelped with fright. "The ladies be in the drawing room."

Jude straightened her back and pasted a thankful smile on her face before turning and facing a young servant—no older than Payton. "Oh, heavens. This is quite the most embarrassing moment in my life." Jude grasped the back of her gown, lowering her stare to the floor before the servant. "I fear my dress has been torn. I am in no condition for polite conversation. I was hoping to locate the ladies' retiring room to see if my gown could be mended."

The girl's smile turned to a frown of concern. "The ladies' room be down that hall." She nodded in the direction Jude had come from—where the women's talking could still be heard. "I jus' go an' collect me mending kit to fix ye right up."

Jude felt a pang of remorse at misleading the girl. "That would be ever so kind of you."

The servant's smile returned and she headed toward the kitchens.

Her time was now significantly reduced. It would not take the girl long to journey to her sleeping quarters, collect her mending kit, and return before the girl found Sam waiting in the retiring room.

There was no way around it—Jude grabbed her skirt and lifted the material high, dashing up the stairs two at a time. She gave credit to her sisters for her skill at climbing stairs quickly, for they'd raced up and down them at Craven House in their youth. Hitting the first landing, she turned and hurried up the final flight, skidding to a halt outside the double doors she'd admired from below.

She glanced over her shoulder to the empty foyer below and whipped back around, grabbing the knob. The door slid open on well-oiled hinges, revealing a massive room that fairly sparkled with all the gilded adornments on the chandeliers, wall fixtures, chairs, and other room decorations. The room oozed wealth, privilege, and prestige—so much so, that Jude had a hard time drawing breath at the sight.

The marble floor was polished until it shone and she feared to slip when she set one slippered foot on it. The drapery was pulled back allowing the moonlight to invade the room, glistening off every surface, lending some visibility in the darkness.

It had escaped her mind to consider finding a candle to light her path into the room. Thankfully, the space was empty except for chairs lining one wall and the artwork hanging with care in frames of varying sizes. The paintings adorning the center of each wall were far larger than the one she sought, so she concentrated her search on the smaller, less gaudy pieces. She also knew the artist had focused on the landscape—Jude passed two paintings featuring children and one of a large farm animal.

If Sam had sent her on another fool's errand, Jude was going to be peeved.

Rounding the room to the third wall, a landscape came into view—rolling countryside with a cloudless, blue sky and an uneven rock formation cutting two fields in half. It had to be the painting described in the post article several weeks back. It was no larger than a silver serving tray and was housed in a narrow frame. The piece did not appear old or special in any way—it could not be any older than Jude herself. Odd that it was so very valuable.

Taking hold of the painting with both hands, Jude lifted it from the peg it hung on and admired the item up close. Certainly, the area and view captured by the artist was breathtaking, but the actual brushstrokes appeared hurried and disjointed; the exact shape and texture of the rock wall were not fully recognized or portrayed.

Jude would ask Cart his opinion of the piece—if he ever contacted her about the vase. She had half a mind to call on him unannounced, as inappropriate as that may be, but time was running slim. Regardless of what she and her sister did with the painting, it would have to be done quickly.

For now, she only need remove the painting from this house without having the alarm sounded on her— again.

There would be plenty of time to think about Cart and his peculiar behavior when she was out of the duke's townhouse, and she and Sam were safely at home.

Jude tucked the landscape under her arm as she walked from the ballroom and pulled the doors closed behind her without a single noise. She tiptoed to the edge of the landing and peeked over to see if the maid had returned and was looking for her to mend the supposedly torn gown, but the lower floor was empty, to Jude's great pleasure.

She descended the stairs with more caution than when she'd climbed them a few moments before, for fear of dropping the artwork. The front door was only steps away—if she could make the last length without being caught, her night would be a success. Her breathing increased with the anticipation of freedom, especially knowing the painting would not be missed until a servant entered the ballroom—highly unlikely that night.

Pulling the door only wide enough for her and the painting to slip through, Jude closed the heavy front door and surveyed the rounded drive before her. A moment of panic set in when she didn't immediately spot Mr. Curtis and their closed carriage. She craned her neck to see around the line of other coaches but also kept herself hidden in the shadows outside the townhouse.

With great relief, Jude spied Mr. Curtis slumped in the driver's box of their dated carriage. With any luck, the older man would be sound asleep and would not notice Jude slipping the painting into the boot of their carriage for safe passage back to Craven House.

The shadows bordering the drive kept her unrecognizable as she moved past carriage after carriage on her way to the only conveyance without a proper ancestral crest. Jude crept to the back of the Craven House carriage, tilted open the boot, and slid the painting to safety.

"Curse you Samantha for being the pretty, social sister," she muttered. It wasn't Sam's fault she'd acquired the personable demeanor while Jude had inherited other useful qualities, including her ability to blend in and go unseen in the most crowded of rooms. But for once, she'd enjoy not being the one risking her neck with their schemes. However, Jude knew her skills did not include captivating an audience or distracting partygoers enough to not notice her change of voice when Sam took her place.

Jude slipped into her darkened coach and awaited Sam's return. They'd be on their way shortly...without anyone the wiser.

Chapter Sixteen

Cart counted the large cracks in the polished floor, following each groove until it met another and branched off into even more connecting networks of cracks. The indentations had been swept and polished so many times over the years, that if people brought their fingers to trace the lines, no hollow depressions could be detected. He knew this to be fact because he'd posed the theory to Theo several years ago and they'd spent an afternoon with their hands flat upon the ground, proving Cart's assumption.

The building, Montagu House, had been built over a hundred years prior, commissioned by the Duke of Montagu and then abandoned—gifted as part of the Act of Parliament in 1753 and established the British Museum, which opened in 1759. It was a fascinating tale of a father's legacy being abandoned by a son in favor of a more fashionable living in Whitehall.

The son had actually done all of England a great favor with his actions. Now, the massive building housed books, manuscripts, coins, and drawings of unbelievable history. Over the past two decades, the museum had even acquired the Rosetta Stone, Townley's collection of sculptures, and the Parthenon sculptures. Montagu House held an overpowering draw for Cart, due to the main fact that it was a free place of learning. It enabled him to introduce Theo to all sorts of antiquities that many people would never encounter in their lives.

A few years prior, Lord Cummings, an acquaintance from Eton, had reached out to Cart, letting Cart know he had accepted a new post as curator. Since then, Cart had been invited to the museum to dine with Cummings after-hours and partake in examinations of new acquisitions—and restorations of older pieces. It had only fueled Cart's desire for a path in the academics and antiquities field.

Today was one such day, however, where Cummings had requested Cart's attendance during museum hours to help identify the exact place and date a coal drawing had been created. It was precisely the thing Cart would have taken great pleasure and satisfaction in doing only short days ago. But this day, Cart was unable to focus, especially as the minutes passed without Cummings arriving in the grand entrance to collect and escort Cart into the secured rooms of the museum.

He paced, following a particularly jagged crack until it split into three and then selected the ridge that moved back toward the main area—and the many early risers who were flocking to the house of impressive history. It was likely that most were in attendance to see the Parthenon sculptures, as they were the newest display of important note. He was in agreement of their extraordinary presence, with their faceless bodies etched into stone. It was even fabled that long ago, the pieces were not white, but painted in vivid colors, hues that had deteriorated over time.

It was in large measure why Cart felt the way he did about pieces of art of historical nature—they must be preserved, kept in a manner maintaining their beauty for generations to come.

Thankfully, Lord Cummings was of a similar mindset.

It would not injure Cart overly if Cummings forgot their appointment. The atmosphere of the building brought a calm that had eluded him for some time. First, his attraction to Jude—so overwhelming that he'd allowed his guard and common sense to fall. Then, the discovery of the vase…in her possession. He'd immediately jumped to the conclusion that she'd stolen the piece. However, that was completely irrational, much like most of his thoughts of late. Why would a woman of the *ton*, from a solid family, have need to steal a vase?

There was no logic in that conclusion—and Cart prided himself on his logic.

He'd spent much time scrutinizing the alternatives. How had the vase come to be in her possession? It was possible she'd been duped into purchasing a stolen piece. But why buy it only to turn around and sell it? And, if she'd bought it from someone, who? And why the fabricated story of it being found in a stable? She'd avoided his questions on the topic—and he'd allowed it.

He was too close to the situation. To her. She was dulling his senses, leading him to believe that what seemed to be, wasn't at all.

He couldn't allow that.

Looking up, he realized he'd wandered into a more densely populated portion of the museum, one that housed small objects of Greek origin, unearthed a decade before when a group of explorers had stumbled upon a city buried by a mudslide or rock split five hundred years prior. It had perfectly preserved pottery, coins, tools, and fabrics used by a community previously unknown to the museum.

The exhibit was fascinating, but Cart had studied everything in great detail over the years. One of his habitual pastimes was standing against the wall, unnoticed, watching the people who came and went as they discovered the wonders of the museum. He'd brought Theo with him several times in the last year, but she tired of watching others and not stepping forward to discuss the exhibits with them. Cart was resigned to blending into the background. His sibling, however, was more the social butterfly. He could not fault her for that. Many times, he longed to be the one who sought out company and did not lock himself away as a recluse, a misfit of society.

Cart backed against a wall, hidden from view by a large statue as people streamed into the room. Their voices echoed off the elevated ceilings and he picked up on bits and pieces of conversation. It pleased him greatly to be able to hear people's thoughts on the pieces without having to join their company. One man thought a coin must certainly be crafted of pure brass and, therefore, be almost worthless except for its historical value. Little did the man know that the brass layer only covered the solid gold below.

Another woman admired a fabric—deteriorated by its time beneath hundreds of pounds of dirt and debris—commenting on the basic nature of the coloring. If only she knew that each thread had been hand dyed by crushed berries and insects to gain what little pigment it had, she'd be astounded.

But Cart kept to himself, listening but not interfering. Every museumgoer was entitled to their own experience—whether that led to increased interest in art and antiquities or a personal confirmation of the primitive nature of past cultures was irrelevant.

Mercifully, human nature and beliefs did not fascinate him. He didn't feel compelled to dispute their irrational and illogical notions of history.

A light laugh followed by a much deeper chuckle drew Cart's attention from a group of young men who found it amusing to grope a nude male statue to a more familiar grouping of ladies. At first, he thought his mind so preoccupied with thoughts of her that he'd imagined her into existence. But that would not explain the accompaniment of Miss Samantha and Miss Payton by her side.

Here of all places—one of Cart's greatest sanctuaries and a refuge of sorts.

He moved slightly right to hide from their view behind the statue at the exhibit's entrance.

He knew he should have slipped from the room, sent his regrets to Cummings on their missed appointment, and returned home—or anywhere besides the museum—but he found himself stuck, needing to see her and judge her true nature without her notice. He knew above all others that people could acclimate their outward appearance to successfully fulfill another's perception of them.

As much as he loathed admitting it, that was precisely what Jude had done—used Cart's interests, habits, and personality against him. It was exactly the thing he'd feared since his uncle's disappearance and Cart's return to London.

Jude was attired in a simple dress of pale yellow with black boots and an unobtrusive hat, while her twin was adorned in a bold blue gown of a shiny material with black, elbow length gloves. The subject of twins was something Cart hadn't given any attention to studying, but the correlation between two such similar-appearing individuals with utter lack of parallel oneness did, indeed, intrigue him.

"Can we go now?" Jude's youngest sister asked, slumping on a bench in the middle of the room. "My feet hurt and there are likely over a dozen things I'd rather be doing."

"We just arrived," Jude called over her shoulder without taking her eyes off the crude drawing she inspected. "Besides, I did not make the pair of you accompany me."

"You know Garrett would not allow you to leave the house unattended," Miss Samantha huffed, sitting next to Miss Payton on the bench. "We were not given the liberty of choice in our afternoon distraction."

Cart wanted to laugh at the scowl Jude sent over her shoulder until he remembered her less than honest possession of the vase belonging to Lord Gunther.

"Do you not love the authentic coal strokes of this drawing?" Jude asked her sisters. "The artist had only rudimentary tools, yet crafted such an elegantly abstract picture." When neither of the women answered, Jude turned a sharp look on the pair. "Come now, do appear a bit interested or I shall endeavor to spend until closing inspecting every item, painting, and sculpture in this museum."

"Oh, the man's adept skill at capturing the precise light in his dreary life is captivating, dear sister." Miss Samantha sat on the bench, inspecting the painting as if she were a matron of the *ton* inspecting a young debutante's acceptability for Almacks. "What would we do with all our extra time if we weren't trapped here taking in all these stunningly ancient masterpieces?"

The sisters were certainly amusing in their antics, much like Cart assumed he and Theo would be had they not been born over ten years apart. His sibling would be in line with Jude, spending hours exploring every exhibit and discussing each piece in great detail.

Cart yearned to step to Jude's side and enjoy the museum with her. However, that was in no way possible. His confusion over the vase and his particular attraction to her muddled his normally highly functioning brain. It was as if his logical brain weren't making the decisions but rather leaving it to another, more erratic, part of his person.

He should be furious with Jude, demand answers—he was furious with her. That was the main reason he hadn't contacted her since the library. He could not trust his actions and feelings when she was close. It was as if all that he'd built his life around— honesty, integrity, and learning—didn't matter when she smiled at him or when his finger brushed her arm. For the first time in years, he was faced with a situation—a person—he could not analyze. Not her or his reactions to her. He knew where the facts in the situation pointed, but his gut was screaming something different.

He hid in the shadows and watched the way her dress swirled about her feet as she hurriedly moved from one museum treasure to another in the room—as though if she didn't make it to each, read the placards, and move on, they'd start disappearing before she'd had a chance to study them all.

The way she floated around the room with a smile on her face, calling important details over her shoulder and moving around other museum attendees with words of greeting, showed how much she appreciated everything. It was a rare sight, to see someone as enthralled in the displays as she.

He watched as the trio moved on to the next room of exhibits. He stepped from his hiding spot, craving to follow their retreating forms, but he could not. He hadn't decided what to do about the vase or about her. Certainly his client, Lord Gunther, deserved to have the piece back, but if today proved anything, it was that he was far more confused about Jude's fate in the entire debacle.

"Simon?" Cummings called. Cart turned with a smile, taking in his friend—a youngest son and, therefore, afforded a life in a career he had a great passion for. "Hope I did not keep you waiting overly long."

"Of course not, I was enjoying the exhibit."

The man's brow rose as he looked over Cart's shoulder at the women moving farther into the museum. "An exhibit, yes?"

Cart wasn't prepared to talk about Jude or his complicated feelings for her with anyone—especially Cummings. "True, you know I revel in the time spent watching others experience the museum."

"As do I," Cummings agreed, nodding. "If you would come by more often than every fortnight or so, you'd see her far more frequently."

Cart shot a sideways glance at Cummings and stepped before one of the small glass cases to study the hammer and weaved basket within. "How long have you been watching me?"

"Oh, long enough to know you weren't studying the exhibits—but another, much more alive display."

Cart narrowed his eyes and took in his friend's smug smile as he slipped his hands into his pockets and rolled to the balls of his feet and back again, satisfied with himself.

"That is preposterous."

"I disagree, Simon—errr, my lord—Cart." He stepped beside the display and pretended to read the card as he continued. "It is only human nature. Obviously, something you've never been afflicted with before."

"Do they come often?"

"You are certainly to the point where you've been outed." Cummings made a show of raising his brows in shock and then rolling his eyes when Cart did not find the humor in his actions. "*They* do not come often, but the redhead—one of the redheads anyways—comes every few days. Sometimes accompanied by her twin or the younger girl—other times with a fair-haired, petite woman. Yet others, she comes alone. I've needed to shoo her out on several occasions when I've found her wandering the exhibits long after closing."

There were many questions running through Cart's mind. Did she leave with anything? Who escorted her when she was without her siblings? Did she put herself in jeopardy walking alone without a chaperone?

But that was not Cart's reasoning for accepting Cummings' invitation to assist in the restoration and assessment currently underway at the museum.

"I visited Lewis Stanford's shop this morning and purchased the items you requested." Cummings aimlessly walked to the next tiny glass box, holding a child's toy of rusted metal with dirt still clinging to its surface. "I bought them in the name of the museum, so the man was more than happy to come to a fair price since his name would be listed on the exhibit when it comes to display."

"I thank you for your kindness, my friend." Cart followed him as he paced to yet another display, moving around a pair of aging matrons dressed in full London finery, their hat plumage hanging dangerously close to a glass case as they leaned over to inspect the piece. "I will gather my funds and purchase the pieces back when I can."

"I will have them sent round to your home."

"That is not necessary." Cart shook his head at his friend's generosity. "I will feel better about getting them when I have collected the coin necessary to buy them back."

When he'd delivered the trunk of treasured pieces to Stanford's and collected the money needed by his mother, Cart had never imagined seeing any of the antiquities again, but when Cummings had invited him for this time at the museum, he'd asked a great favor of the man. Thankfully, he'd agreed and purchased the entire trunk back from Stanford.

"I know you will make good on the debt, Cartwright." Cummings patted him on the shoulder. "You've never failed me before. Not during our time at Eton nor after."

"I appreciate our good standing."

"Then I hope to see you around more," Cummings paused before turning to Cart. "Mayhap you'd be interested in consulting with the museum in the future. It is a paid position, not much, but a small stipend."

"I do not know…"

"Come now, it is more than enough to collect your chest."

"I will have to think about it," Cart answered. "I have much going on right now."

"I hope you will." Cummings seemed pleased with his answer—that Cart would truly consider the opportunity. He was correct, Cart needed the money and he desperately wanted to gain back his chest. "Shall we retire to the back?"

Cart made a hurried glance about the room, but Jude and her sisters were nowhere to be seen—likely deep within the museum by now. "Yes, I think that would be best. We can discuss the position at length."

Chapter Seventeen

Jude walked arm in arm with her sisters. The pair was being far more jovial after their departure from the museum and Payton's insistence they stop for an ice on the walk home. Jude had agreed, knowing that the distraction was very welcome. Delaying their return to Craven House and the troubles that awaited her there was highly agreeable to her. It was unlikely that Lord Cartwright had sent any word to her on the vase in the short time she'd been away and she'd be lying if she said she wasn't worried. And fearful.

She'd become comfortable in the months following her theft from Lord Gunther's townhouse. After the initial few weeks when no one had come to apprehend her or Sam, they'd begun moving in society once again as if it had never happened.

It was supposed to be only once—the payout being enough to settle some of the debts Marce faced at Craven House and provide the necessities to continue their sister's good work. But they'd thus far been unsuccessful in ridding themselves of the piece, which made it necessary for Jude to accept far less than they'd originally anticipated for the vase.

Things were a mess and Jude blamed herself.

Sam continued, unaffected by their misdeeds. Unfortunately, Jude did not have that luxury. And now, she'd been forced to bring Lord Cartwright into their dubious dealings. Her family's well-being should be of the utmost importance to her—that they continue to have a home, meals to eat, and their aging servants not be thrown to the streets. Instead, Jude couldn't stop dwelling on how this would affect Cart if he recognized the vase as stolen. Or worse yet, have someone see the stolen vase in his home.

She wanted to push aside her concern for the man, barely more than a stranger to her while her family had been close at hand her entire life. It only made sense that they should be her priority, not some gentleman she'd dared to kiss—once—and had gotten little response from since. He likely thought her a woman of loose moral character to be so brazen as to kiss a man in a public park where anyone could see.

They rounded the corner to see Craven House, a carriage in the drive, and Jude's stomach sank. Marce had returned, and she hadn't been able to gather the money they needed. She'd failed once again.

"Who could possibly be coming to call at this time of day?" Sam asked. "It is far past the acceptable hour for visiting."

The conveyance before her was certainly not as new and well-sprung as the carriages that collected Marce each year without fail. The exterior was in need of a good scrubbing and the horses at the front were past their prime.

Walking past the horses, Jude saw a small figure standing at their door, preparing to knock.

A spark of familiarity spiked within Jude.

She knew the petite figure with her long, dark plaits hanging down her back, a crisp white apron tied about her. Her dress hung only to her mid-calf, with impeccable white stockings beneath, disappearing into soft kid boots.

This was not as it should be. Jude feared something was most assuredly amiss.

"May I help you?" Jude called to the figure, who turned, a frightened, wide-eyed look upon her face—an expression matching the one she'd seen when she'd fled Cart's house.

"Are you Miss Judith Pengarden?" she asked, her voice high with nervousness.

"I am." Jude wanted to deny the question, turn around and walk back down their drive—and not have the confrontation that she knew was coming. "How may I be of service?"

The girl looked between Jude's two sisters, turning a pleading look on Jude. "May we have a moment alone?"

The girl was not planning to expose Jude in her drive. At least, not yet. "Certainly," Jude said, turning a smile to Sam, who stared back in question. "Please, take Payton inside, Sister. I will attend you shortly."

Sam must have realized who the girl was and hurried inside with their youngest sibling in tow. As much as Jude would have appreciated Sam by her side, it was imperative that Payton not find out what they'd been up to—she'd go to Garrett with the findings, no questions asked. Jude couldn't allow that to happen. She was too close to being rid of the vase and able to provide Marce with the much-needed money.

"Would you like to come in?" Jude asked. The girl shifted from foot to foot with unease. "We can talk in the drawing room."

The girl looked between the open front door of Craven House and her waiting carriage. "No," she stammered. "I will only be a minute. May we speak here?"

Jude had no idea what intentions the girl had with coming here, yet she obviously knew who Jude was. "Of course." Though she agreed to speak with her, Jude most assuredly was not going to start the conversation.

"What are your intentions with my brother?"

Jude took a small step back, stunned. She'd expected accusations about breaking into the girl's home, followed by her intentions to alert the magistrate, but not this.

"I do not believe we have officially met," Jude said hesitantly. If she were going to discuss her personal affairs, then it was only proper they had a formal introduction. "You must be Lady Theodora." When the girl nodded, she continued. "As you know, I am Miss Judith Pengarden."

"It is a pleasure to meet you…again."

Jude could not ignore the reference to their only brief encounter. The girl assessed her with a shrewd stare, much like Cart's.

"Now that we have officially met, I will ask again," Theodora said in measure words. "What are your intentions with Lord Cartwright, my brother?"

This was usually done the other way around, with a father or eldest male relative inquiring of a gentleman his intentions toward a woman—but this situation was no less hostile.

"I know who you are, what you have done, but I do not know why." Theodora paused, allowing Jude to speak.

"I do apologize for frightening you that night." She hoped an apology would weaken the severe set of the girl's grim expression. "It was not my intention—"

"That night does not concern me. Well, not specifically that night," she corrected. "I have noticed my brother has a certain affection for you. He's begun to daydream, idly spending hours looking into thin air, and neglecting his normal passions. It is highly disconcerting to me."

"I can see how that would be troubling," Jude agreed, at a loss for what to say next.

"Very troubling, indeed," Theodora nodded. "Which, by the way, I do not see as a horrible thing. My brother... Well, he has spent many years attending to my mother and me, while pushing his true desires and interests to the side. Now, he seems taken with you." She paused once more, scanning Jude from head to toe. "And while you are a stunning creature of great elegance and charm—much like the great poets write sonnet after sonnet about—I need to know your intentions with him. I will not see him hurt and I fear I will not always be close to care for him."

Lady Theodora spoke like a woman three times her age; maturity, intellect, and poise dripped from her every word. She could sit in any salon in London and interact with the social decorum expected of her. It was an impressive feat that Jude struggled with herself.

The hard truth was that Jude couldn't answer the girl's question. From her heart, she could most assuredly tell the young lady she had nothing but honorable intentions where Cart was concerned. However, in her mind, Jude knew she was taking advantage of him in many ways.

"We have many similar interests," Jude confessed, thinking of her day at the museum—longing for Cart to be there instead of her sisters. They would have enjoyed walking between the exhibits, pausing to discuss any painting, sculpture, or artifact that garnered their notice. Cart would have had unlimited tidbits of knowledge to share with her, as he did each time they met. And maybe, she might know something of note that he didn't. "I have enjoyed spending time with him."

"That is all?" Theodora questioned, placing her hands on her hips, daring Jude to lie. "Only an acquaintance you've delighted in spending time with?"

Jude eyed the girl, keeping her mouth shut. This was Cart's little sister. If anyone deserved answers, it was she. But Jude couldn't bring herself to share with Cart her true feelings, how could she open up to a girl she'd only just met?

"Just so," Jude said curtly. "And, if it pleases, I hope to continue an acquaintance with him." Her words softened as she went on. She had nothing against this girl—and would certainly like her if they continued their association. "Has your interest in me and Cart—Lord Cartwright—been quenched?"

Jude could tell by the girl's tilted head as she continued to assess Jude that her questions hadn't been fully answered, but finally, Theodora shrugged. "Do call me Theo—everyone does, to my mother's horror. But note that I will soon be departing for school, away from London, and I will be unable to keep an eye on my brother. Do not hurt him. He does not know I have come—and it would behoove you to keep this little visit between us." She lifted her hand, holding out an envelope to Jude—one she hadn't noticed the girl held. "I believe this is for you. A man delivered it while I prepared to knock earlier."

The girl swirled around, giving Jude a swift dismissal as she ascended into her carriage. Her driver closed the door behind her and took his seat, quickly sending the conveyance into movement.

Leaving Jude to stare at the missive in her hand— clearly marked, *Notice: Delinquency.*

While Jude needed to think over Theo's abrupt visit and thinly veiled threat upon her departure, there were more important things at hand—namely, the correspondence she now held. The first she'd been able to properly inspect that Mr. Curtis or her sister had not grabbed immediately and disappeared with.

Jude's hands shook a bit, though she didn't know if it was because of the harrowing encounter with Theo or the letter she held.

Chapter Eighteen

The door squeaked open and Cart listened without removing his gaze from the paper before him as light feet entered the room. "Simon?"

"What?" Cart glanced up from the letter he'd been writing, glaring at Theo, who stood at the open door of his study, wringing her hands nervously. He worked hard to remove the frown he knew covered his face and likely frightened his dear sister. He was unused to such drastic changes in his mood. Only days ago, he thought himself in love, but now he knew he was the biggest fool in all of England—and possibly abroad. "My apologies, Theo. Please, come in."

She hurried to the chair before his desk, as if fearing if she dallied he would tell her to leave. For once, there was no book tucked under her arm, no ancient tomes pressed to her nose, no tutor following behind her asking questions of literature, history, or science.

Something was severely wrong, for with all this, she would not make eye contact with him, deeming the scuffed floor beneath her feet more worthy of her attention.

"Where have you been?" he inquired, relaxing his stern tone from a moment before. "When I returned home earlier, it was said you were out 'on an errand'."

"I was," Theo confirmed, stumbling over the words. "But I returned quickly."

He'd wondered what errand a twelve-year-old girl could possibly undertake, but it was likely their mother had dragged her along to pay another social visit to some matron of good standing.

"Very well." He would not press her for details— he hadn't the time. There was much on his mind, least of which was his female relations' whereabouts every minute of the day. Besides, Theo was the one person in his life that he could trust above all others. He watched over her and showered her with as much attention as possible—and in return, she adored him.

Cart tried to refocus, but Theo's unnatural stillness before him drew his attention once more. She neither blinked nor fussed.

"What plagues you, puppet?" he asked. It was a name his father had used—not in an affectionate way, but more to do with the babe who used to hang all over him.

She kept her eyes focused on the floor and Cart realized she was far more upset than he'd thought. Gauging another's emotional responses and cues had never been Cart's strong suit.

"May I ask you a question?" Her voice was timid, something he'd never wish for her. The meek were often taken advantage of. As Cart had discovered long ago.

"You may ask me anything," he said with more force than he'd intended. "Theodora, please, you know that no subject is prohibited with us." They'd become so close since his return to London—he'd left a mere child, but had returned to find his only sibling had grown to the cusp of womanhood—a beauty with an intellect rivalled by no other woman in his acquaintance, but one... "I am your brother. I care for you and your happiness above all else. You do not appear happy at the moment, which vexes me greatly."

"I am not unhappy, only concerned." Theo's forehead scrunched with unease as she continued to wring her hands. "However, I do not want to upset you by prying into your personal affairs. As you have repeated over and over, they are none of my or Momma's concern."

Cart had requested his mother stay far away from his personal life, but never had he said the same to Theo. "I am certain your concerns will not be seen as prying." He removed his spectacles and set them aside, allowing him better focus on her across the large expanse of his desk.

"Was it Miss Judith you met with at the library?"

"Yes, why?" The question puzzled him. He hadn't remembered speaking her name to anyone, though he knew his sister's tendency for listening in on his meetings, especially when it had anything to do with antiquities.

"May I ask where you met her?" Theo glanced down at her hands, sensing she had, indeed, overstepped her boundaries. "It is only...I do not..."

"We met at a garden party not long ago," he answered. "We had a mutual fondness for all things historical and collectible."

"Oh." She stood, keeping her gaze on the floor. "I will leave you to your work."

"Theo, come back," he called when she turned to depart. "Please, sit. Miss Judith and I are only acquaintances, nothing more." Most assuredly nothing more; their relationship moving from acquaintances to little more than a woman he'd thought he knew at some point in the past. Though watching her traverse the exhibit at the British Museum earlier in the day had shown him a new side to her. At least, she hadn't lied about her interest in history.

"But you like her? Enjoy her company?" Theo persisted, still behind the chair she'd vacated.

"Of course, she is an educated person, and you know I am drawn to people of an enlightened nature." He'd thought Jude educated in academia, but it turned out she was only refined in the art of thievery.

The wound from her duplicity was still too new and too raw for Cart to discuss without his chest seizing in pain and regret—pain due to the loss of someone he'd cared for and regret that it was so simple for others to fool him.

"You risked her encountering Momma when she visited not long ago."

"Come out and ask what you truly seek to know, Theo." Cart sighed, folding his hands on his desk, covering the letter he'd been attempting to write to Lord Gunther—wishing all conversation of Jude to cease.

"I should be going." Theo shuffled her feet and looked at the open door behind her. He'd never witnessed his sister so apprehensive.

"Sit." His command boomed loudly and Cart's first instinct was to apologize for his forceful tone, but he would not. Something was wrong in his household—with his dear sister—and he would find out exactly what it was. So many things appeared out of his control lately—namely, Miss Judith's behavior—but members of his family were not. "Explain your troubles."

Theo drug her feet as she rounded the chair once more, sitting heavily, the chair sliding back a few inches and scraping the polished wood floor. "Do you care for her?"

"That is none of your concern."

"But it is," Theo argued.

"It is not, I assure you." He paused, massaging the bridge of his nose to calm himself. "She will not come between you and me." That was Cart's only guess as to why Theo had taken an interest in Jude—a negative interest that he'd have said was unfounded only a few short days before. "Besides, ours is not a friendship that will endure."

"That is sad to hear, dear brother."

"And why is that?" Cart understood why he would see Jude only once more and then remove the woman and any thoughts of her from his life, but Theo's interest baffled him.

"It is unimportant if you say your association will not last," she said matter-of-factly, even nodding her head with the final word.

It never ceased to amaze Cart at how adult-like Theo was at only twelve years of age. She spoke with the grace and manners of a woman twice her years.

"And if our association is extended?" Not that Cart was ready to overlook or forgive Jude her thievery. In reality, he'd pondered his options for turning her in to the magistrate to stand charges for her crime, but he'd quickly discarded the idea. No matter her deplorable actions, he would not see her sent to the tower, nor jailed among other common lawbreakers. He hadn't even the gall to ask her point blank if she were the one to actually steal the vase from Gunther's home. "Not that I am saying it will, but enlighten me as to how that would affect you."

"I had no intention of telling you after she visited the other day." Theo paused, making eye contact with him before continuing. "It's evident that you care very much for her—and she in return." It wasn't a question but a statement—one he would not refute. Mainly because he was unsure how he felt about Jude.

And what Theo knew of Jude's feelings for him.

The rational part of him knew he should cut his ties with her, walk away before he became embroiled in whatever plot was underway. However, the part of him that had been awakened by her—their conversations and their kiss—pled with him to hold fast to her, keep her close.

Cart had never been at such odds with himself.

Decisions—and the path that followed—had always been clear to him. It was not as simple or uncomplicated with Jude.

And if he were honest, Cart wanted nothing less than for Jude to be uncomplicated. It was her complexity that drew him—and held his attention, whether good or bad.

"She is the one who broke into our home," Theo mumbled.

Cart sat up straighter and shook his head. He must have heard her incorrectly—after everything he'd witnessed with her thus far, and now this? "Please, say that again."

"It was Miss Judith whom I saw flee through the drawing room that night."

"You must be mistaken," Cart hissed. "Never once did you tell me a woman broke into our home."

"What would the point have been?" Theo asked, pained at the hurt she knew she'd caused her brother. "Momma ordered me to keep silent on the matter—that nothing good would come from word spreading that we had been victimized once again. She fears we are already the laughing stock of London and that this news would prove the gossips correct in calling us that."

"Then why tell me now?" he heard himself ask, but his temper was flared to such a severe degree, that he had little control over his words.

"I think there may be more to her than that…though I didn't know at first."

Cart counted to ten in his head, beseeching his anger to subside before he said something that would damage his close relationship with Theo. "You allow me to worry about the gossips, you are just a child." It was extremely disheartening to hear his sister agonize over society's opinion of the Montgomery family. "Now, let us revisit your thoughts on Jude…err, Miss Judith being the woman who entered our home—which is a horrible thing to do, by the way."

"It is more than just a thought, dear brother," she said, slumping into her chair. "I have verified my first assumption and found my original notion to be true and correct."

Cart wanted to smile at her ploy of using the scientific method and basic hypothetical construct to convince him of her statement. "And how did you double check your hypothesis?"

At his question, Theo did not hold back her grin. "I convinced you to allow me to tag along when you went to the library to meet her again."

"You little minx." He'd thought he'd been the one to come up with the notion of her accompanying him. Yet another example of how easily he was manipulated. The thought stung, knowing he was no wiser to people's tricks than five years ago.

"It is far worse than that," Theo admitted.

"How could it be any worse?"

"I visited her home today."

"Theo." Cart felt his anger increase further. "Why would you do that?"

"That is not the important part, Simon," she rushed to say. "There was a man there as I arrived. He thought I was a member of Jude's family and handed me a note meant for someone in her household."

"Why should this diminish my fury over her actions?" Deep down, Cart hoped Theo could offer some valid excuse for Jude's actions.

"I certainly did not open private correspondence meant for another."

"Of course, you refrained from such actions," he said. "But what did you see?"

"The letter was clearly marked with the words *Final Notice: Delinquency. Debts due immediately.* I do not know who the missive was from but it is certainly of an important nature, is it not?"

Cart nodded.

"Simon," Theo continued, "I know you have plans for me to go away for a proper schooling."

"I do."

"And I also heard Momma speak of her intent to travel."

"Yes," Cart confirmed. "I was taken aback by her decision to refrain from society for a time. It was not something I thought she ever wanted."

"With Momma away—and me at school—I fear what you will do." She stared at him intently for the first time since entering the room, taking in his reactions to her concerns. "I care for you and I worry about your future."

"You are sounding more and more like our mother each day, puppet."

"You cannot base your entire future around inanimate objects when there are so many living, breathing things in the world," Theo said.

Cart wanted to push her concerns to the wayside, convince her they were not valid concerns at all. But he knew his tendency to surround himself with unmoving things—for those things could never hurt him.

"Tell me I will not have to worry about you while I'm gone, because, if I do, then I will refuse to go."

"You cannot do that, I will not allow it, Theo," he retorted. "Besides, it is I who will worry over your future, not the other way around. I am your elder brother—it is my task to secure your future—and Mother's."

"But not at the expense of your own." Theo shook her head as if he'd shared the saddest news she'd yet heard. "Promise me you will listen to Miss Judith—truly hear her words and try to understand her actions."

"I am undecided on that at this moment." Cart didn't want to hear what that woman had to say—he could not think of one valid reason she could put forth to justify her stealing into his home.

"But if she comes to you…"

"I will hear her out, puppet." Cart massaged the back of his neck, a headache threatening to take over.

"Maybe not wait for her to come to you."

"I appreciate your sisterly concern, Theo." It was the one aspect of their relationship he cherished the most. They wanted the best for one another, with no reservations.

"So, what do you plan to do?" Theo raised her brow as if challenging Cart to make a decision on his course of action.

Little did she know Cart had been debating his next move for the past several days—and her confession did not make his choice any easier. Or clearer.

# # #

After Theo had departed his study, Cart tore up the letter he'd been drafting to Lord Gunther, deciding to deliver the news by servant.

It had taken him approximately twenty-nine minutes to collect his nerve, his overcoat, and hail a hackney to deliver him to Lord Gunther's stoop.

It had taken him exactly twenty-nine seconds to regret his actions, but it was far too late for a change of course as he paced Lord Gunther's private receiving room, awaiting the lord's arrival. Cart counted his footfalls as he walked from one side of the room to the furthest edge, close to the windows overlooking the rear gardens. It took him fourteen strides to cross the span of the area, though normally it would be closer to eighteen. But with his increased agitation, his normal gait was widened considerably.

His tension stemmed from his wild notion of how to retrieve Lord Gunther's vase—and keep Jude's hand in it all secret, taking away any risk she'd be detained and punished for the theft, and giving her the pounds she clearly needed so badly. There was no possible way he could gather the fifty pounds she requested to purchase the vase, especially with the coin he'd handed to his mother only days before. He needed Gunther's wealth…there was no other option that he could deduce.

He was still reeling from Theo's revelation. He was unsure if he could bring himself to accept the dire nature of his purported association with Jude—she'd lied to him, she'd used him, and he'd allowed her to do it. And even with all that, he'd set out to help her.

She was to blame for his inability to reason a solution to his current problem—a problem that was also, conveniently, caused by her.

"Lord Cartwright," Lord Gunther's voice boomed behind him. "Did we have a meeting scheduled for today? I was not expecting you."

Cart swallowed the urge to tell Gunther everything—where to find his precious vase and who was to blame for this entire debacle. Instead, he pulled a folded note from his inside coat pocket and presented it to the man.

"What is this?" Gunther asked as he took hold of it, turning it over in is hand as if he had no intention of reading it.

"Forgive my intrusion, but I received this missive only a short time ago and thought it urgent enough to come straight away," Cart lied, the deception rolling easily off his tongue. That was a fact he would need to analyze later. At length. "It is known I have been searching for the vase and someone has come forth with information."

"Who is it?" Gunther grunted, unfolding the note. "I will send for the magistrate immediately." Before Cart could dissuade him, Gunther pulled the bell cord to summon a servant.

"My lord—" Cart attempted to stop Lord Gunther as he read the note.

"This note is not signed." He waved the paper in the air. "This tells us nothing except that someone claims to have my vase—no name, no directions, nothing of use. What is going on, Cartwright?"

Cart focused on holding eye contact, refusing to look away and confirming the man's suspicions. "I am as puzzled as you, my lord," said Cart, shaking his head to further solidify his words. Inside, Cart was angrier than he'd ever remembered being, even directly after his uncle's misdeeds were exposed, but he could not allow Jude and her family to suffer. Jude was a liar, a deceitful woman, but what kind of gentleman would Cart be to allow a woman in need to go without help? "It arrived this morning. My butler tells me it was delivered by a hired messenger, who knew nothing of import and was directed not to await a reply to the letter."

Startled, Cart realized even if his uncle had come to him after all he'd done, Cart would have accepted him and done what he could to help the man.

"And this person only requests fifty pounds for the return of it?" When Cart nodded in confirmation, Gunther took to pacing the same path Cart had only moments before. "How do we know this person has the vase? Or that once they have the funds, it will be returned?"

"We do not know," Cart replied with all honesty, except he did know the person who held the vase, and did not doubt she would hand it over when she received payment. He refused to believe she'd duped him without good reason. "If you so desire, I will handle the transaction and take all the responsibility. I will take the ransom and exchange it for the vase—if there is no vase, then we are back to where we were before I arrived today, your fifty pounds still in hand."

He hoped his confident demeanor was enough to convince Gunther to trust that all would be as it should.

Cart waited in silence as the man continued to pace back and forth. Cart longing to do the same. Instead, he focused on the decorative paper covering the wall on each side of the hearth, counting the many swirls and committing the complex pattern to memory. It was useless information to retain but brought a form of tranquility to him—something he could control, the numbers, the speed of his counting, and the consistency of the pattern. After several minutes, he was certain he could close his eyes and draw the swirling pattern from memory.

"I will have my man of business send the banknotes by tomorrow morning." He handed the letter back to Cart, who slipped it into his pocket, knowing it would be tossed in his own hearth as soon as he returned to his townhouse. "Please inform me when things are done." The man clasped Cart's shoulder and squeezed. "I do thank you for all you are doing."

At what point had Cart compromised his integrity so far that he felt only a small degree of the guilt that should weigh him down at this point?

Cart took a small step away from the man, causing Gunther's hand to fall back to his side.

"Antiquities are my passion." The statement was as true as it had been before he'd had the misfortune of meeting Miss Judith and would be just as true after she was out of his life and forgotten. "The passion extends to my own collecting and the safeguarding of all things of a historical nature."

The older man nodded as Cart spoke, clearly encouraged by his declaration.

"Then I will wish you Godspeed, Lord Cartwright."

Cart bowed stiffly, accepting the man's good wishes, though he didn't deserve them. "I know my way out. Good day, my lord."

As he fled Lord Gunther's townhouse, he noticed his strides were no longer sure and wide, but short and hurried—almost as if he were running away from something. When, in fact, he sensed he was running toward something. Or rather, *someone*.

His sense of obligation toward Jude knew no bounds—and bordered on irrational. He was now determined to extricate her from the predicament she'd placed herself in.

With the money, she should have no reason to steal…and he would have her word that she'd never put herself in harm's way again.

Chapter Nineteen

"I've had enough," Jude declared, throwing her cards face up on the table.

"That is not fair," Payton whined. "You must finish the hand. It is the way of things."

"You are only jealous that Jude has won nearly every hand when you fancy yourself a master at cards," Sam said with a chuckle, not bothering to look up from the gossip sheet she read.

"How dare you!" Payton pushed from her seat and launched herself at Sam where she lounged on a settee a few feet away.

"Do pipe down," Sam said flippantly.

"Tsk, tsk," Garrett said, wrapping his arms around Payton's waist as she flew through the air toward Jude's twin. "Do not be a spoilsport. She won fair and square almost a dozen rounds ago."

"Any player can demand the right to win back their coin before another player leaves the table," Payton quoted the rules followed at gentlemen's card rooms, such as White's and their own home, Craven House. "Is that not so, Garrett?" She squirmed to break free from his hold, her eyes still locked on Sam, who reclined with ease but had set the paper aside in case Garrett's hold should fail.

"It is, you little minx—" He released his youngest sibling but kept a firm hold on her wrist. "However, you were given the opportunity to turn your luck around. That was four rounds ago."

"Before you lost a month's worth of allowance, I might add," Sam continued, brushing an invisible piece of dust from her skirt as if unworried Payton would leap for her again. "But I will make certain Jude buys some pretty hair ribbons with your coin. Something that would suit our auburn locks—and unfavorable to hair of a darker color."

Jude smirked, knowing their bickering was for nothing as each girl always slipped their allowance back into Marce's office when their sister was otherwise occupied. Marce never mentioned the returned coin, and neither did Sam, Jude or Payton address the issue.

"Cheats!" Payton screamed, wrenching from Garrett's hold. "You are all thieving cheats!"

"Payton." The commanding boom in Garrett's voice even had Jude whipping her stare to him. "That is not only unfair, but also unsportsmanlike of you. That will not be repeated again, inside—or outside—of this house."

Jude had never noticed his severe similarity to his only full sibling, Marce, until that exact moment. The tone and sternness of his command matched that of their eldest sister, though Payton was not to be deterred from her tantrum.

"The pair of you"—Payton pointed first to Jude and then Sam, where she now busied herself inspecting her shortly trimmed nails—"are conniving—"

"I said, *enough*!" Garrett's nostrils flared and Jude waited for him to lose his temper completely. "The three of you are like a rabid pack of dogs. When will you ever learn to trust those in your family? It is people outside that circle who will do you harm."

Jude glanced between Sam and Payton, each staring at their brother without a thing to say. Even Payton's anger subsided as his words sank in.

"You have each other and that is far more than most have," he continued. "This petty bickering is pointless and will get none of you anywhere. And all over a few hands of cards. Despicable."

Again, Jude was led to believe that Garrett's meaning went far deeper than any of them could understand. She suspected it had much to do with Garrett's older half-brother. The man had refused any association with Marce or Garrett after their mutual father died and he'd inherited the estate, throwing Marce, Garrett, and their mother out in the cold on the very same day.

But, Garrett and Marce had said long ago that the man was dead to them, and that their mother had made sure they all had a secure home which would never be taken from them.

"Payton," Jude said, standing from the table. "I had no intention of collecting on our wager."

"It has naught to do with the coin." Payton slouched back into her chair. "I have been working very hard…and it seems I am just not an adequate player."

"What do you mean you've been working hard?" Garrett asked from the sideboard where he poured another drink.

"She thinks she can count cards." Sam had no remorse telling Payton's secret obsession to Garrett as she grabbed the gossip rag again and spread it across her lap. "I have told her it is a waste of time, for when she marries, it will all be for nothing. Her time would be better spent on reading the sheets."

"Why?" Payton collected the discarded cards and prepared to shuffle them. "So I can study all the eligible men and select a target?"

"Target," Jude laughed at Payton's choice of word—a very accurate term, indeed.

"That is not at all what I am doing," Sam huffed. "I only seek to avoid getting embroiled with an unfavorable man, especially one known to be a rakehell."

"Because you can be the only rakehell in a relationship?" Payton continued to poke, paying Sam back for her harsh words earlier. "You do not need to know names, only pick a man old enough to be your father…"

Jude covered her mouth to stifle her chuckle at Payton's precocious comment, happy for the moment of distraction and allowing it to take her mind off the fact that Cart had kept his distance.

"Ladies," Garrett said after he'd drained yet another tumbler of port fortified with a spot of brandy—cringing at the foul taste. "Do not kill one another on my watch."

A solid pounding sounded from the front of the house.

They all glanced at the tall clock in the corner. It was barely past midday and certainly none of them were expecting anyone. It was rare that anyone came calling at Craven House, especially since Ellie had married Lord Chastain.

"Guests shouldn't be arriving for many more hours," Garrett mused aloud as they listened for the front door to shut after Mr. Curtis answered the knock. "Which of you is in trouble?"

He jested, but Jude quickly looked to Sam, who shrugged her shoulders in response. Neither had left the house since the night before. When they'd arrived home, Garrett had been duly occupied, so much so that he'd still failed to notice the new painting hanging in their foyer, small as it was. Hidden in plain sight seemed to be their family's greatest secret—even Marce saw no reason to hide her chest of coins.

Jude hoped their luck held and it wasn't the magistrate seeking either of them. Or another letter demanding money for unsettled debts.

But when Curtis stepped into the room and looked at her directly, Jude feared her time outside the confines of the magistrate's quarters was about to end. In her mind, she thought through all the things she'd request to take with her: her comb and brush set—not that she was vain in any way, but her hair became knotted fairly easily—and her warm blanket crafted so many years ago by their housekeeper for Jude had always loathed the cold. Maybe a few books to keep her occupied during her time away. Sad, but that was about all she possessed, besides her clothes, and she'd certainly have no place for her armoire of fancy gowns and kid gloves. Not where she was going. Everything else would remain here at Craven House.

"Miss Judith," Curtis nodded as if he somehow knew he was personally sending her to the tower—if she were so lucky to gain entrance into such a fine housing for thieves, she'd likely be relegated to far worse accommodations at Newgate. "Ye have a visitor. Would ye be like'n' me ta show him here?"

Jude glanced at Garrett, his interest piqued at the surprise visitor. Then to Sam, who'd gone back to her reading, showing no interest. Payton began shuffling her cards once more, hoping one of her siblings would slip into the chair that Jude had vacated.

"I am expecting no one." Though in all truth, she knew who awaited her in the foyer—and had quite possibly brought the fifty pounds she'd requested for the vase. "I will meet with him in Marce's receiving room."

It was located toward the front of the house, but also not far from the side entrance of Craven House. It allowed her sister's special guests to come and go without fear of being seen from the street.

"I shall return," Jude casually called over her shoulder. With great luck, none of her siblings made to follow her as she walked from the room where Mr. Curtis waited just outside.

He held a small card out to her before continuing, "He said ta give ye this."

Jude was relieved that Curtis hadn't announced the man's name to everyone.

Looking down, she found what she'd expected to see.

The Earl of Cartwright

Simon Montgomery

It was written in bold, heavy script, obviously printed by the finest calligrapher in London. There were no flourishes or fancy lettering. Exactly what she'd expect from Cart—never an overdone or fanciful man, with the exception of his cravat.

"Do ye want me ta show him ta the room, Miss Judith?"

"No, thank you, Mr. Curtis," Jude said, placing her hand on the elderly man's arm in reassurance. "I will meet him in the foyer and show him myself."

"I will have tea brought round."

While Jude would enjoy nothing more than an afternoon spent with Cart, comfortably chatting and debating topics of mutual interest, she also knew she needed to exchange the vase for the banknotes and have Cart out of the house before Garrett decided to look into her guest. Or heaven help her, Craven House's card room began to receive guests for the evening's gathering.

She also sought to hide Craven House's true nature, as it would reflect poorly on her if Cart didn't understand the reasoning behind Marce's nightly endeavors.

Though, it was possible Lord Cartwright already knew Craven House's secret and even darker past and chose to overlook it. That was more than Jude could hope for any man of the *ton* to do.

Curtis nodded and turned in the direction of the kitchens, leaving Jude to make her way to the foyer. As she moved soundlessly down the hall, she heard Cart mumbling—possibly numbers...

"Lord Cartwright," Jude greeted him formally in case someone lurked close. "Lovely of you to call."

He bowed before her—a little too stiffly and a bit too low. "Miss Judith."

When he said not another word, his eyes roaming the entry, Jude continued, "I had expected word from you a few days ago."

"Ah, well, some things take time," he replied.

As like at the library, something was not right with Cart.

"We can talk more in here." Jude swept her arm in the direction of Marce's private receiving room. "Right this way."

"Of course, Miss Judith," Cart said, taking the first step in the direction Jude had motioned. He began to talk as they walked toward the room, a bit of normalcy returning—whatever normal was for Lord Cartwright. "My sincerest apologies for not calling sooner—"

Abruptly, his words cut off and he stopped in his tracks, focusing on the small painting hanging on the wall.

"My lord?" Jude asked as his eyes narrowed on the landscape and his hand rose to touch it.

"This painting…"

"It is breathtaking, is it not?"

"It was not here on my last visit."

"No," she confessed. "It is newly acquired."

"I..cannot…where…"

He seemed as captivated with it as she'd been when she'd taken it. "Can you imagine a place so beautiful in all of the world?"

Jude's unease grew as he clearly recognized the painting—the one she'd taken only the night before.

"I can," Cart replied.

"And to think, it is in England." Jude stepped to his side, taking her eyes off him and looking at the painting that held his complete attention. She would be lying if she said it didn't bother her to have mere objects overtake his attention so completely, but she sensed it was more than just the beauty of the painting that captured him. It was as if he were looking at something entirely familiar to him while she'd become something he didn't recognize.

"I came here to try and save you, Miss Judith." Sadness crept into this voice, as if he'd lost something truly valuable. "But I see I cannot."

"What do you mean, my lord?" He could not know that she'd taken the painting only days before in an attempt to salvage their plan to help Marce. The air around them electrified—and Jude felt their attachment unravel. What good would it do to deny stealing the painting? Instead, she would say nothing.

They stood side by side, neither looking at the other, their voices kept even as if they spoke over tea. Panic infused every limb in her body.

"You are a thief." If she hadn't locked her knees at the accusation, she'd have been knocked over by the hushed fury in the statement. "A common thief. I should have sounded the alarm on you at the first warning sign. I should have known you for what you truly are when I'd seen Lord Gunther's stolen vase in your possession."

Jude sucked in a breath, unable to speak as her heart about pounded out of her chest.

"You knew?" she asked. He'd known all this time, yet he hadn't called the magistrate on her and had even offered to purchase the vase.

"Where did you get this painting?" Venom dripped from his every word, a rage Jude had never thought him capable of.

She could only shake her head—in denial, in remorse, in utter disbelief that all the good she was trying to do was being brought down in this manner, by the one man she thought could one day understand her.

"I said, *where* did you get this painting?" His voice rose with anger, bouncing off the walls and traveling deeper into the house.

If she didn't calm him soon, Garrett and her sisters would come running.

"Lord Cartwright, please…"

"Please, what?" He finally turned toward her, the painting forgotten. "Please do not expose you for the thief you are? Please do not send for the authorities? Please do not ask how a painting—commissioned by my father before his death—came to reside on your wall? You ask much of me, Miss Judith."

"I did not—" Thankfully, he cut off her, stopping yet another lie from crossing her lips.

"You are not the victim here." His chin lifted and he glared down his nose at her as if expecting her to disagree.

But all of his words were true.

# # #

Cart was shaking—not outwardly, but internally he'd been shaken to his core by the depths of her deceitful nature. He'd prayed her possession of the vase had some other reasonable explanation. Something his rational mind could grasp and reconcile; anything that would enable him to process and understand her devious activities and return to the time—not that long ago—when he thought her a woman of perfection.

He glared into her moss-green eyes, noticing for the first time the hazel flecks sprinkled within. But he couldn't allow this new discovery to dim his fury. He wouldn't allow it to take away from the hurt he felt at her treachery.

"Do I even know you?" He kept his stare intense and she seemed to wilt before him. "Has it all been a ruse to make me look the fool?"

She only shook her head again as water gathered in her eyes, threatening to spill over.

He would not let her feminine tactics dissuade him from gaining the answer he sought, the answers he needed to move forward—in whichever direction those answers led him.

"Are you interested in antiquities or is it only a means to line your pockets?" Cart had witnessed her passion for history firsthand at the museum but even now, he could not trust his eyes. Cart had so many questions rising to the surface. "What more do you have hidden within these walls?"

His hand shot out and grasped her elbow as he pulled her farther from the foyer. He needed answers and shouting at her in the foyer was not the way or the place to attain them. "Come, let us seek a bit of privacy to discuss your felonious behavior at length."

"No." She planted her feet and jerked Cart to a stop only feet down the hallway off the foyer. "I did not do this to hurt you."

Cart tightened his grip on her arm and pulled her close, his face mere inches from hers. "The bloody hell you did not."

"Cart…" The word came on a sob. "I assure you…"

"Your assurances and promises mean nothing," he hissed. "Did you think to make me look the bigger fool than I already do to society?"

"This has nothing to do with—"

At that, Cart laughed, a maniacal chuckle that scared even him. It was clear that if he did not rein in his emotions, he'd lose the upper hand with her. "It has everything to do with me."

He'd been taken advantage of by so many people in his short life: his uncle, his mother, and now, Jude. And he'd been unaware of any of it until it was too late.

She pulled away and he released her arm. "If you will only listen to me."

He snorted. "Listen to what…your half-truths and outright lies?"

There was nothing more she could say. Nothing she'd ever told him had been grounded in truth. The things Theo had shared about Jude's family meant nothing to him now. He was wrong to have hoped for the best with her. He'd actually put himself in peril to untangle the mess she'd made for herself.

"Tell me, does your family know about all of this?" When her eyes widened, he continued, "Your twin, very likely. I should call for the magistrate on the pair of you.

A bit of time spent locked in a room to think about your actions would do you well, I am sure."

He should have seen her for what she was long before she'd showed him the vase and certainly before he'd seen his family's picture hanging upon her wall. Right out in the open as if to rub her skill in his face. And he'd been so blinded by her that he hadn't noticed the painting on his first visit to Craven House.

Cart could not control his feelings or trust his instincts where Jude was concerned, that much was grounded in fact.

And to break into his home and scare Theo so, then try to win her forgiveness—what game did Jude play?

"I suppose you have had your sights set on me for some time," Cart mused aloud.

"Until Lady Haversham's garden party, I had no idea of your existence. I swear." It was her turn to grab his arm, lightly pulling him toward the privacy of a room, but he would not allow it.

A room with a closed door would only lead to a private moment. Cart did not trust himself to be completely secluded with the woman before him.

"You think I can ever trust another word that comes out of your mouth?" He was speaking only in questions and accusations, instead of his usual facts and logic. Everything about Jude had him throwing reason and caution to the wind. "I highly doubt you can give me a sensible explanation for how you came to possess a stolen vase or my family's precious heirloom."

"Can you at least give me the opportunity?" she asked. "You owe me at least that much."

"I owe you?" His voice thundered down the hall and into the foyer, unrecognizable even to him as Jude shrank away from him. "Let me make one thing clear. I owe you nothing. You are in possession of something belonging to my family with no plausible explanation, you sought to embroil me in illicit dealings, and most of all, you called into jeopardy my integrity. And then, if that wasn't enough, you pulled my sister into all of this. Not only have you hurt my standing within the antiquities community but in society as a whole. This not only harms me—I could care less about my standing with the *ton*—but you have brought a new kind of peril upon my sister. Society will judge her by the actions of her brother. I will not have her life ruined by a scandal she had no involvement in. Do you hear me?"

The offer from Cummings to consult at the British Museum raced through his mind, certainly an offer he'd be unable to accept.

"What is going on here?" a male voice yelled behind him. "Step away from my sister, you scoundrel!"

Cart took a breath, realizing at some point his hands had balled into fists at his sides. As he released them, he held Jude's eyes, needing her to see his rage at her deceit.

"I said unhand my sister. Now!"

"This is not over, Miss Judith," Cart spat before turning and removing his father's painting.

"What are you doing?" the other man asked.

Cart only stared the man down, daring him to stop Cart's retrieval of his family's painting. Though he did recognize him as the man who'd departed the night watchman's house with Jude and Marce. Her brother, certainly.

He paused before Jude's brother, knowing he owed this man something, even if it wasn't the complete truth. "My apologies for disrupting your household, sir, but it would behoove you to keep a better watch on your sister."

"Why...I..." the man stammered.

But Cart didn't pause for further explanation. Tucking the framed portrait under his arm, he walked to the foyer and directly out the door, ignoring the many people standing stunned at his angry departure.

With finality, Cart slammed the door behind him.

Ending his association with Miss Judith and promising to himself he'd never again speak her name—or embark on a single path that would benefit her in any way.

And there was one thing Cart could trust in...his own promises.

Chapter Twenty

"Who in the bloody hell was that?" Garrett demanded, striding toward her.

Jude wanted to flee. A chance to be alone to think through all that Cart had said—all that he'd accused her of. The paintings, the vase, the ancient books—they were all objects, things…things could be replaced and no one had ever been hurt by her thieving. She'd never thought her actions could wound others for all she'd done was relieve them of pieces they scarcely noticed. However, Cart was hurt—deeply.

But she could no longer delude herself into thinking that was true—for Cart was certainly hurt. Jude slipped her hand into her skirt pocket and touched his calling card, the paper feeling rough and uneven against her skin.

"He is Lord Cartwright," Sam called from wherever she stood out of sight.

Jude never meant to hurt anyone, especially Lord Cartwright—though that was not entirely true…she knew the possibility of injuring him and had taken the risk with very little remorse or forethought. Jude hadn't spent time pondering the lasting consequences of Cart being found in possession of stolen art, nor had she truly absorbed the magnitude of the harm they were inflicting on people.

"And why did he call on Jude only to yell at her—in her own home?" Garrett posed the question to the household at large, suspecting someone would give him an answer, though it wasn't likely to be Jude. "Then to walk out with a painting from our wall? The man is certainly senseless. Someone had better start giving me the answers I seek."

Instead, Jude whirled around and started for Marce's private salon and the vase.

"Come back here!" Garrett yelled. "Do not walk away from me."

But Jude had faced the ultimate wrath of Cart—and that had frightened her far more than her brother's false bravado.

"I will speak with her," Sam called to Garrett, following Jude down the hall.

A favorable thing, because Jude was going to need her twin's help if she was going to return the vase to Lord Gunther's and make things right with Cart.

"Close the door," Jude said curtly when Sam followed her into the room.

"What is going on?"

Jude had kept much from Sam of late, including her meetings with Cart, and especially their kiss and Jude's growing attraction for the man.

"We are returning the vase."

"What?" Sam asked with bewilderment. "That is not possible. What will happen to our home?"

"All hope of selling the vase is gone and Lord Cartwright is more than prepared to send for the authorities." It was a threat that Jude was certain he'd never follow through on, but one that would ensure Sam's assistance. Sam was too vain and self-involved to ever suffer the risk of being taken to Newgate—for any amount of money. "Hurry, we do not have time—it is likely the magistrate has already been sent for and could be knocking on our door at any moment. There will be naught Garrett or Marce can do for us then."

Sam continued to watch her, paralyzed with fear, as Jude collected the vase and peeked out the door. "Garrett is gone. We can leave through the side door, but I will need your assistance to return this without getting caught."

Her twin only nodded.

"You must keep Lord Gunther occupied—and his servants, as well."

"How in heavens do you expect me to do that?" Sam squeaked.

"You are always most comfortable being the center of attention," Jude reassured her. "I am certain you will find a way to distract his household long enough for me to slip the vase back into the house."

"But what if I fail?"

"That is not an option." Jude set the vase aside and pulled Sam close, wrapping her arms about her sister's stiff frame. "We do this last thing and it is over. All of it is over. We let things happen as they will. If Marce runs out of ideas for supporting Craven House, then we will find other ways—legitimate ways—to help."

Theodora had obviously shared her visit to Craven House with her brother, infuriating him all the more, which Jude understood. She'd lied to the young girl, just as she'd been doing to Cart this entire time.

Sam pulled back and stared at Jude, their eyes perfect mirrors. Jude knew their depths held far different truths. "Let us get this over with," Sam sighed. "Make sure we do not get caught."

"I will do all in my power, I assure you of that."

After slipping out the side entrance, the walk to Lord Gunther's townhouse passed uneventfully, even though Jude noticed Sam glancing over her shoulder as if waiting for the magistrate to pounce on them at any moment.

Jude was a bit more at ease, knowing that Cart could not—*would* not—do that to her, at least not before allowing himself to calm down, and possibly giving her an opportunity to explain. He was not a man who made decisions rashly without immense thought beforehand, though his erratic behavior made her fear she did not know him as well as she assumed.

Even if he gave her a day, he would not overlook her crimes for long, and would eventually do what she knew to be the only thing that would appease his need for justice—he would turn her over to the magistrate.

Hopefully, long enough to return the vase and prove to Cart she was not the horrid woman she appeared to be.

Jude hid around the corner of the townhouse as Sam raised her hand and knocked on Lord Gunther's door. She hoped he was in residence. Otherwise, their ruse would be far more complicated.

The door opened and Sam handed the butler her card. "I am here to see Lord Gunther. Is he receiving this afternoon?" Sam's voice appeared a bit strained and high-pitched, but the servant didn't seem to notice as the door opened wider to allow her twin entrance.

Now, Jude waited. Sam had assured her she could create enough distraction for Jude to slip into the house unseen if given five minutes. If there was one thing her twin excelled at, it was gaining the complete attention of a room. But to also divert a household of servants? It seemed more than even Sam was capable of.

True to her word, Jude heard a female scream and then the sound of something large crashing to the ground within—and then the shattering of glass. Next came the frantic shrieks of several other women, likely maids hurrying about.

Jude crept to the front door and pressed her ear to it. She heard loud footfalls deep within the house, but none directly opposite the door. She glanced over her shoulder to make sure no one was watching her. Thankfully, the front stoop was concealed by overgrown ivy and other potted plants, making it impossible for anyone to see anything other than her feet unless they were close by.

The door opened easily and Jude entered the deserted foyer. The vase was tucked safely in her satchel. She glanced around the entry to spy a suitable place to set the vase; somewhere it would be noticed immediately, and its return announced to Cart. Certainly the table beside the front entrance was far too visible and obvious.

She moved farther into the foyer as another round of footfalls and hurried calls sounded within the house.

Jude wasn't certain what scheme Sam had concocted to keep the household in a frenzy, but she was eternally grateful for it.

Two other tables in the foyer were overly cluttered with flower arrangements or other odds and ends, leaving no room for the vase without Jude needing to move the objects to different locations. It was her intent to have the vase appear as if it'd never been taken from Lord Gunther's, only misplaced within the large house.

Down a hall to her left, Jude heard Sam's voice. "I am most fine. I must have fainted—oh, look at this dreadful mess I have created. You must forgive my appalling manners, my lord."

Jude was running out of time. She scanned the area again, spotting a small shelf mounted on the wall with only a small, framed portrait occupying space. Transferring an object the size of her palm was far more agreeable than an entire table housing a statue, plant, and candle display.

Taking the vase from her bag, Jude grabbed the picture and replaced it with the delicately painted ceramic pot, rotating it to show its most stunning side to the room at large—needing the vase to be found quickly. Satisfied, she quickly moved to the table bordering the front door and shifted a statue of a woman reading to a gaggle of children at her knee.

Jude paused for a second, pondering the value of the piece before shaking her head, remembering that was exactly what had gotten her into the current situation she was in.

Setting the portrait next to the statue, Jude cracked the door and slipped out as she heard voices returning to the foyer. "You certainly do not need to call for a doctor, my lord. I will be just the thing after a short rest. I am sorry to have disrupted your day."

"You will call again—or allow me to call upon you?" Jude heard a man ask as she closed the door without a sound and hurried down the steps to await Sam's departure.

She'd only just pressed herself against the wall of the townhouse when the door opened again. Glancing around the corner of the structure, Jude watched her sister walk out of Lord Gunther's, a weary smile on her face with her palm pressed to her forehead.

"My carriage is only just down the road," Sam said, removing her hand from her forehead to point in the direction of several parked carriages down the lane. She even waved in their direction to convince the man. "See my coachman? He is ready for my departure. I bid you good day, my lord."

Lord Gunther must have agreed that Sam could see herself to her waiting coach—or that her lowly status did not require accompaniment—for the door closed and Sam hurried down the stairs to where Jude waited.

Sam's hand was once again pressed to her forehead, pain clearly etched on her face.

"Whatever did you do?" Jude asked, her brow furrowing with concern.

"You said you needed a distraction grand enough to draw the entire household—so, I fainted," Sam confided, wincing.

"What happened to your head?" Jude reached forward to remove Sam's hand.

"I wagered that fainting would not be enough, so I decided a bit more theatrics were necessary." Sam pulled her hand away revealing a bump that was already starting to bruise. "So, I took a painting off the wall and a side table down with my fall. I think my wager paid off and I very well may be set for the stage. How much do you think I could earn working at the playhouse?"

"Oh, Sam." Jude lightly touched the bump. "I did not mean for you to injure yourself in any of this. We must return home and have a compress readied, or your face is likely to turn all shades of blue by morning."

Sam brushed Jude's hand away. "I assure you, I will heal and the pain will last far less time than if we are taken by the magistrate."

Jude had never imagined her twin would risk her own safety for her. It was far more than Jude could have asked, even though their scheming had been a joint endeavor from the start.

"Very true, Sister," Jude conceded. "Let us be away from here."

"But," Sam said, slipping her arm around Jude as they started toward Craven House. "If Lord Gunther follows through on his promise to call on me, you will take my place. The man is certainly not to my liking."

"Agreed." Jude would do anything, if only Lord Cartwright would learn of the vase's return and forgive Jude her transgressions. Even if it meant they never saw one another again, it was unbearable to imagine him thinking the worst of her forever.

Chapter Twenty-One

Anger infusing every bone in his body, Cart leapt from his carriage before it had fully stopped in front of Lord Gunther's townhouse. Even his trip home to return his family's painting to its rightful place hadn't diminished his rage at Jude and the situation she'd placed him in. At some point, he'd made his decision regarding what to do—it might not be the most thought out conclusion, but it was a solid path he was dedicated to taking.

It was simple. He'd return Lord Gunther's money, give him the name of the woman who'd stolen his vase, and let him handle the situation as he saw fit. That way, Cart was not responsible for Jude's fate. The consequences of her actions rested solely on her shoulders, not any decision Cart made—or didn't make. Undoubtedly, he believed she deserved some sort of punishment for her illicit activities, but did that include being detained by the magistrate? It was not for Cart to say or decide.

He was removing himself from the entire situation—and Jude's ultimate fate. He could not jeopardize his own future for a woman who could not be honest with him.

When he'd shut the door to Craven House behind him, it was for good. Miss Judith had to be cut permanently from his life, especially if he were to regain some semblance of his normal self. It was similar to his course of action after his uncle, Julian, had absconded from England with much of his family's fortune in tow. Cart had moved past the scandalous family betrayal by doing just that—moving on, not dwelling on what he could have done to prevent it all. He'd simply made the decision to never allow it to happen again.

And he'd failed once again. But this time around, he had the chance to make sure all of society didn't witness his fall from grace.

A man who spent two hours reading the London paper in the morning instead of tying an intricate cravat. A man who dedicated time to learning, not debating the appropriate social hour to call on a woman. A man devoted to restoring his family's prestige and traditions as opposed to squandering money on frivolous niceties deemed necessary by society, such as the calling cards he'd sent for the previous week.

That was the man Cart needed to return to.

Sensible, self-assured, decisive.

He bounded up the steps to Lord Gunther's townhouse with his fist prepared to knock, but the front door swung open to reveal Lord Gunther himself.

A very furious Lord Gunther.

"Lord Gunther—" Cart said, his words cutting short at Gunther's narrowed stare.

"Cartwright," he hissed. "I am surprised you would show your face here again."

"Excuse me?" Cart stood on the stoop as the man made no move to invite him inside. "Is all as it should be?"

"As it should be? Far from it!" With each word, Gunther jabbed his finger at Cart's chest. "You think I am a bloody dullard? You think you can take advantage of me in such a manner and get away with it?"

Unease filled Cart at the man's harsh words. Something had happened since he'd met with the man and asked for the money Jude requested for the vase. "My lord, I am unsure what you speak of."

Gunther took another step toward Cart, forcing him to back down the steps. "You think you can come into my home and lie to me—take my money and disappear."

"I have not disappeared, my lord," Cart reassured the man. "I am here, with your banknotes." He patted his coat's breast pocket where the envelope resided. "If you will allow me to come in, I will explain everything."

"I have no doubt you have had ample time to concoct another harebrained scheme to foist on me."

"My lord, please," Cart said, raising his hands in surrender. "Let us retire to your office and discuss whatever has happened to negatively affect your opinion of me."

Gunther stepped aside and Cart entered, following the man through the entry toward the hall that led to his study.

"Sit," Gunther commanded, closing the door soundly behind him.

As Cart made to sit, his eyes alighted on the object atop Gunther's desk.

"The vase," Cart whispered.

"Yes, the vase!" Lord Gunther boomed as he moved behind the desk and sat.

Cart still stood, too shocked to say or do anything.

"Would you care to explain how the vase appeared in my home?" He raised his brow in question. "I can assure you, my servants searched every square inch of this house before I contacted you to help find the stolen piece. Imagine my utter astonishment when I walked a guest out earlier today and turned to see it—sitting right on a shelf off my entry."

"How?" Cart was far more dazed than irate. He'd left Craven House less than two hours before, with the intention of telling Lord Gunther everything and laying himself at the man's mercy. And somehow, Jude had beaten him to it. The woman was infuriating and meddlesome. "My lord, I was coming today to return your money."

Gunther entwined his fingers, creating a steeple, and then re-folding them, all while keeping his hardened stare on Cart. "I am sure that was your intent."

"I can assure you, it was."

"And what of this note you received, offering the vase in exchange for fifty pounds?"

He'd known since he'd used his left hand to scribble the note that he'd one day come to regret it— today was that day. And from Lord Gunther's angry demeanor, that day may also be tomorrow and the day after.

"I am as puzzled as you are." Cart sat heavily in the seat Gunther had offered him. "After receiving no further communication from the individual purportedly possessing the vase, I came today to return your funds and discuss other options for finding the piece." To show his honorable intentions, he removed the envelope from his pocket and set in on the desk. With two fingers, Cart pushed the envelope toward Gunther, who only stared at it—making no move to take it and count its contents. "You see, I was on my way to discuss things with you. Possibly the person never had the vase and, therefore, had no intention of meeting with me for the exchange."

"That still does not answer how the thing turned up in my home." Gunther sighed. "I am overjoyed to have it back in my possession, do not misunderstand me, but it all seems a bit too convenient—and you are the one person at the center of it all."

"I agree it appears odd, but let us focus on its reappearance and not dwell on the other stuff." Cart directed the conversation away from who could have possibly taken the vase—and then returned it without being discovered. The woman had some gall, indeed. He'd arrived with the intent of explaining to Gunther exactly the con he'd been a part of, but somehow, Cart was ending up protecting Jude once again. Though he'd sworn to himself he would not. "If that will be all, my lord." Cart stood, pushing his chair back on the hardwood floor. "I will be going."

Gunther also stood. "Do not mistake my aims, Cartwright. I plan to look into this matter further and find out what happened. And as of now, nothing appears honorable on your part. It is certainly advantageous that you hold a title, but once everything becomes apparent, that may be the only thing you have in your favor."

"I will certainly be investigating this, as well," Cart said in response to the man's threat. And Cart knew the only place to find the answers he sought—the one place he'd promised himself to never go again, no matter how badly he longed to see the woman within. "I will show myself out."

"You should do that," Gunther said in way of dismissal, nodding to Cart before he turned and left.

Another convenient coincidence, certainly, Craven House was a short walk from Lord Gunther's townhouse, far closer than Cart's home was.

To focus his thoughts and calm his irritation at Jude, he began counting the steps as he walked, leaving his carriage behind. The fading evening light gave way to a far cooler night breeze as Cart moved down the sparsely crowded street. The farther he walked, the fewer carriages drove past him and the number of people on foot lessened. It was the time of day when most of society was arriving at their nightly entertainment—the dinner hours quickly approaching.

Cart ignored his own stomach's rumbling, realizing he hadn't eaten a bite since his morning repast with Theo.

With only eight hundred and thirty-four strides, Cart rounded a corner and Craven House came into view, every room on the ground floor had lights ablaze.

Jude hadn't told him her family was entertaining that night and the household had appeared quiet when he'd been there earlier in the day—not that he'd been very aware of his surroundings due to his incessant anger with her. It was very unlikely that she'd share her plans for the evening with him, as he'd not given her much opportunity to speak.

But he was prepared to do just that, allow her to speak—say her piece before he gave her an ultimatum.

Stop her criminal activities or he'd turn her over the magistrate himself.

She could not continue as she was without being caught at some point. If that happened, Cart would be unable to help her. It mattered naught that it had been Jude who'd broken into his home, it had been Jude who'd lied to him about where she'd gotten the vase, it had been Jude who'd given him false hope for his future.

There must be consequences for her actions—a debt to be paid.

He shouldn't care about her—or her safety—but the fact remained that he did...far more than he'd realized.

The stark realization was that his safety was in jeopardy because of his feelings for her.

His rational brain knew no woman who'd been proven a liar was deserving of any feeling but scorn from him. Then Cart thought of the pure kiss they'd shared. There'd been no hiding for either of them in that moment. She hadn't been discouraged by his peculiar tendencies or that on their previous stroll he'd ended up face down in a pond with mud saturating his clothes and boots. He hadn't questioned her mysterious appearance at Lady Haversham's garden party—completely disrupting his well-ordered life.

Everything about him and his priorities had shifted since meeting Jude. So much so, that he barely recognized who he'd become. The worst part was not knowing if it had changed him for the better…or for the worse.

A carriage pulled into the rounded drive in front of him and three men departed the conveyance, each dressed in far better-tailored coats than his own, their boots polished until they shone from the light spilling from the open carriage door. One man even made use of a cane, making him appear decidedly distinguished. Cart had never pondered the use of a cane…odd that a man who looked virile enough would weaken his presence by use of a walking aid.

Cart kept a close eye on the trio as they approached the door, which swung open without them knocking to announce their arrival.

The men were expected guests, but who exactly had they arrived to see?

Cart's awareness of the men grew as they chuckled at something said by whoever greeted them at the door. The person stayed just out of sight for Cart. He felt his judgment slipping, a primal need to follow the men into the house and demand to know the reasoning for their attendance at Jude's home taking hold.

He'd never been a man to puff his chest and demand anything of others. That all changed when Jude was involved. These men did not belong at Craven House. And certainly, they did not belong anywhere near Jude. They appeared the high-stepping peacocks that were all too prevalent in society these days. He would not be astonished to find the trio was known scoundrels.

Without further thought, Cart marched to the open door just as the butler pushed it closed, nearly smashing Cart's nose. Instead of knocking—as any other gentleman worth his title would do—Cart took firm hold of the doorknob and pushed it open once more, stepping over the threshold unannounced.

It was not until he stood solidly in the house with the three men turning to greet him and several others—servants by their dress, gawking at his impromptu arrival—that Cart comprehended the overwhelming feeling coursing through his body and taking over his actions.

Jealousy.

Red-hot jealousy ran through him as one of the men stepped forward to greet him.

"Lord Cartwright?" the man asked with a grin.

Cart didn't say a word, not trusting his temper to remain within if he spoke.

"Gideon, Duke of Davies," the dark-haired man said by way of reception. "We have not had the pleasure of meeting, though I have heard of your great work from Lord Barton. I am happy to make your acquaintance. This is Lord Humberton and Sir Giles."

Cart nodded to the three men as their names were called.

"Lord Cartwright is an academic man known for his vast knowledge of antiquities," Davies said to the room at large. "We missed one another by only a short year at Eton."

"Good evening, my lord," Sir Giles bowed. "Will you join us for a round at the card table?"

Giles' invitation did nothing to dampen Cart's foul mood. "I am here to see Miss Judith, but thank you for the invitation to play. Maybe another time."

"I will be sending for her, my lord," the older man, Curtis, called to him and shuffled down the corridor away from the great amount of noise emanation from a room to Cart's right.

"It was good to see you, Cartwright." Davies patted his shoulder in camaraderie and moved toward the celebration. "Who is ready to lose their treasured money to me? Giles, I hope you collected your pin money from your wife before coming out tonight."

Cart watched the men as they disappeared down the hallway, laughter floating back toward him. He would never understand the gesture of slamming another man on the shoulder to show kinship. It seemed more of a punishment than a means of showing another you cared.

Around him, the servants returned to their tasks—none stopping to greet him or pay him any mind. That pleased him more than having to engage in idle talk of inconsequential subjects with strangers while he awaited Jude's arrival in the foyer.

He noticed no new painting hung where he'd removed his father's artwork earlier in the day. At least she hadn't departed Lord Gunther's and immediately located another precious object to steal. It was ludicrous to think she had actually been able to get away with stealing the vase and returning it, all while escaping notice.

Her ability to enter his home without remorse, her guilt being so great as to drive her back out irked him. She'd visited his home and performed as if it had been her first time within.

"Lord Cartwright." Cart swung around to the main stairs as Jude rushed down, casting a nervous glance around the entry. "What are you doing here?"

His anger returned quickly. "I find it insulting that you should need ask such a question."

Jude took hold of his arm and pulled him in the direction Curtis had left, away from the laughter and boisterous noises coming from deeper in the house. "Please, come with me to Marce's private room. We can talk there without interruption."

It was the same room she'd attempted to lead him to earlier in the day—thankfully, at the moment, his mind was not consumed with taking her into his arms and kissing her soundly. Cart acquiesced and allowed her to lead him down the hall.

When the door shut behind them, Cart instantly moved away from her, needing the distance to keep his thoughts straight. This was his final-final time seeing her. To avoid the need to return, it was imperative that he say all he need say before walking out the door.

"Why would you risk yourself once again to return that blasted vase?"

"You gave me no choice, my lord," she said, throwing her arms wide in defeat. He did not relish her accepting defeat, but in this situation, it was a necessity. "I am not the horrible person you think I am. And the only way for me to show you that was to return it to Lord Gunther's home."

"And what did that prove, except that you are foolhardier than I'd suspected?" he accused.

"It was to prove I care."

"About what, exactly?" Cart challenged. "Your need to possess things that belong to others? Your need to prove your skill as a thief? The need to see if you can evade the magistrate's noose once more?"

"None of those things matter to me!" she shouted, taking a step toward him. He held up his palm to stop her.

"Then what?"

"That I care about you." Her confession should have meant something, cooled his fury at her, or had least given him pause about her true motives, but it did none of those things. It only convinced him that along with being a skilled thief, she was experienced as a manipulator, as well. "Cart, I have had an affection for you since the moment I noticed you making your way across the lawn at Lady Haversham's garden party."

A lie, for certain. Using his emotions and feelings for her against him.

Her soul was as white-cold as her delicate, porcelain skin.

For a brief moment, Cart only wanted to flee, get as far from her as was humanly possible. He could never understand a woman like her. Jude's motivations were foreign to him; a perpetuated cycle of misuse and deception brought upon him by a woman who most certainly lacked a heart. Even their kiss was tainted forever in his memory by her dishonest nature.

Chapter Twenty-Two

Jude hadn't planned to see Cart until she was ready to tell him everything: her family's past, their current struggles, and how his abrupt entrance into her life had changed everything she'd thought she wanted for her future.

It had been important for her to settle all the chaos in her life before making her amends with him. She owed him that much. Jude knew she owed him far more than that, possibly far more than she had to give. But first, she'd decided to resolve and remedy everything once and for all, truly be done with her past as a thief and come to terms with knowing it was something she could never revisit. It was something she'd never desired to do in the first place, yet her options for helping her family were almost nonexistent.

She could not seek employment in the workhouses, Marce would never allow it. She was reluctant to leave her family to pursue a life dedicated to being a tutor, children's maid, or a hired companion, though that fate looked far more desirable than being sent to Newgate or the Tower. It was only now, faced with Cart's scorn for her, she realized her options were far more prevalent than she'd first thought. Her fingers were more than skilled enough to gain work mending clothes. Or she could have sold some of her finer gowns. She shouldn't have grasped on to the first notion for helping her family, but thought of another way, a less criminal way, to keep her family's home—but she'd needed the money quickly. Her plan hadn't worked out in the slightest and she'd likely have made more money hiring herself out as a lady's companion.

Anything to avoid standing here while the man she cared for stared daggers at her, apparently so angry he stood across the room from her. He obviously found her so repellant he couldn't be within several feet of her.

"I know you have no reason to believe anything I've said," Jude's voice cracked with hurt, the anguish inside finally pushing its way out. "But I swear I have been honest with you. About my feelings, at least." She looked away, her hair falling before her face, unable to maintain eye contact as the many things she'd been less than truthful about filled her thoughts. They far outnumbered the things she'd been honest about.

She turned back to him as he turned from her and began to pace the small room, his mouth moving as if he recited a poem or counted but no sound passed his lips.

His lips.

Jude glanced away once more, knowing nothing good would come of her being lost in the sight of his lips or the broadness of his shoulders. Or the way his light brown hair fell forward across his forehead, much like her much darker, auburn hair had moments ago. Or the way that, even now, the bridge of his nose showed tiny indentions where his spectacles sat when he worked.

Why hadn't she noticed all these subtle things before?

Before it was too late.

"You broke into my home, Jude." His expression was blank, unreadable. "You frightened my little sister half to death."

"I can explain that," Jude rushed to say. "It was a mistake. A misunderstanding."

"I'm beginning to believe our entire relationship is a mistake, which for me,"—he paused before continuing—"is far worse than any misunderstanding."

"Do not say that, Simon." Jude was unsure where that had come from. She had used his given name as opposed to his preferred shortened title. She wanted to prove to him that they knew one another past the point of formalities or even socially acceptable pet names. She wanted to believe she knew him deeper than that—and that he recognized her depth at the same level. "We have been far more than that…our kiss—"

"Do not dare hurl that back in my face. You have already made it clear that it was another mistake you regretted. I suppose you are going to claim I took advantage of you, ruined your chances of a favorable match."

"Of course not." That had never crossed her mind. "I would never—"

"Then what about the kiss?" he asked. "Was it as false as everything else? It would not surprise me if you planned the entire ordeal, laughing behind my back with your sisters at the gullible way I reacted to your attentions."

"They know nothing of it." Jude needed him to believe her, to understand everything that had happened between them. "It was a moment for us and us alone."

"So, I am not worthy enough to mention to your family?"

"You are talking in circles, Cart," Jude said. "If I mention our kiss to anyone, it is because I seek to ensnare you in a marriage trap, but if I don't share the news of our kiss, then I am embarrassed by our association." Her head was spinning, so much going through her mind. There was far more than she'd be able to share with him in the time they had.

Cart's head fell to his palms. He scrubbed his face as if he could brush away all that had happened, but he couldn't…and they both seemed to gather that undeniable fact.

"You cannot have it both ways." Jude took a step toward him, hoping he'd let her close. She needed to be near him—more than she needed anything in her life…ever. "Tell me what I can do to fix all of this."

"You can do nothing," he said, dashing all her hopes. "Lord Gunther plans to ruin my reputation. No more will I be trusted to do the one thing I love, the one thing that brings me ultimate happiness."

"He cannot do that."

"He undoubtedly can, Judith," Cart seethed.

"How? He knows nothing."

"I tried to help you," he admitted. "I drafted a note requesting the fifty pounds in exchange for the vase. I collected the fifty pounds from Lord Gunther and then, mysteriously, the vase reappeared in his home."

"But—"

"And now, Gunther thinks me a fraud and a lord not worthy of his place." Cart's shoulders sagged, the gravity of the situation finally bearing down on him. "He will ruin me—my family."

"You are not a fraud, Cart," she said.

"I know that, but he does not."

"It is a misunderstanding…"

"No," Cart said, clenching his fists at his sides as he moved toward the door. "It was another mistake. I thought I could help you—save you from yourself…but I was gravely mistaken. And the only ones who will suffer are me and my family."

"No." Jude shook her head back and forth with such force she became lightheaded. "I did not mean for that to happen. I did not intend for any of this to happen."

"Sometimes intent has little bearing on consequences. You will do well to take that bud of wisdom to heart, Miss Judith Pengarden."

"Do not go." Jude tried to step before him to block his departure, anything to keep him here—and talking. If only they continued to discuss everything, it would work out, and they could reach an understanding. "Please, Simon."

But he navigated around her.

"What is going on here?" Garrett asked from the now open doorway. "I thought I threw you out earlier."

Her brother stood, blocking Cart's retreat as he eyed the pair.

"Garrett, please," Jude pleaded. "Allow us some privacy to speak."

"I will do nothing of the sort—"

"Do not fret," Cart cut in. "I have nothing further to say and will take my leave. Good day to you both."

Jude watched as Garrett stepped aside and allowed Cart room to pass by him before he moved back to block her from chasing after him.

"Move, Garrett." Jude pushed against his chest, begging him to permit her to follow.

"No, let him depart."

Jude pounded her fist against her brother's chest, her frustration turning to a deep-seated ache within her, threatening to consume her entirely if she weren't able to stop Cart from leaving. Unbidden tears rolled down her cheeks as she laid her head against Garrett's shoulder, her fight draining from her.

Her brother stroked her hair as she cried, her shoulders shaking with each wrenching sob. "Shhhh," he soothed. "All is not lost."

He had no notion what had transpired between her and Cart, but his words did lend her comfort. If Cart never forgave her, at least she had her siblings and Craven House. Though Jude wouldn't give up. She would make Cart hear her out.

Jude cringed when she heard the front door slam as Cart left.

She couldn't help but fear she'd never see him again, never have the chance to explain herself further. The way things were left was not the sole thing she wanted him to remember if they never crossed paths again.

As the moments dragged on, Jude calmed, her tears drying up and her sobs lessening. The sounds of Craven House's nightly card tables invaded Marce's private receiving room, bringing with it the reality of where

Jude was and how she'd mucked everything up. It also brought the sense that she could fix things with Lord Cartwright. It would take work.

Something she rarely shied away from.

Lifting her head from Garrett's shoulder, she said, "Thank you. I am sorry you were privy to my moment of weakness."

"My dear sister," Garrett said, pushing her to arm's length so he could stare directly at her. "That was not weakness but the starting point of a growing strength within you."

It seemed every man she encountered this day was full of wisdom while she struggled to grasp the simplest notions.

"Now remind me again, who was that man?" Garrett frowned. "And how are you acquainted with him?"

"His name is Simon, Lord Cartwright," Jude confessed. It was so much like Garrett. He didn't remember Sam naming Cart just hours ago. "We met at Lady Haversham's garden party not long ago."

"Why do I get the notion that you care for this man as more than a mere friend...?" His voice trailed off, expecting a response but not pushing her to admit anything immediately. She remained silent. "It is not my intention to pry, but as the eldest male family member, it is my duty to see that no harm comes to you."

Jude giggled, permitting the last of her hopelessness to fade as the sound filled the room.

"Oh, you think I am jesting?" Garrett asked, his brow knitting as he stood a bit taller and gave her his most serious glare. "I am very much concerned with your future, Judith."

"My future." She stifled another laugh. "If there is one other Craven House member whose life is in more shambles than mine, it is you, Garrett. As you can see, we are in no position to help one another."

He broke eye contact and stomped to the windows. "This is no joke, Jude. I understand I have never been the most solid and sturdy member of this family, but, damn it, you are my sister. If he hurt you, then I will avenge your honor."

Avenge her honor, Jude pondered. Did she have any honor worth avenging?

"It is I who hurt him."

"Not you," he disputed, swinging back to face her, an utter expression of denial on his face. "You are kind, thoughtful and, by far, the most compassionate of us all."

It was exactly those qualities that had gotten Jude in the position she was in.

"Be that as it may," she continued, "it is all my fault."

"What did you do? Maybe I can help? Not fix everything, but offer advice." He started pacing again. "If Marce were here, she'd know how to solve all of this."

"I do not know even where to begin with all I've done to cause Lord Cartwright harm."

"How about his most serious grievance with you…" he prodded. "We can start there."

"I stole from him." Jude moved farther into the room and plopped down on the lounge facing the hearth. "Not directly, though I tried that, as well, but he found me in possession of a painting belonging to his family. I also lied to him. About several things."

"That was what he took back this morning?" His nostrils flared with his agitation. When Jude nodded, he continued, "I cannot believe all this has been happening right under Marce's nose. She is going to be so enraged at your actions. Why would you ever think you could escape trouble?"

"It has all been a terrible thing—"

"You're bloody right it has," he seethed. "What do you need that kind of money for?"

"It was to help Marce pay the debts she owes for Craven House," she confessed, happy that Garrett must now finally understand why she did what she did. "If I sold the painting, I would have given the money to Marce."

"Whatever led you to believe Marce needed you to put yourself at risk?" he asked, stunned.

"The notices have been arriving for unsettled debts," she said. How could he not see that what she'd been doing was for all of them?

"Where do you think Marce is right now?" He recoiled, his eyes holding no emotion, his anger having fled at some point to be replaced by contempt. When Jude shook her head, he continued, "She is collecting on a debt owed to her and will make right with everything as soon as she returns to London. You have overstepped yourself and created much trouble, Judith."

His continued use of her full name brought tears to her eyes once more.

A tear fled down her cheek and she held back a sob. She'd unintentionally hurt so many people she cared for.

"You said he is Lord Cartwright—an earl, correct?" His demeanor softened once more as Jude fought to hold her emotions back.

"Yes. Do you know him?" The question escaped on a cry.

Garrett kept quiet as he pondered the name, a frown creasing his face as he tapped his chin with his forefinger. "Not personally, but, yes, I remember hearing something about his family several years ago."

"Well?" Jude glared, waiting for him to continue.

"I do not know for certain," he said, sitting on the lounge next to her. "…and I'd need to speak with Marce to be sure, but I believe the papers were full of rampant gossip about his uncle stealing off for France not long before Lord Cartwright's majority—bleeding the estate's coffers dry before his departure. I believe while the man was away at university, his uncle sold off precious family heirlooms, furniture, and even a property not entailed to the Earldom, if the gossip rags are to be believed."

If Jude's heart could sink further than it already had, it was likely lying at her feet at this moment.

"It is said his estate was on the brink of ruin and he was facing debtor's prison for his uncle's misdeeds."

Cart had had everything taken from him without his knowledge or the opportunity to defend himself or his title—and Jude had done the same.

"No," she sighed.

"Yes, it is only recently that he has begun to restore his family name and holdings," Garrett mused. He set his hand on hers, squeezing it gently. "There is word that he has taken on a paying position to do that." Normally, her brother would scoff at the notion of a gentleman of the *ton* being associated with the working class. Now, she only heard sadness in his tone.

And Cart was going to lose everything he'd worked to accomplish because of her.

He had every right to despise her.

Chapter Twenty-Three

Tainted Bloodline.

Cart read the headline for the fifth time, unable to process how any reputable news source would write such a scathing story—about him. It was disgusting, it was degrading, and worst of all, it held some truth.

Tossing the morning post aside, Cart picked up his fork and pushed the cold, forgotten food around on his plate. He should eat something. He was famished, but couldn't bring himself to take so much as a bite when he arrived home the previous evening. He could feel his stores of energy within his body depleting with each breath he took. He'd been so frustrated with the situation, with Jude, that he hadn't slept at all.

He'd gone over and over how he'd been so oblivious to her deceptions. After all these years being back in London after his father's passing and his uncle misuse of the estate, Cart thought he would have noticed something was wrong. He should have been able to stop Uncle Julian from destroying all his ancestors had built, but the truth was plain before him. Much like with Jude, Cart would have been completely ignorant to his uncle's activities.

Maybe his bloodline was tainted, or more accurately, *he* was tainted.

He set his fork down and a maid appeared out of nowhere to collect his dishes, still piled high with Cook's usual morning meal.

Lord Gunther had been justified in distributing the details of the vase's disappearance and reappearance. That it meant Cart was named as the antiquities contractor who was charged with finding the vase was unfortunate, especially since all the sordid details pertaining to the ransom note and money demanded for the vase's return were also included in the story. All of London was likely reading the story as if it were a modern day crime tale, complete with the vase's mysterious reappearance at Lord Gunther's townhouse. The only part the post did not see fit to report on was that the ransom money had been returned to Lord Gunther. Suspiciously, that tidbit of information had been left out entirely.

He could only imagine the shame this would bring upon his family—Theo especially. Cart had been interviewing boarding schools for her to attend until her coming out season. The chance that any school in good standing would accept her now with the family's scandalous past—and present—was unlikely. She was an innocent in all this.

Curse Jude for setting her sights on him, for drawing him in with her brilliant mind and, mostly, for making him believe he could have more following their kiss.

It was not all her doing, though. Cart knew that much.

His irrational behavior and impaired judgment may have been the direct result of their association but he was responsible for his own actions and reactions. He had never been that randy fool who threw caution to the wind and seized the day, his father used to say. His life had been one of study, learning, reflection, and action, but he'd lost sight of that where Jude was concerned.

And he would suffer the consequences.

"Simon!" Lady Cartwright screeched, sailing into the dining room.

Cart wished he'd kept his plate to busy himself during her tirade.

"I have received a note this morning."

"Oh," Cart said, a serene expression masking his dour mood. "Do tell me more."

"You will not believe this," she continued as if he hadn't spoken. A servant jumped forward to pull out her chair and another set a dish with toasted bread and marmalade before her. She did not so much as pause to show her appreciation. "My attention and attendance are no longer required at Chrissely's House. Can you believe that, Simon?"

He racked his brain for what Chrissely's House was, though its name did not even vaguely sound familiar.

"My charity for the salvation of impure women of dubious standings," she said around a bite of bread. "They cannot do this. I assure you, I will be a force to be reckoned with. If they think to dismiss me with no grounds after my many years of service, dedication—and money—they are mistaken."

"My money," Cart mumbled. It was an insult his mother didn't deserve. "Besides, you were only telling me a fortnight ago that you plan to depart London after the season."

"Your father's money," she refuted. When Cart only snorted, grabbed the post, and feigned disinterest, Lady Cartwright huffed. "At any rate, I cannot fathom what I have done to deserve the dismissal. My husband—your father—was a powerful man. You"—she looked at her only son, a pained expression on her face—"are an earl, as well. They cannot do this to me, no matter what my future plans are."

Her meaning was not lost on Cart. His own mother still saw him as a failure, a man not worthy of the Cartwright title. She thought him a dimwitted, gullible, easily swayed man without the sense needed to lead his family.

Once she set eyes on the morning post, all her accusations would be grounded in fact, at least where society was concerned.

"What do you suggest?" she queried, sipping her tea.

She never asked for his opinion, let alone assistance with an actual dilemma she was trying to solve. "What do I suggest about what?" Cart played as if he were uncertain of what she spoke.

"Chrissely's House," she said. Her teacup returned to the table, the delicate china hitting the saucer with more force than usual. "I have half a mind to write a contemptuous letter of rebuttal and send it to each of the chairwomen. That would show them I am not one to trifle with."

A small part of him longed to agree and allow her to draft the letters and send them off with much fanfare, but it would only hurt Theo further. "Mother, are you not involved with several other charities of equal import?"

"Why, yes," she scoffed. "What sort of fashionable lady would I be if I did not use my influence to help the less fortunate?"

"What sort, indeed?"

"You are not taking this seriously, Simon." She set her intense stare on him. The same look would have sent him cowering under his bed as a youth, but now he felt only pity for her. "I am trying to set forth a favorable example for Theodora, well, as favorable as possible on the measly allowance you allot to me."

"You know we are both on a similar allowance—I can argue you far outspend me and Theo combined." His pocketbook was likely to suffer further when his mother left for her travels. Cart shook the paper to straighten the crease and located a story he'd been reading before noticing the article naming Lord C_wright as the man Lord Gunther had found disfavor with. Thankfully, they hadn't printed his name in its entirety, but it was certain to be enough for many to guess at whom the post alluded to. "Besides, you have done nothing, it is I who have offended the powers that be in society and gained us a mention in the post."

The room grew silent. And still. No sound of his mother chewing her meal, sipping her tea or grasping her table knife to stab him. For the last, he should feel fortunate. Not that a knife to his hand would be amiss, as it would at least give him a measure of distraction.

"What have you done to tarnish this family further?" she seethed.

Her words were no more than a whispered accusation. Far more dangerous than when she loudly proclaimed her allegations to anyone who would listen. This question was meant solely for him, not for those around them to ponder all the shameful things Cart had done.

If he were wise, he'd leave the post for her to read and walk from the room. He could maybe spend the day at White's in their reading room. They hadn't obtained new, worthwhile reading stock in months, but the distance would prove wise when his mother began her assault on his character. The disdainful looks he'd receive at White's would be no less brutal than his mother's onslaught of cruel claims.

On the other hand, running away may very well suit him best—not to his gentlemen's club, but farther away. Outside society's reach and far from Lady Cartwright. Certainly then, people would forget him and the mockery he'd made of himself. With time, Theo's connection to Cart would become blurred and the *ton* would forget her association with him. By the time she was presented to society, he would be a distant memory for everyone involved. The last lingering remembrances of a commonly held name, but nothing more.

"Do not make me ask you again, Simon Montgomery," she hissed. "You may very well be Lord Cartwright, an earl in your own right, but I am still your mother—and the matriarch of this family."

His mother? Cart wanted to laugh at the term.

How nice it would have been to have a mother after his father had died suddenly. She hadn't even sent for him at Eton.

How reassuring it would have been to have his mother by his side when he found out about his uncle's duplicity. Lady Cartwright had treated him with outright scorn since his return from university—her plans to journey outside of London, no matter the cost to him, were worth the peace to his household.

How he'd delight in a mother who would commend his many accomplishments in restoring the family coffers. Yet his mother continued to think her only son a dullard, a man not fit to take the helm of the Cartwright legacy.

He was innocent in everything Lady Cartwright held him accountable for.

His Uncle Julian's siphoning from the Cartwright estate had likely started long before Cart's father passed away. Though he'd pored over every estate ledger since his return from Eton, Cart had seen no entry embellished or any funds taken without authorization by his man of business.

But still—everything had been gone.

And the only person left to take the blame was Cart.

He was beyond tired of taking the blame. Utterly exhausted. There was not a person in all of England who'd cast the culpability of his family's ruin on a mere boy, which was what he'd been when it had all occurred.

It had to stop.

"Here, you can read for yourself, Mother." He calmly folded the post with the shaming article front and center before handing it to Lady Cartwright. "But, keep your venomous outbursts about my suitability as an earl to yourself. I am uninterested in your wallowing and self-pity over your cursed relations."

Cart made to stand, a servant appearing to pull his chair back. He should feel victorious, vilified for finally speaking his mind to his mother instead of cowering in her presence.

Instead, he felt empty—and alone.

Not a single soul to call friend.

He was dead set against bringing Theo into any of this, as he knew the strained living arrangements did not escape her notice as it was.

As if conjured from his very thoughts, his younger sibling entered the room, her nose pressed so close to a book that she nearly collided with Cart as he attempted his dignified retreat from the dining area before his mother finished reading the article detailing his downfall.

"Simon," she called, not bothering to look up to see if he was even in the room. "There is something dreadfully wrong—" She ran into his outstretched palm. "Oof!"

"Slow down, puppet," he said. "What can you find dreadfully wrong in a book"—he tilted the book up to see the cover—"that's nearly a hundred years old?"

She gave him a knowing smile, as if proud to find something erroneous in a book Cart had studied a dozen times. "This, look here." Theo pointed to the page before her, lowering the book so Cart could inspect what she'd been reviewing. "See this map?"

"Yes, it is a map of England, done by Robert Morden around 1695."

Her narrowed look told him she was impressed by his skill at pinpointing the name of the mapmaker in questions. "Do you see anything off about this page?"

"Heavens, Theo," he sighed, lifting the heavy book of maps from her outstretched hands. "It is a map, likely traced from the original by one of Morden's many assistants."

"Please, take a closer look, Simon," she pleaded, her excitement at finding something unique showing in her voice.

His mother hadn't seen fit to berate him as yet, so Cart took a closer look at the map, following the edge of England all the way around. He briefly inspected the name of each shire, followed by the outlying areas including the channel. Nothing seemed amiss—or maybe it was that he'd been overly distracted of late. It only followed suit that his mind was not as sharp as it had once been.

Whatever Theo meant for him to find, he could not spot it. "I give up, Theo. What have you found?"

"Look!" Her small index finger landed on the bold script across their great country...and it was labeled Angland. She giggled in triumph at her keen observation skills. "I can hardly believe this."

"Something our dear Simon didn't notice?" Lady Cartwright fairly cooed from the table behind him. "Oh, Theodora, do pull your head from the clouds—if it weren't for me, we'd be living in the poorhouse."

"Mother," Cart warned. They'd agreed long ago to keep their animosity between them and out of hearing range of Theo. "Theo, that is fascinating!"

"My lord?" Squires called from the doorway. "This just arrived for you."

On the silver platter, a single cream envelope was perched. No writing to signify whom it was from.

"It arrived by courier only moments ago," Squires answered Cart's unasked question. "The man did not indicate a response was needed and left before I could ask his direction."

"Thank you, Squires." Cart lifted the letter from the platter.

"Lady Theodora, your languages tutor has arrived and awaits you in the schoolroom." Squires tucked the empty tray under his arm, bowed, and departed the room, likely returning to his post at the front door.

"Puppet," Cart said, tugging on her loose plait. "Hurry now to your studies."

With a quick smile, Theo bounced from the room, overjoyed to have impressed Cart.

"Simon?" Lady Cartwright called from the table.

He glanced over to see his mother still studying the post. "Yes?"

"I think it best you find a school for Theodora with all haste."

"I agree, Mother." For the first time in many years, they were in agreement on something. "I will increase my efforts to locate a school for Theo."

"Very good, and with this new development, it may be for the best if I distance myself from London with similar haste."

Cart walked from the room, his disbelief over his mother conceding to a boarding school for Theo only overshadowed by her last words: distancing herself from London—and very soon.

Her disapproval of him was so ingrained in her every action and thought, he'd lost sight of their bond—

a bond that he'd considered irrevocably broken years before.

And now she would leave him to his own follies—abandon him to repair the damage he'd done by his association with Jude. For once, he agreed it was something he deserved.

Cart continued to his study, the letter almost forgotten in his hand when he looked down and saw the missive addressed not to him, but the magistrate.

Chapter Twenty-Four

Jude sat waiting, her hands resting lightly on her lap, her hair perfectly pinned, and a smile on her face. She'd meant her grin to be bright and reassuring. But as the hours passed, she felt it slip from lively and content to anxious and exhausted. Sam had pointed out the dark crescent moon shaped circles below each of her eyes— the one sign of her fatigue that she was unable to mask.

Slumber, the deep regenerating kind, was impossible to attain when so many things weighed heavily on a person. Her exhaustion notwithstanding, Jude knew she'd made the correct decision—for possibly the first time in a long time.

And she was resigned to accept the consequences.

Lord Cartwright's words had bounced around in her head all night—intent had little bearing on consequences. It was true beyond any fact that Jude knew.

The morning post had only solidified her decision made the night before. Cart's name had been thinly veiled. Unfortunately, Lord Gunther's accusations and insinuations hadn't been. She was thankful her letter had departed in Mr. Curtis' capable hands before she'd taken a light repast and moved to the front salon to await her fate. If she'd read the many horrid things Gunther had offered to the gossip columnist as fodder for the scandal-ready *beau monde*, then she would have paid the elderly man a visit, and…well…she would have done something she would have had no remorse over.

She was not prone to violent acts of aggression. All the same, Jude had clenched her fist several times that morning and punched it at the empty air in front of her, wishing it was Gunther.

The man had gotten his vase back—and his fifty pounds. Why couldn't he have left well enough alone? If she weren't trying desperately to change her ways, she'd have stolen back into his home and taken the blasted antique again.

Lord Gunther should count himself fortunate for Cart's intervention in Jude's life.

She glanced to the ticking clock by the door. Almost noonday.

What was taking so dreadfully long for them to arrive?

She'd planned things perfectly—Sam and Payton had been invited to tea with Lady Chastain and her sister, Mrs. Jakeston. Garrett had left this morning while all of her sisters were abed and would not return until later in the day. She'd even sent the housekeeper on a fool's errand for a plum jam supposedly awaiting Jude at the market. Mr. Curtis was the only servant present, though he worked in the stables most mornings.

The perspiration at her brow grew thick once more and Jude retrieved her kerchief from her pocket before hastily wiping the moisture away.

Her foot tapped an erratic beat on the floor, the noise muffled by the rug underfoot.

She'd selected her sturdy riding boots with the hard sole. The laces were tied tightly, constricting her ankle. Her frenzied heartbeat coursed through her body, causing her lower leg to ache at the top of her tightly-laced boot.

Closing her eyes, Jude allowed the smells and sounds of her family home to wash over her, to invade and ingrain themselves in her subconscious. The aroma of warm bread in the kitchen drifted through the house. A loud creak could be heard every so often as the floorboards settled under the weight of the house. If she sat very still, Jude could even feel a light draft across her face from an open window across the room.

Everything about her home was safe…secure…and as it had always been.

It was a chaotic home, but one filled with love and loyalty.

The Craven House siblings were known for their banter and bickering, but they were a fiercely loyal group.

Jude would not change that for the world—not for a treasure trove of coins or a fancy title and home or the opportunity to travel the world.

But, there *was* something worth giving up her home and family for.

Love.

She'd cried most of the night at the mere thought of the word.

Certainly, she loved her family. For sure, she loved her home. And yes, she loved her fancy gowns and mingling amongst London's *beau monde*.

It was only in the last several hours that Jude had come to the realization that she loved one thing more than all the rest combined—and that petrified her.

Not the love itself, but knowing she'd caused heartache and pain that would always stand in the way of her claiming that great love.

Because of her actions, that love would be forever out of her reach.

Her gloved hands shook where they were clasped in her lap.

If Marce were here, she'd never allow Jude to do what she was doing. It was her way to swoop in and rescue her younger siblings, even from their own foolish mistakes.

Her sister was due to return home from her trip any day—possibly any minute. If Jude were going through with her plan, then she need do it immediately. She needed to confess all her wrongdoings to the magistrate immediately and clear Cart's name—remove the blame and scandal that would befall his family because of her.

Jude was resigned to let Lord Cartwright go, to never see him again, but he needed to know how much he meant to her. Their entire relationship was not a mistake. She did not regret a moment of it.

If she could go back, she would have fallen in that pond with him—and remained there as they laughed at their social blunder. She would have invited him to meet her at the library for an afternoon of exploring all the secrets the place held hidden within. She would have extended an invite to dine with her family, play a round of whist with Payton, and retire to another room with Garrett to discuss current affairs and drink heavy tumblers of fine spirits. They would have taken to the dance floor at some fashionable matron's grand ball, turning heads and causing a stir at their regal pairing—Jude with her tall, slender frame and strikingly bright red hair, and Cart with his elaborately tied neckcloth, intelligent air, and artfully combed golden-brown hair. They would laugh the night away, discussing all manner of things deemed unsuitable for a mere woman. Others would flock to their sides as Cart told stories of their most treasured acquisitions.

They would be the talk of all of London—not for their wealth or title, but because of their love for one another.

It was all hopes and wishes.

She would never enter a ballroom on his arm. Nor would they travel and see the many wonders of the world together. Neither would they so much as share a meal in each other's company.

The clock chimed loudly. Twelve times.

Outside, the sun would be directly overhead and the fog of the morning hours would be dissipating. People would venture out shortly, destined for Hyde Park, Rotten Row, or Bond Street. Their hours would be filled with selecting the perfect fabric for a new gown, ordering the perfect stationery for letter writing, strolling with acquaintances, and meeting with fellow aristocrats at their fencing clubs.

For so many, their day was only just beginning, but for Jude, her life as she knew it would be ending before long.

She only awaited the knock at her front door—if they even paused to announce their arrival instead of just swarming the house looking for her.

A part of her wanted the wait to be over, an ending to her fate clearly written.

A loud knock finally sounded through the house, a solid fist banging intensely on the door.

They were not going to burst in, after all.

Jude stood, her hands moving down the front of her skirt to smooth out any wrinkles. Next, she glanced into the tiny mirror on the wall to verify her hair was still properly pinned, a mass of auburn curls secured atop her head with only a few tendrils escaping the knit. The ache in her ankles faded with her movement.

In the background, the pounding upon the door continued unabated.

A small traveling case sat by the door in case they allowed her to bring anything with her. It held her writing supplies, warm woolen stockings, her brush, and a night shift. Nothing of relative value, but each essential to her—and far more than she deserved to have.

Her eyes watered, but she blinked the tears back. She would never again awaken in the bed next to Sam or spend her evenings bickering with Payton over a card found suspiciously on the floor. There were so many things still to learn, such as where Garrett went when he wasn't at Craven House, or how far Marce traveled each year for her excursion.

And that was only the beginning.

The day would never come when she'd have the time to properly get to know Theodora. From their short encounter, Jude sensed the girl was much like her brother while retaining her own individuality. Gone was her opportunity to meet the formidable Lady Cartwright, his mother.

Cart had barely begun to show her all his many collected treasures.

Her fingers rose to touch her lips and she could almost feel Cart's mouth pressed to hers, commanding yet yielding to her. The feel of his hands pressed against her back, holding her close with nothing more than an inch separating them. His hesitant smile after they'd kissed was truly what had captivated her most—it was as if he'd discovered a new treasure, one worth more than all he'd gathered before.

For a brief time, Jude believed she was that treasure to him.

The one thing a person would give up everything else for.

Love.

Cart was exactly that to her.

So much so, she was willing to give up her freedom to show him how much he meant to her.

The time had come—and the pounding on the door had not lessened, nor would it after what she'd done.

Jude trudged from the salon, pausing before the thick wooden front door.

With a deep inhale, she took hold of the knob, preparing to pull the door wide.

Something in her told her she'd made a terrible mistake, that she should run—leave Craven House behind her and distance herself from the fate that awaited her if she opened the door.

"Judith Pengarden," a familiar voice shouted from the far side. "Open this door immediately or I shall be forced to break it down."

Her confusion was quickly replaced by relief as her hand fell from the knob and her shoulders sagged.

It took everything she had not to fling the door wide and jump into his arms.

The relief that initially filled her when she heard his voice faded to trepidation.

Cart wasn't supposed to be here. He wasn't meant to witness her further humiliation—maybe he'd come to make sure she got what she deserved. The idea of him watching the magistrate take her away from her home, likely enjoying her disgrace, wounded Jude to her core. He was not a heartless or cruel man.

Though she'd hurt him deeply. The stark fact made only more glaring with Garrett's news of Cart's past. He'd been injured by a man who should have cherished him. His own flesh and blood. Jude couldn't imagine the emotions that must have overtaken him at Jude's deception.

She laid the palm of her hand against the solid door as Cart started pounding again.

She wanted to let him in, not only into the house, but also into her life. Bare her soul to him. She could trust him to treat her heart with care, but after all she'd done, how could he expect her to do the same?

This time, she allowed the tears to fall, etching a path down her cheeks. Dripping off her chin and jawline. The lucky ones landing at the collar of her gown, while the rest continued to the floor, small droplets pooling at her feet.

"I heard you walk to the door," he shouted over the sound of his fist slamming against the door. "Your footfalls are as recognizable as your voice. Open the door, Jude."

If she opened the door and gave him entrance, she'd never follow through with turning herself over for her crimes—and then he'd by no means see how much she truly cared for him. It was the only way.

"Go away, Cart," she whispered. When his pounding abruptly stopped, she knew he'd either heard her or sensed she'd spoken. They had that connection, the pair of them. Or maybe it was only that he was attuned to her in a very uncanny way. Jude didn't understand it—nor did she need to. She loved him—far more than she loved anything. There was nothing she wouldn't give up to confirm that love. "Please, leave me be."

"I most certainly will not," he said, his voice returning to normal volume. "You are being irrational and impulsive."

He knew nothing of what she was thinking or how many hours she'd toiled over her choices before coming to the conclusion she had—far longer than she'd debated stealing that blasted vase or Cart's family's painting. He was the typical man who thought no woman shrewd enough to make a decision for herself about her future.

"You know nothing of my decisions," she responded.

"You are going to get yourself into far worse trouble if you continue in this manner."

"Why are you here?"

"To stop you from continuing down this foolish path," he said. "You are putting yourself in great jeopardy."

He thought to stop her from continuing in her thievery. That must be it. Did he think her so callous that she hadn't been gravely affected by how her actions had hurt him? That she could continue her life as if it had never happened—to either of them?

Her hand fell from the door.

"I will not leave," he said again. "By my estimate, I have at least forty-eight hours until my hunger will become taxing. I can sit on this stoop all day—and night—if that is what it takes."

Jude envisioned her sisters returning home to find Cart sitting at their entrance. Or worse yet, if he were still there when guests arrived this evening for cards. Her gut told her Garrett would demand he leave long before then.

But none of that would come to pass, for the magistrate would arrive and take her away before the sun set.

Chapter Twenty-Five

Cart's hand had begun to throb after only several moments of slamming his fist against the wooden door of Craven House. Now, it was devoid of feeling and hanging limply at his side. He needed to be within the house so he could dissuade her, show her that all was not as dire as she suspected.

The time he'd wasted staring at the envelope before opening it could have been too long.

"Jude." His gravelly voice conveyed the pain he'd tried to keep inside. "I am not going away. Take the time you need, but I will be waiting. Right here."

Cart leaned his back against the door and slid to the ground, not caring if his white linen shirt became soiled with dirt or if his trousers creased. He pulled the letter from his pocket and read it once more:

Dear Sir Featherstone, JP,

I, Miss Judith Pengarden, am responsible for the theft—and return—of Lord Gunther's cherished vase. I am aware that my actions were wrong and am ready to take full responsibility for everything. No one else knew of my crimes.

She'd signed the letter with a hasty *J*.

Featherstone, the magistrate responsible for several miles surrounding his townhouse. The letter had not been meant for him and he shuddered to think what senseless scheme she'd concocted. This was a serious confession to a crime that would not go unpunished if Lord Gunther's anger at Cart told him anything.

Jude and her entire family would be ostracized and publicly shamed for her offenses. Even if Jude escaped without going to Newgate, she'd never escape the scandal. Her chances of finding a match—or employment—would be zero. And society had a long and detailed memory about such things. Her name and portrait would circulate in every newspaper and gossip rag for months to come. Her invitations to soirees and dinners would disappear as no hostess would risk having a thief in their midst. Yes, she may appear the mysterious creature for a time, but that too would fade. She would be relegated to a life in the shadows, obscurity her only way of any life at all.

And for what?

To clear Cart's name—certainly not. Cart was a peer, an earl. It was likely many would view him differently, maybe even whisper behind his back about his culpability in the Gunther fiasco, but that gossip would fade far quicker than if Jude were to see charges for her crimes. There would be lasting consequences for Cart, but nothing that time could not mend. He'd returned the fifty pounds to Gunther and, truly, the lord's only recourse was to go to the post with the sensationalized story. That was all it was—no magistrate could offer any proof that Cart was in any way involved with the theft and return of the vase.

As far as society's opinion of Cart went, he had no interest in it. Besides a few men he'd met at university and his many business acquaintances, all of society—and their lofty brashness—could go straight to the devil.

He'd overreacted at the situation and had treated Jude horribly. He'd come to terms with that before seeing his name in the post this morning. The slanderous article about him hadn't changed his opinion either.

Everything had been out of his control since he'd met Jude—and it was exactly what he'd needed. Life was not about controlling every aspect of your life, so much so that not a thing excited you or created any surprise. His life had been mundane and routine since returning home from Eton. He'd thought if he created an environment free from anything out of the ordinary, each day progressing as the one before it with order and consistency, then life would not return to the hectic time directly following his return from university. He would keep a firm grasp on his life and continue to be in control of his family's future. He would ensure his sister never go through the turmoil he'd been forced to endure and never need give up something she held dear.

He'd always assumed he thrived on consistency; counting his steps, making his calculations, and studying any topic that proved out of his grasp.

The whirlwind and change that came with Jude should have solidified that fact in his mind.

Instead, it had him questioning his life thus far. Order, consistency, and routine would lead to a bleak future with little pleasure and, certainly, no surprises.

It was not the way he wanted to continue, for once he secured a school for Theo, that would leave only him and his mother…and his collecting. With his sister away, it only left him to appreciate all he'd attained. His mother would gladly sell every piece of his treasured collection.

But not Jude.

She may have been dishonest about the reasoning behind her interest in him, but he'd observed her passion for art and history firsthand—just as he'd witnessed her reaction to their kiss in Hyde Park. She'd been as affected by their intimacy as he—that was something neither of them could have falsified.

"Jude."

"Yes." Her voice sounded mere inches away, as if she, too, sat against the door.

"You are so unpredictable," Cart conceded.

"I know, but—"

"And cunning," he continued, cutting her off. "And extraordinary…and breathtaking…and intelligent…and everything. You, Judith Pengarden, are everything."

"I am also a liar," she sighed. He could almost hear her tears falling. "And a thief…"

Cart had no response to her words. She was both of those things, but it changed nothing about his feelings for her.

"Why?" It was the question he'd never asked because he feared the answer would crush him further. "Why do you do it?"

"Did it," she said. "I have no plans to steal again."

"Why?" he asked again.

"For my family," she confessed. "Marce toils endlessly, day and night. She works to take care of us, to care for any woman who comes to Craven House seeking a safe haven, and she lives no life of her own. None of this is what any woman would choose for her future, but she never complains."

"She knows of everything?" Cart could not believe her eldest sister would allow Jude to put herself in harm's way for any measly amount of money.

"No. Samantha and I came up with the ploy to help Marce."

"And she takes the money without question of where it came from?"

Jude chuckled lightly. "Heavens no, we'd planned to slip the money into her private chambers or add it to the money brought in from the card room. She hasn't a clue—about any of this.

"Do you remember the first time we met?" he asked. He wasn't sure why he mentioned it and doubted she remembered him at all.

"Yes, of course," she said. "Lady Haversham's party…"

"No, before that." She didn't remember and Cart would be lying if he didn't admit, at least to himself, that it stung. "You bumped into me outside the night watchman's residence—the morning after you broke into my home."

If he'd only taken better notice, questioned her reasons for being there, and hadn't been duped by her attentions at Lady Haversham's garden party, maybe they wouldn't be in their current situation.

"It was you?" she asked. "I told Sam you looked familiar that day at the party. And I truly didn't mean to break into your home. I was directed to your home, thinking it was Lord Asherton's residence."

While he was unsure if he believed her, the reasoning behind her actions made sense to him now.

Cart pondered the name, unfamiliar with the man or his direction.

# # #

"He has, purportedly is in possession, several Bible leaves of unimaginable value." Jude tilted her head back against the door, unsure why she needed to share that piece of information as it only made her look like more of a horrid person. "Not that it has any bearing on my current situation."

"I cannot help you if you turn yourself over to the magistrate."

She sucked in a breath. "How do you know?"

"A letter was delivered to my home—and I am certain it was not meant for me."

"It was not," she replied. Curse Mr. Curtis and his meddling ways. She'd thought he found something needing attention in the stables and that was the reason she hadn't seen or heard from him since he departed earlier to deliver her missive. He'd known Cart would come and discourage her from her decision when he read the letter.

"Cart," she whispered. "This is something I have to do."

"You need do nothing of the sort," he challenged, his voice rising in frustration.

"I am sorry. Sorry for everything I have done. Sorry for the hurt I've caused you," she said on a sob. It was too much to hold in any longer. He was finally allowing her to speak, to explain herself, and all she could do was cry. "I never meant to wound you—or your family. I swear it. I had no intention of misleading you when we met. It was only that Sam saw an opportunity to be rid of that cursed vase and still gain a small portion of the money we'd planned. It was to be our final time, I promise that, but everything was so muddled at that point." Jude took a deep breath to focus her thoughts. He could return to anger at any moment and depart. She need say her piece before he was gone. "I need to prove how truly remorseful I am. I know you may never fully believe me and that forgiveness is something I do not deserve, but neither does your family deserve the shame and disgrace caused by my actions."

He was so silent on the other side of the door. Not even his breathing could be heard.

Jude feared he'd had enough of her rationalizations and left.

"All this time, on no occasion, did I think about how this would affect anyone else—except my own family," she continued, unable to stop even if Cart no longer listened. "I am a selfish person, Cart, but I want to change. I need to change, even if that means revealing my secret to the magistrate and my family. My intent was never to hurt anyone and my punishment will be losing the love and loyalty of so many people. You included."

"Maybe your penance can be served without losing anything."

She was relieved to hear him finally speak. "It was you who told me that intent does not dictate consequences."

"Sometimes I am not a smart man," he confided with a small, weak laugh. "Sometimes, more times than I will admit, I have little notion of what I speak, especially with social interactions and, worst of all, emotions. Neither is concrete and definitive—but ever-changing and growing."

"You think the magnitude of my actions does not justify severe consequences?" she asked. "I hurt you and that should receive the stiffest punishment imaginable."

"I am only a person, Jude." She heard him move, his booted feet hitting the ground as he stood. "Why would hurting me—out of everyone—be the most important and dire to you?"

She knew the words were going to pass her lips and Jude didn't even attempt to hush them. "Because I love you."

"Open the door, Jude."

She couldn't face him, not now, not after her confession.

She could not take it if he said he didn't feel the same. She couldn't take it if he said that he couldn't look past the hurt she'd caused and her deception. Cart should hold his family and their well-being before anyone and she'd tarnished them before society. His sister deserved better than to have people talking behind her back about Cart's past.

"Please," he begged.

But it would make everything easier to accept if she faced him now and heard directly from his mouth that he did not feel the same for her.

It would make the lonely hours to come more bearable, to know that her feelings were not reciprocated and that Cart had spoken his piece and moved on from her.

Her future was unsure, but she would not take him down with her. He deserved years of happiness—a family, friends, and acceptance—she could not give him any of that, not where she was going.

A clean break—with no ties or obligations to one another.

Surely, Cart sought the same thing.

Closure. With no secrets or regrets left unsaid.

Beyond this moment, she and Cart were guaranteed nothing.

With trembling hands, Jude moved and turned the key in the lock.

Cart pushed the door wide as she stepped back, dressed as gentlemanly as ever with his fine linen shirt, crisp cravat, and gleaming Hessians. His hair was the only thing out of place, as if he'd run his hands through it many times while he begged her to open the door.

His face was a mask of confusion and pain.

The exact emotions that coursed through Jude.

"You have been crying." His fingers brushed her cheek, taking with the swipe her tears. If only it were so simple to wipe away all the bad things between them. "Come now," he said, taking her hand. Their palms met and their fingers intertwined, fitting perfectly. "No tears."

"I don't think I am capable of stopping them." They stood facing one another, less than a foot separating them, their hands still clasped. "Saying goodbye is so much harder than I ever dreamt it would be." Which was the exact reason she'd planned to never have this moment with him. Once the magistrate took her away, she'd made up her mind to deny him a chance to visit her, not that she'd held much hope that he would ever come for her.

Saying goodbye was admitting things were over and done with—all that she'd experienced in their short time together would be gone and all she'd be left with would be memories. Wonderful memories. She would hold them tightly, relive them often, and never allow them to fade. All at the same time, Cart would go on. Certainly, he would remember the woman who'd betrayed him with her lies. The woman who'd drawn him in with a passionate kiss, the woman who'd stayed by his side after he fell into a pond before hordes of people—and the woman he could never trust. Because of Jude, he would remain guarded with every new person he met; assessing their motivations and trying to decipher if their intentions were pure.

She had done this to him—and she could never forgive herself.

She stared into his brown eyes, noticing his confusion had faded and the tight line of his mouth had relaxed.

"Miss Judith Pengarden," he said, an unasked question in his tone.

"Yes, Lord Cartwright." She despised the use of formal names between the pair of them, but she desperately wanted him to stay, to keep talking...but most of all, to never let her go.

"I am going to kiss you now." His hand squeezed hers, pulling her the short distance to him. His other arm wrapped about her waist, dragging her even closer as his lips captured hers.

Jude hadn't time to say anything or utter a protest, though that was the furthest thing from her mind.

At the moment, she simply concentrated on keeping pace with him—his kiss was far more demanding this time. There was nothing tentative or hesitant in the way his mouth pressed solidly against hers, coaxing her lips to part as his tongue brushed lightly along her bottom lip. She could feel his hand massaging her lower back.

Finally, his lips left hers and she sucked in a deep breath as he placed small kisses along her jaw, collecting any stray tears that may have hung on. He released her hand and brought his to her cheek, his fingers stroking the opposite side he'd kissed, then gently caressing down her neck.

A moan escaped Jude as she tried to keep control of her senses.

His lips reached her ear and he nibbled at her lobe before tracing a path back to her parted lips. Their mouths met again as if they were used to one another and fit together as perfectly as their hands had. Their tongues danced as their lips found a rhythm all their own.

Jude wanted this to last forever.

"I did not mean for any of this to happen, but I am so grateful for all that transpired—leading to you." Jude laid her entire self before him, no longer willing to hide anything. She would not hide who she was or what she wanted. And she'd never wanted anything more than the man before her.

"I have been misled, deceived, and hurt in my past," he breathed, his lips still so close to hers. Jude couldn't move, was afraid she'd stop his words from coming, but she needed, desperately, to hear them—just as he needed to hear hers. "I feared you had done the same—used me to gain only what you sought."

"Never."

"I have come to live my life based on facts, numbers, proven theories, and known conclusions—but you are none of those things. I cannot house you in a small box nor do I have explanations for the immense responsibility and adoration I feel for you, despite all you have done. I cannot reconcile any of it, not to my own satisfaction or yours. I should walk away. I should put you from my life and my mind—yet, each time I try, I find I cannot. Every thought I have revolves around you. Your presence banishes the mere thought of rational thinking from my mind. You are a temptress, and I find myself powerless to resist."

"I did not know anything of you or your family's past when we met," she confided. "You must believe me."

"Never did I believe you were the callous woman your actions pointed to."

She cringed at the term callous, as she'd never meant to harm him in anyway. "I'd only sought to help my family...and yes, I fully regret the way I went about it and the injury I caused you, especially."

In Cart's arms—there was no other place she could be happy and content. His embrace was strong and commanding. But Jude sensed he would never restrict her or try to tame her in any way.

Too soon, he pulled back. Jude felt the giant void between them return, even though his arms still held her.

"You would turn yourself over to the magistrate just to show me you love me?" His question was asked in a tone of complete bewilderment, his eyes searching hers for the truth of the matter. "You would give up your family, your freedom, and your future to prove to me how repentant you are?"

"No," Jude shook her head vehemently. She wanted no other misunderstandings between them. Not ever again. "I would give that all up for you…only you. Not to prove any point or show my remorse, but to see you look at me like you are right now."

His face clouded with confusion once more and he pulled slightly away from her. "How is that?"

"Like I am the only thing in the room you notice, even with a treasured vase close at hand or a scepter forged of the strongest steel." Jude paused, remembering each moment she'd noticed the stare. "As if you are sopping wet and covered in pond muck to your knees, but still can barely take your gaze from me to notice the crowd of onlookers."

"I was mortified in that moment," he confessed, a blush traveling up from his shirt collar. "My saving grace, if I remember correctly, was a pair of moss-green doe eyes that kept locked with mine, at least until I was able to crawl from the water. Were there so many people staring?"

Jude laughed at his wide-eyed expression, horror written all over his face. "No, certainly not that many. Only a hundred or so of London's upper crust."

They'd so easily reverted to their light, teasing companionship. Something Jude cherished more than anything. It gave her hope. Not that he'd forgiven her, but that maybe he one day would. and they could establish some sort of friendship beyond the forgiveness a kiss promised. Longing for anything more was destined to crush her.

"What in the devil is he doing back here again?" Garrett's deep voice thundered from behind Cart. "And why are his hands touching your backside?"

Cart tensed at the gruff words.

"Oh, Garrett," a familiar and comforting voice scolded. "Do stop your peacocking and strutting. I am certain our Samantha can explain everything if you'll only calm yourself."

"That is not Samantha!" Garrett flung his hands wildly as if wondering why he was the only person in the room reacting to the scene before him.

Jude stared as Marce's eyes widened and then narrowed. "Judith Pengarden—you will explain posthaste, but first, Garrett, close that door before all of London witnesses the embrace in our foyer."

Chapter Twenty-Six

Cart accepted a tumbler of spirits, uncertain what specific liquor it contained but fearful of declining Jude's brother's offer of a drink. It was not often he partook in drinking anything stronger than a sherry as it inhibited the mind and further decelerated his judgment capabilities. Not a fact widely accepted, but one that Cart had seen firsthand with his father.

The group had retired to a room completely unfamiliar to him. It housed the household ledgers and many other books, including a small desk, clearly designed for the delicate frame of a female, as opposed to a full-grown man. In other households, it might be referred to as an office of sorts, but the shockingly feminine shades of lavender and sea green dispelled the notion immediately.

The color palate was so overpowering and distracting Cart could not see himself being able to concentrate on anything academic in this room. Even now, his eye was drawn to a small lamp upon the white desk, its shade embellished with green tassels and a gaudy, jeweled trim. The fixture appeared completely unsuitable to hold a candle without burning the entire house down. He should mention something to Jude's sister about it before departing—if he made it out of this room with his skin still attached.

With the pacing and angry muttering coming from Garrett, Cart would bet *against* his survival. Not that he was a betting man. No, he chose to invest in facts and logic. At the moment, logic and his gut instinct were in alignment.

The only thing giving him some semblance of ease was Jude's eldest sister, who'd immediately embraced Jude after Cart had let her go and then led her to this room, leaving Cart with only two options: depart semi-unnoticed or follow them.

There was only one place Cart wanted to be—at Jude's side.

Despite all she'd done, everything she'd been less than truthful about, she'd done what she had to do to help her family. Cart could not fault her for that. He'd done the same since returning from university. He'd embraced what most of society saw as distastefully gauche. With much effort and energy, he'd worked hard. Though he wasn't toiling in a field or building structures, he was using his skill and knowledge gained by countless hours of learning to achieve the level of an esteemed antiquities expert. No small feat in the world of academia. If Cart had been afforded the luxury of choosing his own path in life, he'd likely work for a museum or university where he could continue studying the precious pieces he adored.

Possibly even participate in an excursion to foreign lands in search of rare new artifacts.

But as a peer, that was not an option for him—and he was resigned to that fact.

He'd dedicated himself to making his entire household a place of learning. Theo was awarded the finest tutors he could find, even though it meant more shillings than he had. Cart not only searched for his own family heirlooms, but he'd amassed a rather impressive collection of other fine artifacts and paintings, as well.

The hope was that the future Earl of Cartwright, after Simon was long forgotten, would continue in his stead and preserve all matters of historical import.

It was only since meeting Jude that Cart had realized what a lonely existence he'd settled on for himself. No amount of possessions in the world could alleviate or replace that of a companion. Though not just any companion would do any longer. He'd survived with Theo for company all these years, but it was her time to live her own life, explore what England had to offer, and decide on her own path—which left Cart to pick up the pieces.

The most strategic piece was right in front of him—a woman he'd known, somewhere deep inside, was meant for him and him alone. A woman who had drawn him from his mundane and routine existence with barely any effort. A woman willing to give up her entire life—family, home, and future—for him.

It was a dedication he'd never imagined possible, especially directed at him.

Certainly he'd seen the immense love his parents had shared and his mother had never recovered from his father's sudden passing. But he'd also witnessed the aftermath of that love—his mother's domineering, shrewish, harsh demeanor where she'd become withdrawn and nothing like the woman who'd raised him.

Those were the consequences of love.

He'd studied every aspect of it. His parents shared a great love. But when his father was lost far too soon, his mother suffered from it. Love harmed far more people than it helped.

Or, at least, that'd been the outcome of facts in his short study of the matter called love.

He didn't want that for himself or Jude.

However, somewhere along the way—during their short journey—Cart had made a new discovery.

Loving Jude—every wonderful, exciting, and unsettling aspect of her—was worth years of pain, heartbreak, and bitterness he might experience if he ever lost her.

Their journey together would be worth far more than any artifact, painting, or ancient tome he could collect.

But how to express that to her?

"Marce, Judith," Garrett roared. "Leave Lord Cartwright and me to speak in private."

"No, Garrett, I love you but—"

Garrett held up his hand, halting Jude's protest. "This is a discussion for gentlemen. I will handle this and let you know what terms we reach."

Terms?

"Terms?" Jude called, mirroring Cart's thoughts, not for the first time. "I am not livestock to be bartered and sold, Brother. Marce, say something!" She turned to her sister for help.

Cart was not privy to their family's inner workings, but he'd always suspected Marce, the Madame of Craven House, to be in control, ever since the moment he'd passed them leaving the night watchman's residence.

"Jude," Cart started, uncertain how she'd react to what he had to say. "Mayhap your brother and I—"

"Absolutely not." Jude moved to his side. "This—all of this—is between us. No one else."

"We have not all properly met," Marce said, stepping forward and taking control of the situation. "It is very good to see you again, Lord Cartwright. Might I introduce my brother, Lord Garrett. Garrett Davenport, Lord Cartwright—but I believe many call him Cart."

"Cartwright," Lord Garrett growled. "If the women seek to be present, then I will ask you for them…what are your intentions with my sister?"

Cart recognized Lord Garrett for what he was, a brother terrified for his younger sister. It was a feeling Cart could well understand, being an elder brother himself. But appeasing the anger that came along with his feelings of terror was another thing entirely.

"My intentions?" he asked, setting his untouched tumbler on a small table. Cart sensed the coming conversation would take all of his wit to endure. "I…well…"

"Lord Cartwright." Jude placed her hand on his arm and he turned to look into her deep green eyes. Within them, he noticed her emotions were as unsettled as his own, rolling like the green hills of his family estates. "You do not answer to him."

"My coming words will not be directed specifically at him, nor to your sister, though I highly respect her supervision of your care and well-being." Cart paused to calm his nerves. What came next would change his life—and hers, he hoped—for the better. "Miss Judith Pengarden," he said, taking hold of both her hands and looking only at her. The others in the room faded as he lost himself in her face, her small smile, and the way she tried to hide her irritation with everyone present. "We have not had an acquaintance of great longevity and complete openness. At the basest nature of our association, I believe we have come to know one another at a level many others do not achieve in many decades' time."

"What does any of that mean, Cartwright?" Lord Garrett asked before draining his tumbler. "You are one of the strangest men I have ever met."

"Shhhh," Marce hissed. "Be quiet and take notes, my dear brother. I believe you are witnessing what many would call a proposal of the most romantic kind—one you can only read about from the greatest poets of our time."

Cart heard their voices, but they faded into the background. All he could see was Jude, smiling at him with the most honesty he'd ever seen in her.

And that was all he needed to keep speaking…

Chapter Twenty-Seven

Jude stood, enthralled by his words, by his tone, by his every breath. She'd never witnessed Cart in such an imperious way—he was forceful in his stare and confident in the way he held her hands, firmly, but with gentleness only he possessed.

Somewhere behind her—and far away—Jude sensed the door to Craven House's office open and close as Garrett and Marce left, giving them the privacy she needed.

She was ready to give Cart everything—but telling her sister and brother what she and Sam had been doing all these months was too much, but with Cart by her side, maybe one day she could.

"Miss Judith Pengarden," Cart started again, never once taking his eyes from her as his hands released her and framed her face. "Nothing in my life has prepared me for you. You are everything I am not—cunning, adventurous, spontaneous, fearless. I could recite your qualities all day and never run out of words. But your best quality is that you scare me to death…you force me to recognize all that is lacking within myself."

"You are not lacking," she protested, eyes wide.

"Not outwardly, but in my heart." Cart didn't know how to make her understand something he was barely realizing himself. He raised their clasped hands and untangled their fingers before placing her palm on his chest. "Do you feel that?" he asked. When she nodded, wordlessly, he continued. "That is my heart beating. It beats more solidly than it ever has before…because of you. I feel alive, not lost in my studies of ancient things. I am here, I am present…and that is all thanks to you. The change I feel within is all because of you, Jude."

"But I lied about so many things." It was the one thing she regretted about everything and, eventually, it would be the only thing that stood between them. His heart continued to beat beneath her hand—steady and sure. "How can I be responsible for any of this change?"

"You may not have been completely honest with me, but like you said before, our connection goes far deeper than the surface. Beneath both of our shortcomings, we are linked on a level more primitive and transcendent than I knew existed. You never once noticed my oddities and I see the woman behind your actions."

His words were too much to hope for, Jude knew. "I have brought scandal to your family—tarnished your good name even beyond that of your uncle."

"How do you know of that?" His face clouded and she sensed him retreating, but she would not allow it.

"Garrett told me of your uncle's deception, his lies, and his disappearance." She pulled her hand from his chest and moved his palm to hers. "Feel my heartbeat as I tell you this...I have never met someone with more compassion and understanding as you, Cart. For a rational man, you are able to look past the facts of our situation and truly appreciate my actions. I never, in a million years, sought to hurt you—in any way." She knew her heart sped up as she confessed her innermost thoughts, the beat surely felt by his hand. "I would give anything to go back and start over. I would also, if you demanded it, give myself up for my crimes. I would clear your family name by taking responsibility for everything."

"That will never be what I want." He lifted her fingers to his lips. "There is a time when happiness is far more important than anything else. If I am happy, my family will be happy, and society will see that happiness and hopefully celebrate with us."

Us. Jude didn't know what to say. The same thing continued to swirl through her mind. She'd tried to ignore it, push it from her thoughts, but it was the one thing that kept returning. "I thought you said our entire relationship was a mistake..."

"Yes, but if you'll remember, I also said that intent has little bearing on consequences—well, your intent was to use me to rid yourself of a certain stolen vase...but the consequences are nothing either of us could have foreseen."

She looked at him, her eyes questioning his words—and their meaning. For a brief second, Jude feared her heart had stopped. She wanted nothing more than for him to stop talking, for if he did that, the damning words she feared were coming would never be spoken. She could hold this moment in her memory forever, banishing all that followed. She looked to where his lips once against brushed her knuckles.

"Look at me, Judith," he commanded.

"I cannot risk it." She didn't want him to say anything further. Her heart would continue to beat with all he'd said previously, but if her love was not returned, his words of dismissal would crush her—it was a thing she'd never recover from. Her will would be gone, her flame extinguished.

"I will say what I have to say regardless, Jude."

"Does it have to end this way?" she asked.

"Judith," he sighed. She would never, in all her life, tire of her name on his lips, and she feared this would be the last. "Your intent may have been dishonest, but the consequences are pure and sincere…and completely out of your control."

"I cannot hear more—"

He released her fingers and tilted her chin to look her in the eyes, but she shut them tightly. "But you will, you owe me that much."

She could not disagree with that as she opened her eyes once more to see his intense stare.

"The consequences are that I have fallen deeply in love with you—every part of you. The part that makes me question every decision I've made in my life. The part that terrifies me at the prospect of things taking over my life that aren't routine or even vaguely known to me. The part that dispels all my previous notions about love and its power over people. I will gladly give love the influence to control my every move with you." He finally paused, a tenderness entering his gaze.

"You—and this love I am dedicated to explore—are worth more than any antiquity or artifact."

Jude knew the vast meaning behind his words. Not only was she more important than any of his precious collectibles, but he was also telling her she was far more significant than the scandal created by her transgressions. He was willing to put all of their troubles behind them and face the future—whatever it entailed—together, side by side.

"What I am trying to tell you, Jude, is that I will gladly give up everything I possess to have you by my side."

He was running out of words to express all he wanted to say, Jude knew. It was, by far, the most she'd ever heard him speak when it had nothing to do with his passion for objects and collecting.

"Lord Cartwright." Jude blinked several times to banish the pesky tears that threatened to overwhelm her once more. "Never will I command you to give up anything."

For the first time since arriving in the office, his confidence shook and Jude saw the doubt in his eyes.

"I will fight my way through everything and everyone to remain at your side from this day forward."

Obviously, it was the only thing he need hear, because the words had barely left her mouth before his lips were on hers—sealing their pact.

A life together.

An unbreakable love.

An eternity in each other's arms.

Epilogue

Jude entered Cart's home for what felt like the first time—and they were late.

"Squires," Cart's voice boomed as he strode confidently into the foyer to greet her and her family. "May I present Miss Judith Pengarden. Jude, this is my trusted butler, Mr. Squires."

They looked at one another, smirks on both their faces. Jude had visited several times and interacted with many of Cart's staff—the last time only being the afternoon before on their way to Lord Gunther's townhouse. But this time was clearly different.

"Miss Judith," the elderly man said as he bowed before her. "It is an honor to meet our future countess. We all welcome you and your family."

"And may I present Lady Marce Davenport, Lord Garrett, Miss Samantha Pengarden, and finally, Miss Payton Samuels." It was a mouthful and Jude felt a measure of surprise and great satisfaction that Cart had spent the time to learn her family's many names—and not question their inconsistencies. They still had much to learn about one another, each with their own secrets, longings, and hopes to share. Thankfully, they had many years to accomplish everything.

The man acknowledged each in turn before motioning toward the hall Cart had come from. "Lady Cartwright and Lady Theodora await you all in the dining room."

"My apologies for our late arrival," Jude rushed to say. "I do hope we have not ruined dinner for everyone."

"Certainly not, Miss Judith," Squires confided. "It has been refreshing to have an evening not within Lady Cartwright's complete control."

"Now, my man," Cart chuckled, stepping to Jude's side and offering his arm to escort her to their waiting meal. "We have had our fun at my mother's discomfort, but let us not keep her waiting a moment longer."

Garrett stepped to Marce's side to escort her, while Sam and Payton linked arms.

"Right this way," Squires called, starting toward the dining hall.

Cart hesitated, allowing Jude's siblings to precede them across the foyer.

"My lord?" Jude questioned his reluctance to follow, dreading he'd changed his mind about their coming betrothal announcement. "Is something amiss?"

He looked at her like she longed for him to gaze at her every day forever. "Actually, everything is perfectly as it should be—and you look radiant this evening. I cannot remember a time when my life has been more perfect."

She felt her cheeks redden at the pride—and love—in his words.

"Are you certain our meeting with Lord Gunther went as planned?" She'd known she'd have to take responsibility for her actions at some point, and thankfully, Lord Gunther had agreed to meet with them the day before. "While he listened intently—and understood it had all been a misunderstanding, do you think the damage has been repaired?"

Cart smiled, his happiness taking over his entire person. "Did you not see the Post today?" At Jude's questioning look, he continued, "Lord Gunther spoke with the Post again—as I think he takes great pleasure in doing—and remanded his former statement, further announcing Lord Cartwright, that is me—" Cart raised his brows in surprise. "—as his new associate for acquiring three new pieces for his collection."

It was all too good to be true. "And he certainly wants something in return."

"Partly, to see his name in the Post once again," Cart paused, a rakish grim overtaking his face, putting Jude on alert. "Oh, and to be invited to our wedding—in hopes of furthering his acquaintance with the fair and lovely—his words, mind you—Miss Samantha Pengarden."

They both laughed, the sweet, unrestrained melody echoing through the halls of the Cartwright townhouse.

As they both sobered, Cart took in her exquisite dress, his eyes traveling from her head to her toes and back again, clearly admiring the gown Marce had insisted she commission for her younger sibling in celebration of her betrothal dinner.

Jude had chosen a dress of a bolder color than was her normal custom. The satin was a vibrant, deep green that made her auburn hair appear on fire and her eyes glow. It had never been her choice to stand out within a crowd, but with the ruby and diamond ring bestowed upon her by her future husband, Jude knew no other color would do it justice.

"Are you ready to meet the formidable woman that is my mother?" he asked.

Jude straightened her shoulders and lifted her chin a notch, hoping to convince not only him but herself that she was up to the challenge of meeting her future mother-in-law and Theodora, another sister to add to her growing list of admired and cherished female relations.

"But remember," Cart leaned close and whispered. "I love you, I adore everything about you, and you are the one I chose for my future."

His proclamation seemed to hold some meaning Jude couldn't entirely grasp, but when he placed a chaste kiss to her cheek—the meaning made no difference.

He loved her. And more than anything, she loved him.

Nothing else mattered. Not how this evening played out, nor how society reacted to their sudden betrothal and upcoming marriage.

"A house of ill repute?" a voice shrieked from the direction Squires had led her siblings. "You are a what? Simon! This is unacceptable and not proper…you live in a den of iniquity?"

Cart raised a brow in question.

"Craven House is not what it appears, but certainly something we have yet to discuss, my lord."

"Then I look forward to many days—and nights—exploring all the topics of conversation we have yet to converse about." His smile returned, quick and sure, something she was rapidly getting used to seeing. Gone was his pensive, distant nature—replaced with a man who was constantly present, no longer lost in his own thoughts, but living each moment for her, with her. "Shall we, my love?"

She inclined her head and they moved toward the dining hall as Cart's mother's call for assistance continued. Payton's and Sam's laughter drifted to greet Jude and she knew, with Cart by her side and the support of her siblings, she and Cart would live a life full of love and happiness.

Far more than a common thief such as she deserved.

But her final—and most important—task was complete.

Miss Judith Pengarden had successfully stolen her earl—Simon Montgomery, Lord Cartwright.

But many would suggest that it was Lord Cartwright who'd stolen Miss Judith's heart long before she'd taken his.

Books By Christina McKnight:

Craven House Series
The Thief Steals Her Earl
The Mistress Enchants Her Marquis – Coming
December 2016
The Madame Catches Her Duke – Coming 2017
The Gambler Wagers Her Baron – Coming 2017

A Lady Forsaken Series
Shunned No More, A Lady Forsaken (Book One)
Forgotten No More, A Lady Forsaken (Book Two)
Scorned Ever More, A Lady Forsaken (Book Three)
Christmas Ever More, A Lady Forsaken (Novella)
Hidden No More, A Lady Forsaken (Book Four)

Available at all retailers!
Standalone Title
The Siege of Lady Aloria, A de Wolfe Pack Novella

Coming Soon!
Theodora, Lady Archer's Creed (Book One)
Adeline, Lady Archer's Creed (Book Three)

About the Author:

Christina McKnight is a book lover turned writer. From a young age, her mother encouraged her to tell her own stories. She's been writing ever since.

Christina enjoys a quiet life in Northern California with her family, her wine, and lots of coffee. Oh, and her books . . . don't forget her books! Most days, she can be found writing, reading, or traveling the great state of California.

Follow her on Twitter: @CMcKnightWriter
Keep up to date on her releases: www.christinamcknight.com
Like Christina's FB Author page: ChristinaMcKnightWriter

Author's Notes

Thank you for reading *The Thief Steals Her Earl, Craven House Series (Book One)*.

If you enjoyed *The Thief Steals Her Earl*, be sure to write a brief review at
Amazon, Barnes and Noble, or Goodreads.

I'd love to hear from you!
You can contact me at:
Christina@christinamcknight.com

Or write me at:
P O Box 1017
Patterson, CA 95363

www.ChristinaMcKnight.com
Check out my website for giveaways, book reviews, and information on my upcoming projects, or connect with me through social media at:

Twitter: @CMcKnightWriter
Facebook: www.facebook.com/christinamcknightwriter
Goodreads: www.goodreads.com/ChristinaMcKnight

Sign up for my newsletter here:
http://eepurl.com/VP1rP

There are several people I'd like to thank for staying with me through the emotional journey of writing this book.

To Marc, my amazing boyfriend, who continues to stand by my side through the utter chaos that is my creative process. Thank you…your love and dedication never ceases to amaze me. I hope to one day be as selfless and compassionate as you are.

To Lauren Stewart, my critique partner and best friend, you pushed me to explore new avenues of thought I never dreamed possible. If we were in a true relationship, it would be one based on co-dependency, but in a good way. My writing would not be what it is without your comments, criticism, suggestions, and guidance.

I'd also like to thank the wonderful women who've supported me in both my writing career and life, including (but not limited to): Debbie Haston, Angie Stanton, Theresa Baer, Roxanne Stellmacher, Laura Cummings, Dawn Borbon, Suzi Parker, Jennifer Vella, Brandi Johnson, and Latisha Kahn. I know I'm forgetting people…You have all been very patient and wonderfully supportive of my eccentric ways.

A very special thank you to my editor, Chelle Olson with Literally Addicted to Detail, your skill and professionalism surpass all that I expected. Chelle Olson can be contracted by email at literallyaddictedtodetail@yahoo.com.

Also, a special thank you to historical editor, Scott Moreland. Welcome to my team!

And to my proofreader, Anja, thank you for embarking on yet another journey with me.

Cover and wraparound cover design and website design credit to Sweet 'N Spicy Designs.

Finally, thank you for supporting indie authors.

www.ingramcontent.com/pod-product-compliance
Lightning Source LLC
Chambersburg PA
CBHW030415180626
46812CB00005B/2011